GROWING THE CIRCLE

BOOK SIX OF THE GUIDING EMILY SERIES

BARBARA HINSKE

ALSO BY BARBARA HINSKE

Available at Amazon in Print, Audio, and for Kindle

The Rosemont Series

Coming to Rosemont

Weaving the Strands

Uncovering Secrets

Drawing Close

Bringing Them Home

Shelving Doubts

Restoring What Was Lost

No Matter How Far

When Dreams There Be

Waves of Grace

Novellas

The Night Train

The Christmas Club (adapted

for The Hallmark Channel, 2019)

Paws & Pastries

Sweets & Treats

Snowflakes, Cupcakes & Kittens

Tarts & Turnovers

Workout Wishes & Valentine Kisses

Wishes of Home

Wishful Tails

Back in the Pack

Novels in the Guiding Emily Series

Guiding Emily (adapted for The Hallmark Channel, 2023)

The Unexpected Path

Over Every Hurdle

Down the Aisle

From the Heart

Growing the Circle

Novels in the "Who's There?!" Collection

Deadly Parcel

Final Circuit

CONNECT WITH BARBARA HINSKE

Sign up for her newsletter at **BarbaraHinske.com**
    Goodreads.com/BarbaraHinske
    Facebook.com/BHinske
    Instagram/barbarahinskeauthor
    Pinterest.com/BarbaraHinske
    BookBub/Barbara Hinske
    Twitter(X)/Barbara Hinske
    TikTok.com/BarbaraHinske
    Search for **Barbara Hinske on YouTube**
    bhinske@gmail.com

GROWING THE CIRCLE

BOOK SIX OF THE GUIDING EMILY SERIES

BARBARA HINSKE

CASA DEL NORTHERN PUBLISHING

ISBN: 9798991115148 (paperback)

ISBN: 9798991115162 (hardcover)

Library of Congress Control Number: 2025905940

Casa del Northern Publishing

Phoenix, Arizona

To the extraordinary puppy raising, mother/daughter team of Teena and Samantha Tabor, and the incredible Lonny, who they raised and is now a remarkable guide dog. Your commitment to making the world better for others is a beacon of light in this world.

CHAPTER 1

*E*mily Main paused in the doorway of her stepdaughter's bedroom. Diedre's rhythmic breathing told her the girl was asleep.

Emily and her guide dog, Garth, then moved to the next bedroom. Curled up at Zoe's feet lay Sabrina, thumping her tail against the mattress. Her faithful miniature schnauzer was always at Zoe's side.

Emily knew at once that Zoe was not asleep. She crossed the room to the girl's bed and stretched out a hand to find the lumpy form huddled under the covers.

"You're still awake, sweetheart," Emily said. "Everything okay?"

Zoe released the breath she had been holding. "How do you always know?"

"Call it 'mom instinct.' Even though I'm just your guardian—"

"You're my mom," Zoe interrupted.

Emily swallowed the lump in her throat occasioned by those simple words and ran her hand along Zoe's side.

Zoe scooted her body away from the edge of the bed, making room for Emily to settle down next to her.

"You girls have had a busy week. The end of the school year was incredibly hectic. Diedre's out like a light. I thought you would be, too."

Zoe shrugged.

"Grant and I are proud of how you and Diedre managed your transition to your new school. Joining your fourth-grade classes after the Christmas break took a lot of courage. Each of you not only survived, but you thrived. Diedre was a standout in the music program, and you were part of the team that won the school science fair. And you've each got fun plans for the summer."

"I know." Zoe's tone was devoid of enthusiasm.

Emily smoothed the hair away from Zoe's forehead. "What's got you down in the dumps?"

"Fifth grade."

"Well … yes … that's the natural progression. You weren't challenged by any of the fourth-grade curriculum. I thought you'd be looking forward to fifth."

Zoe lifted herself onto one elbow. "We have to move to a new building. We'll be in middle school next year. Instead of being the big kids in elementary, we'll be the little kids again."

Emily slid her arm around Zoe's shoulder and pulled her close. "You handled being a new kid in school extremely well. Those adaptive skills will benefit you when you enter fifth grade." She rested her chin on top of Zoe's head.

"You really think so?"

"I do. The middle school building is on the same campus as your elementary school and the kids you know from fourth grade will be with you in fifth." Emily squeezed Zoe's shoulders. "Everything's going to be fine. I hope you don't spoil your summer worrying about things that won't happen."

"How do I make my mind stop thinking scary thoughts?"

Emily chuckled. "That's the hard part—controlling your own thoughts. Each of us has to do that throughout our lives. It's an essential skill to learn." Emily took a deep breath before continuing. "When I'm worrying about something, I tell myself to *STOP IT! RIGHT NOW!* I even say it out loud."

Zoe popped up onto her knees. "For reals? I've never heard you say that."

"For reals. If other people are around, I say it quietly—but I do say it. Then I force my mind to think about other things. If my thoughts drift back to something I'm worried about, I repeat the entire process."

Zoe bounced on her heels, making the mattress move.

Sabrina got to her feet and jumped off the bed to join Garth in the doorway.

"Would you like to try it?"

"Sure."

"Think the scariest thoughts you can imagine about the first day of fifth grade."

Zoe clamped her eyes shut in concentration.

"When you're ready, say STOP IT! RIGHT NOW! in a firm voice."

Zoe uttered the words in a tremulous voice.

"Let's hear that again—this time with gusto."

Zoe repeated the words at full volume.

Sabrina uttered a muffled woof.

Emily and Zoe laughed. To their surprise, Diedre didn't stir in the next room.

"That's the ticket. Now, settle down under the covers and think about something you're looking forward to."

"Going to Sylvia's with Diedre tomorrow. Martha will be there, and they're going to teach us to become serious cooks." She burrowed into her pillow. "Sylvia said they're calling it Grandmas' Culinary Institute and we're going to learn new skills and recipes all summer long."

"They didn't tell Grant or me about this. What a fun idea. That gives you something happy to think about."

Zoe nodded against her pillow and yawned big.

Emily leaned over and planted a kiss on Zoe's temple. "Sweet dreams, sweet girl." She rose from the bed and, as Sabrina resumed her spot at Zoe's feet, left the room with Garth at her heels.

CHAPTER 2

*G*arth

We've had a week, all right. Running between home, Emily's office, the girls' school, and our favorite pizza parlor, cafés, and coffee shops. We've attended school functions and stopped for ice cream afterward every night for the past three days.

I'm not complaining. I love to be out and about with my Emily. Especially the pizza place—there are frequently tasty scraps of crust on the floor. And they always buy me a pup cup when we go for ice cream. I love peanut butter and banana pup cups.

The worst part is coming home to my buddy Sabrina. She's an ordinary dog—not a guide dog—and not a well-trained ordinary dog at that. She can't go out with us, so she's stuck at the house alone during these long days. I feel guilty after I've had a pup cup. She doesn't let on, but I'm certain she smells it on my breath.

I'm not sure, but I think today was the last day of what my humans call fourth grade. We're expecting our calendar to be less packed, our schedule to be less frenetic. That's what Emily and Grant kept saying to each other.

I'd love for my family to move at a slower pace for a while. I'm not sure what they're doing all the time, but I know each of them is tired, stressed, and on the edge of being cranky.

Sabrina and I put a lot of our energy into keeping everyone on an even keel. I'd been hoping we would get a break from our constant vigilance.

But based on the scene I just witnessed, our efforts are needed more than ever.

I trailed after Emily into our bedroom.

Grant was in the bathroom, brushing his teeth.

Emily knew every inch of our bedroom like the back of her hand. She didn't need my guidance in here. I headed for my bed in the corner of the room, circled three times, and settled in for a good night's sleep.

CHAPTER 3

*E*mily removed her shoes and felt for the open slot in the shoe rack that hung in her closet. She arranged them precisely in their place and followed a similar procedure with her suit and silk blouse. After arranging everything, she pulled her favorite cotton nightgown from its hook on the back of her closet door and slipped it over her head, its soft folds falling to her ankles.

With practiced precision, she made her way to the bathroom, passing Grant in the doorway. He pulled her into a hug, and they clung to each other, swaying slightly. The hug turned into a kiss until she gently pushed herself away from him.

"Don't get any amorous ideas. I think I'll fall asleep the moment my head hits the pillow."

"I'm afraid I'm in the same boat," Grant said. "We can make up for lost time tomorrow since it's Saturday."

Emily walked to the sink and picked up the toothpaste and her toothbrush from their assigned spots.

Grant leaned against the doorframe to the bathroom. "Diedre told me that Ava's parents invited both girls to spend the day tomorrow with Ava. They're going to a matinee movie, followed by bowling, and then dinner."

"Wow! Sounds fun. It's very nice of them. The girls will love it."

"Ava's parents are picking them up at nine. I thought I'd run out for croissants and coffee from our favorite bakery. You can have breakfast in bed, and we can laze around the house the entire day. I'd love for you to stay in that flimsy nightgown of yours."

Emily rinsed her mouth and turned back to her husband. "About that …"

Grant circled her waist with his hands as she tried to move past him. "We agreed—no plans this weekend. Whether or not the girls were home. This family needs downtime."

"I know, I know." Emily inhaled deeply before blowing out a breath. "I messed up my schedule. I thought I agreed to do something on Friday, today. Turns out, the workshop is tomorrow."

"What're you talking about?" Grant dropped his hands and turned toward the bedroom.

"The Foundation for the Blind is hosting a jobseekers workshop this Saturday. It's supposed to prepare recent graduates to look for jobs. They're covering how to find open positions, write a résumé, how to interview, and ways to handle rejection. I'm giving a presentation on interview skills, and I'll lead breakout sessions conducting mock interviews."

"That's all worthwhile, Em, but we agreed to an unplanned weekend." Grant ripped back the covers and got into bed.

"You're upset with me." Emily crossed to her side and climbed in next to him.

"I'm disappointed. We made a promise to each other. There will never be a time when one of us doesn't have to turn down an opportunity to keep a promise to our family."

"As I said, I thought the workshop was on Friday. I scheduled myself for a day out of the office. That was a legitimate mistake." She reached out to him and found him sitting rigidly against the headboard.

"You can't get out of it?"

"No! I don't want to get out of it. I'm an alum of the Foundation, for heaven's sake. They taught me the skills to regain my independent life after I went blind, and I'm extremely grateful. Whenever they request my help, I'm going to say yes." Her tone grew icy. "You've heard me talk about the 70 percent unemployment rate among the employable visually impaired *and* the Herculean effort it is for the blind to find jobs—even though they can do jobs anyone else can do through today's assistive technology."

Grant remained silent.

"I have a chance to provide tangible assistance to people who sorely need it. If I help even one person polish up their interview skills—if I give one person hope—my time will be well spent. I won't walk away from that, Grant."

He ran his hand across the stubble on his chin, then reached for her. "You're doing the right thing, Em. Those people need you. I'm just disappointed we won't have an entire day alone together. I'm sorry I acted like a petulant child."

"I'm disappointed we won't have the whole day to ourselves, too." Emily folded herself into his embrace. "I'll pay more attention to my calendar in the future. Since the girls are spending more time with our mothers this summer, let's take a day off when they're with Sylvia and Martha to stay in bed all day."

"Maybe we can even find two days in our schedules," he murmured as he held her close. He reached out a hand to turn off his bedside light, and they discovered they weren't as tired as they had suspected.

CHAPTER 4

Grant carried Emily's satchel as she and Garth made their way down the front steps to the waiting rideshare. He opened the rear door. Garth jumped in and settled on the floor while Grant placed the satchel on the seat next to where Emily would sit.

"I'm sorry I can't drive you to the Foundation."

"Don't be silly. It's way out by where my mom lives. I'd never have expected you to drive me there." She reached for his face and rose on her tiptoes to kiss him. "Besides, you need to wait here for Ava's family to pick up Zoe and Diedre. What do you plan to do the rest of the day?" Emily stepped back until she felt the opening created by the open car door and lowered herself onto the rear seat.

"I dunno. Maybe I'll install those cabinets I bought for the garage. They've been stacked up for weeks. It's about time I got them hung."

"That chore can wait. I think you should allow yourself a lazy morning. Read the paper, drink coffee, maybe even snooze on the sofa. You've earned it."

"While you're off at the crack of dawn to make an impactful presentation? I don't think so."

Emily reached for the car door and began to swing it shut. "Then knock off after lunch and do something you'll truly enjoy."

Grant put up a hand to impede the door's progress. "What time is your presentation?"

"One o'clock. I'm the first person after lunch. It's a bad time slot. I hope my audience doesn't fall asleep."

"Not a chance," he said. "You're a terrific speaker. They'll be hanging on every word." He let go of the door, and she pulled it shut.

Grant watched the rideshare pull into the street and speed away. He'd hang garage cabinets in the morning and do what Emily suggested in the afternoon. He already knew what he'd genuinely enjoy doing.

EMILY EXCUSED herself from the table where she was having lunch with a group of workshop attendees. She had found the morning sessions informative, interesting, and encouraging. Based on the enthusiastic flow of conversation around their table, she knew these attendees agreed with her assessment.

"I'm the first speaker after lunch," she told the group. "I'd like to review my notes. The morning sessions were first-rate—I've got tough acts to follow."

Her table mates uttered warm goodbyes, and she and Garth left the lunchroom. "Forward, outside," she commanded Garth.

Garth led her to the entrance, and they stepped out into the sunshine of a pristine early-summer day. "Find bench."

Garth led them twenty feet forward before he stopped.

Emily reached out a hand for one of the benches she remembered lined the walkway to the Foundation's entrance. She found what she was looking for and sat. Pulling her tablet from her satchel, she engaged the screen reader to locate her presentation. Emily listened to her notes, pausing them twice to think about her remarks before continuing. Satisfied that she was as prepared as she'd ever be, she reached for her satchel.

She was stowing her tablet in her satchel when a woman with a dog approached. "Excuse me," the woman said. "May I ask about your dog?"

Garth remained stretched out at Emily's feet and ignored the other dog, as he'd been trained to do.

The lab with the woman noticed Garth briefly but didn't try to engage with him or Emily.

"Sure," Emily said. "He's a guide dog. I can tell that you've got a dog with you. Is yours a guide, too?"

"Almost. Lonny is a guide dog in training—he's working right now with his harness and vest on. I'm a trainer at the Guide Dog Center. We came today because my cousin is attending. I'm here to support him."

"That's nice of you. How's Lonny doing with his training?"

"Spectacular. He's smart as a whip, and he has incredible drive. I knew the first time I worked with him he'd successfully complete the program to become a guide."

"That's interesting," Emily replied. "Garth's trainer told me the same thing about him."

"Lonny looks so much like Garth," the woman said. "They're the same pure black, his muzzle is the same shape, and he holds his tail like Garth does. I don't know—there's something intangible that connects these two beautiful boys. That's why I came over—to find out where you got Garth."

A grin slashed across Emily's face. "Garth is from the Guide Dog Center. Just like Lonny." Emily provided the year they had been partnered.

The woman slapped her thigh. "I knew it," she cried. "Lonny is younger than Garth, but there's such a similarity. Maybe they had the same mother or father. I'm going to look it up when I get back to the center."

"That's fun," Emily said. "Lonny may be your ... half-brother... or something, Garth."

Garth remained in the down position but ran his eyes over the dog that was a mirror image of himself.

"When do you expect he'll be ready for a match?" Emily asked.

"We'll be done with training by the end of the month. I know he'll be easy to place. I expect he'll be a working guide in a few months."

Emily got to her feet. "We'd better go. I'm making a presentation on interviewing after lunch. I want to give Garth a comfort break before we begin."

"We'll be in your session. Both my cousin and I are looking forward to it."

"That's good to hear." Emily grabbed Garth's harness. "See you both soon. And best of luck in finishing your training and finding your perfect match, Lonny. If you take after Garth in performance of a guide dog's duties as much as you do in appearance, you're going to improve someone's life more than you'll ever know."

CHAPTER 5

*E*mily stepped to the podium and turned toward the people seated in rows of chairs in front of her. Fifty-nine people had signed up for the workshop. From the hustle and bustle as people filed into the room after lunch, she guessed that most of those signed up were in attendance.

She couldn't know that the person who entered the room right before they closed the doors and slipped into a seat in the back row was Grant.

Garth thumped his tail against the floor in recognition of his family member, but Emily didn't notice.

"Good afternoon, everyone." Emily thanked the person who introduced her and continued. "You've found out about a job you'd love to have. You've completed the application and submitted your résumé. Maybe you've even survived a phone interview. And now you've received the call you were hoping for—they want you to appear for an in-person interview.

"The prospect of an interview is thrilling. You call your friends and family. You let yourself imagine your happy future." Emily hesitated before continuing. "And then reality sets in. You've got to ace an in-person interview!"

A titter of laughter ran around the room.

"Well—fear not. We're going to cover everything you need to know. Four of this morning's speakers and I are going to conduct mock interviews. If that's of interest to you, stay in the room after this session. We'll divide you up and instruct you where your group will move to."

She paused for a moment, standing up straight at the podium, as she visualized her presentation.

"First things first: you want to impress the people interviewing you. Initial impressions matter. So, get a good night's sleep. Wear clothing appropriate for the job, or even one level better. Hair combed, shoes shined.

"Arrive on time. Nothing kills your chances of getting a job more than being late! If you need to make a trial run to the company location, do it. It's your responsibility to get yourself to work.

"I assume you researched the company before you applied for the job, but now it's time to do more research. Learn about their business, products, or corporate culture. The internet will be your friend in this endeavor. Use this information to predict the questions they will ask you so you can prepare great answers ahead of time. You'll also need to come up with insightful questions to ask your interviewer. That will show the interviewer that you're interested in the company and savvy enough to learn about it."

Emily leaned over the podium, her posture relaxed as she warmed to her topic.

"Speaking of questions from the employer, is it okay for them to ask you how you can do this job as a blind person? Show of hands if you think it is."

She waited, giving the attendees time to consider their answer. Hands slowly lifted across the room.

"If you raised your hand, you are correct. Prospective employers can ask what sort of accommodation you need to do the job. They can't ask what caused your blindness, any medical challenges you face, or how you perform other aspects of daily life."

A man in the front row made a loud "pffft" sound.

"I hear you. This can be tricky in an interview. The key is to keep the conversation focused within legal guidelines. Let's take an example that happened to a friend of mine."

Emily coughed and felt for the water bottle she'd been told would be on the shelf in the podium. She found it, unscrewed the cap while listening for the telltale crackle that told her it was a new bottle, and took a sip of water.

"You arrive for your interview ten minutes early, using your white cane to navigate to the reception desk. The receptionist is dumbstruck when you inform her you are there for your interview. But you're blind, she blurts out.

"Yes. And I'm qualified for and capable of doing this job, you reply. I'm early, so I'll take a seat. Can you tell me where the chairs are?

"The receptionist gets out of her chair, walks around her desk, and takes your arm to drag you to a chair in the reception area."

A titter of recognition washes across the room.

"You politely tell her you can find the chair if she tells you which way to turn and how far ahead of you it's located. She ignores you, and you take your seat. This is annoying behavior, but don't let it ruin your mood.

"When someone comes to reception to escort you to your interview, you may go through the entire process again. Remember, you could be the first blind person they've encountered. They may not know the correct protocol, but you do. Calmly tell them they can help by offering you their elbow. Most people want to do the right thing."

Emily took a breath. "You're now in a room with the interviewer. The first words out of the interviewer's mouth are, 'You're blind. How did you get here?' They shouldn't ask that question, but it's common. You can call them out on their error, or you can answer the question. Say something simple like, 'I'm an expert on the city's mass transportation system' or 'I take rideshares everywhere.' If they press for details—how many bus transfers you had to make or how expensive your rideshare is—you can close the topic down by assuring them that you've been traveling independently for years and always get to your destination on time.

"It's good to prepare answers that steer the discussion back to the job opening. If they ask how you can perform the job as a blind person, you should be prepared to mention appropriate assistive technology. Most sighted people don't realize that major software programs are designed to be accessible to the visually impaired, and that there are screen readers and other software and devices that we are adept at using. This is an appropriate area of discussion. Remind them that there are resources available to help determine what accommodations you will need and there are tax breaks available to defray the cost. The average cost of assistive technology for a blind employee is only a one-time expense of $500, so be sure to work that into the conversation."

An alarm on her smart watch beeped. Emily tapped her screen to silence it. "That means we're ready to split up into groups for mock interviews. Gosh—that time went by fast. Thank you for your attention."

The audience erupted into applause. The person who had introduced Emily returned to the podium and began assigning the attendees to groups.

Emily heard Garth get to his feet and felt his tail swishing through the air.

A man made his way up the center aisle to her. He placed his hand on the small of her back and leaned in to whisper in her ear. "Knocked it out of the park. Again. As usual."

"Grant!"

"You should have seen these people. They were drinking in every word."

"What are you doing here? I thought you were spending the afternoon doing something you truly enjoy."

"That's exactly what I did. Watching you light up a room is the absolute best."

Emily flushed with pleasure at his remark.

"Mind if I sit in on your mock interviews? I'm learning a lot. When you're done, I thought we'd grab dinner at that restaurant by Martha's that you love."

Emily grinned. "On one condition: I'm buying dinner."

"You drive a hard bargain, Emily Main. It's a deal."

CHAPTER 6

*G*arth

I lay by Emily's empty chair, obeying her Down, Stay command like the pro I am. Lonny was positioned one chair over next to his trainer. I could tell by the way he breathed that he'd segued into a nap from his Down, Stay command.

I considered following Lonny's lead, but Emily and Grant were at the front of the room. They were doing something I'd never seen before. I was interested.

Emily addressed the small group seated around me. "Before we begin mock interviews, I want to cover the topic of handshakes. I suspect you know most of the etiquette I'm about to share, but I want to make sure. I want everyone to practice shaking hands in an interview because it's an important part of the process."

"My husband, Grant Johnson, is next to me to demonstrate because we have at least one sighted person in the audience. Grant also has sight. Grant—will you show and describe the appropriate way to greet a blind person?"

Grant took over. "I'm extending my hand while addressing the blind person. If I were greeting you, I'd say 'Hello, Emily. It's Grant. I'm extending my hand if you'd like to shake.' "

"Perfect," Emily praised. She located his outstretched hand and shook it. "And if you didn't know me?"

"Instead of saying, 'It's Grant,' I'd introduce myself and proceed with the rest. Since blind people can't see someone smile at them to say hello, a handshake greeting is the best method."

"Exactly. I think I speak for everyone in the blind community when I say we wish everyone would follow this etiquette. Encountering sighted people who know to do this is rare. Chances are the person who is interviewing you won't know to proceed this way."

Emily faced my direction to address the crowd. "Whenever I meet someone—whether at work or socially—I extend my hand first as I give my name. Sometimes this creates an awkward moment. Things get tricky if their hands are full and they have to shift things around to free up a hand to shake mine, but it's the best way to handle things in an interview. What other handshake tips do you have, Grant?"

"Slide your hand into the one you're shaking until both palms are touching. Don't grasp the other person's hand so tightly that it hurts them, but don't allow your hand to feel like a limp fish, either."

The humans around me laughed.

"No one enjoys that sort of handshake."

"You'll all have a chance to practice your handshake when it's your turn to interview," Emily said. "We'll follow the same script for everyone, and we'll learn from each other's mistakes. Grant has graciously agreed to replace me as the interviewer for our group. That'll give me the chance to listen to each interview and offer feedback, without being distracted by acting as the interviewer."

She called the cousin of Lonny's trainer to the front as Grant guided Emily to her seat next to me. As promised, they practiced shaking hands. Both Emily and Grant gave pointers. The mock interview progressed, with Emily and Grant commenting, until the cousin was done and the next person walked to the front of the room. The entire process repeated itself.

My eyelids grew heavy. I looked over at Lonny. He'd rolled onto his side, and his paws twitched. I knew what that meant. He was dreaming, and it included an adventure. He might be chasing a rabbit. That's what I was usually dreaming about when my paws quivered.

I love dreams where rabbit chasing is involved. I rolled onto my side, shut my eyes, and was soon asleep.

I woke when Emily grasped my working harness and called my name. "Okay, Garth. Nap time is over."

I got to my feet. People were filing out of the room. I spotted Lonny as he exited through the door. An involuntary 'woof' escaped my lips. I was instantly ashamed of myself. Guide dogs were not noisy.

"Would you like to go out with Lonny? I think it's time for a comfort break. Follow Grant," Emily commanded.

He led us out of the building to the dog relief station. Emily had been right. That's where Lonny and his trainer were going.

We both took care of business, then engaged in our own form of handshake—a thorough sniffing of the intimate parts of each other's bodies.

His scent was both familiar and comforting. I liked this Lonny. I could tell he feels the same way about me.

Emily and Lonny's trainer concluded their conversation and said goodbye to each other. The trainer commanded Lonny to move forward.

I watched Lonny lead the woman to the curb. She commanded him to move forward into the street, but he refused. One of those silent cars was driving by them. Those were tricky. Emily hears cars in the street, but not these kinds of cars.

If Lonny had followed his trainer's command, the car would have hit them. This was called intelligent disobedience and was one of the hardest and most crucial skills for a guide dog to learn.

My heart swelled with pride. Lonny had executed the behavior perfectly. I watched as his trainer showered him with praise.

Lonny was going to become a guide dog, just like me. I was certain of it. I hoped he'd be paired with someone as special as my Emily.

"Ready to head for the restaurant?" Grant asked Emily.

"Absolutely. I'm starved. Let's retrieve my satchel and get going."

I tore my eyes away from Lonny as I resumed my life's work of guiding Emily.

CHAPTER 7

Sylvia Johnson caught Martha Main's eye across the long family dinner table.

Martha's smile reflected her gratitude for being included in the monthly family dinners that Sylvia hosted for her sons, Grant and Craig, and their families.

Sylvia nodded and smiled back. When her son Grant had married Emily Main, she'd not only gained a lovely daughter-in-law but a new granddaughter in Emily's ward, Zoe, and a best friend in Emily's mother, Martha. That Craig's wife, Gina, had been Emily's best friend cemented the already close family bonds.

Craig picked up the platter of chicken enchiladas and sent them around the table again. "These are great, Mom. They were my favorite when we were growing up."

"Mine, too," Grant chimed in. "You used to keep them in the refrigerator for after-school snacks when we were in high school."

"Our friends wanted to come to our house because there were plenty of your enchiladas," Craig said. "Remember that, Grant?"

"I sure do. You must have made thousands of these while we were in school, Mom."

Sylvia laughed. "You may be right. Even all these years later, I don't need to look at a recipe."

"They're delicious, Sylvia," Martha interjected.

Gina helped herself to another enchilada when the plate came her way. "I'm glad it's family dinner night," Gina said. "Craig and I want to ask about everyone's summer plans."

"Martha and I are hosting the girls here next week. The big thing we'll be doing is teaching them to cook."

"Grandmas' Culinary Institute," the girls chorused in unison.

Gina chuckled. "That's a fabulous idea. I wish I were free to attend. You're both spectacular cooks. I'm sure I'd learn a lot."

Both older women flushed at the compliment.

"Call me any time you have a cooking question," Sylvia said.

"The same goes for me," Martha added.

"What are you girls doing after your week with Sylvia and Martha?" Craig asked.

"I'm going to a summer theater camp at the youth theater," Diedre said.

Gina asked, "Is that the youth theater where you starred in *Mary Poppins Jr.* last spring?"

"Yep. Do you remember our friend Ava?"

"The little girl who stepped into the role of Burt when you took over as Mary Poppins?"

"That's the one. She's going to the program too."

"That's nice to have a friend at the camp," Gina observed.

"I know a bunch of other kids from Mary Poppins who are going, too."

"What about you, Zoe? Are you enrolled in the theater camp?"

Zoe shook her head no. "I'm going to a STEM summer camp. We'll do three experiments each day as a class, and we'll have group and individual activities, too. At least that's what the website says."

"Wow! Grant and I would have loved that when we were your age," Craig said.

Zoe shrugged.

"You're not excited?" Gina asked.

"It's just that I won't know anyone there. Diedre will know everyone in her program."

"You'll be with other brainiacs like yourself," Diedre said. "When you work on projects with other kids, you'll make friends."

Zoe shrugged again.

"Look how quickly you made friends with Ava," Diedre added.

"That's right," Grant interjected. "You introduced Ava to our family. If it weren't for you, Diedre wouldn't have auditioned for *Mary Poppins Jr.*, either." He reached behind Emily to pat Zoe on the back. "It's daunting for anybody to enter a group where they know no one. You're very empathic and know how to make friends."

"I wholeheartedly agree." Martha nodded encouragingly at the girl she loved like a granddaughter.

"What about your family?" Grant asked. "Are the three of you taking a vacation this summer?"

"It's complicated having an infant in tow," Gina said, smiling at Alex as he played contentedly in his travel playpen. "We're renting a large Airbnb in La Jolla the first two weeks of July. My mom and dad are staying with us for the first week. We wanted to invite everyone— including you, Martha—to come the second week."

"Heavens. How big is this place?" Sylvia asked.

"Six bedrooms, plus a sleeping porch," Craig said. "There'll be plenty of room and we're only two blocks from the beach."

"Can we?" Zoe and Diedre asked their parents in unison.

Emily turned toward Grant. "It sounds like fun, but I'm extra busy at work while Dhruv is on paternity leave."

"The girls have their summer camps during that time, too," Grant replied. "Thank you for the offer, but it won't work for us."

"Mom and Martha?" Gina asked.

"I'd love to," Sylvia said.

All eyes at the table turned to Martha.

"I need to check with Doug," she said. "I believe we have plans." She blushed like a schoolgirl as she mentioned Doug Roberts, Gina's uncle. She'd met him at Gina and Craig's wedding, and they'd been dating ever since.

"Emily and I want to take a family trip later in the summer." All eyes turned to Grant. "We'd like the girls to see places they've never been. There are so many natural wonders, museums, and cultural destinations in the United States. We intended to bring it up at dinner tonight. We're also including Sylvia and Martha."

"Gina and Craig—you and Alex are also welcome," Emily interrupted.

"A destination for a middle-school family won't be ideal for an infant." Gina chuckled. "Thank you for including us, but a lazy week at the beach is all we can manage. We'll leave the heavy sightseeing to you."

"I don't have any travel plans this summer, so I'm in," Sylvia said.

"Everyone on the trip will get to pick a favorite activity for us to do during one day of the trip. That way, we'll experience new things and each of us will have a day of the vacation devoted to something they're especially interested in," Emily said.

"That's a genius idea," Sylvia agreed.

"Where are we going?" Zoe asked.

"That'll depend on what everyone's 'one special thing' is," Emily replied. "You and Diedre can think about it next week. Do some internet research. Talk to each other and your grandmothers. You too, Sylvia and Mom. If you're on the trip, you get to pick the activity for one day."

"That's a marvelous idea. I love to tour art museums when I'm on vacation. It doesn't have to be one of the big, famous ones. Smaller, local museums are less crowded and just as interesting. We'll come up with ideas by the end of next week."

"Perfect," Emily said. "Mom? What about you? Will you join us?"

Martha cleared her throat. "That's a kind invitation, and I think your approach is terrific," she said. "If I were going to be around, I'd be happy to go." Everyone put down their knives and forks, waiting for her to continue.

"You're going somewhere, Mom?"

"I've been meaning to tell you," Martha said. "Doug and I are going to London." The room became silent. "For two weeks in August."

Sylvia was the first to speak. "OMG! I knew something was up with you. When were you going to tell us?"

"We made the final decision last night."

"That's wonderful." Gina was the first to weigh in.

"Honey?" Martha faced Emily.

"It's great news," Emily replied. "I'm happy for you. I guess I'm just surprised."

"I've always wanted to go to Europe," Martha said. "I'm extremely excited."

"As you should be," Grant said. "You deserve a big adventure, Martha."

"Mom says Uncle Doug is crazy about you," Gina murmured, a faraway tone in her voice. "He's the nicest man. This sounds so romantic. Strolling arm in arm through Hyde Park; afternoon tea at the Ritz; shopping at Harrods ..."

Diedre giggled. "Gosh, Martha—"

"Okay, everyone," Martha interrupted. "That's enough of that." Martha placed her napkin on the table and rose from her chair. "Who wants a slice of homemade strawberry pie for dessert?"

She headed for the kitchen to serve the pie without waiting for their replies.

CHAPTER 8

Stephanie Patel lowered the sleeping baby into her crib. She held her breath as she gingerly slid her hands out from beneath her, waiting for Amelia to wail again.

Amelia puckered her lips and swiped across her face with a balled fist.

Please stay asleep. Stephanie sent up the silent prayer. She and Dhruv had returned from the pediatrician an hour earlier, after a sleepless night spent trying to comfort their infant daughter.

The doctor had diagnosed an ear infection and sent them home with a prescription for an antibiotic and recommended a painkiller. Stephanie had waited in the car while Dhruv filled the prescription and they'd given Amelia her first dose right there in the parking lot.

Amelia had fallen asleep in the car on the way home but resumed crying the moment they removed her from her car seat. They brought her inside and gave her a dose of painkiller.

Stephanie volunteered to rock Amelia until the painkiller took effect, and she insisted Dhruv take a nap. As tired as Stephanie was, she knew Dhruv was more sleep-deprived than she was.

He'd burned the midnight oil the previous several nights, working on a project for his employer. Dhruv was on paternity leave but continued to handle the project for one of his business units. The manager of the unit didn't want to work with anyone other than Dhruv. Emily, Dhruv's manager, had been assigned to this unit while he was on leave, but the unit manager had contacted Dhruv directly on his personal cell phone. Dhruv knew that his being out on leave created a hardship for his team. Amelia slept most of the time—when she wasn't sick—so Dhruv continued working on the project.

Dhruv had taken Stephanie up on her offer and fallen asleep on the sofa the moment he lay down.

Amelia's brow relaxed, and she brought her hand to her side, without batting at her ear. Her cheek rose and fell with her rhythmic breathing.

Stephanie released the breath she'd been holding and tiptoed out of the room, colliding with Dhruv in the hallway.

He steadied her and they both froze, listening for sounds from Amelia's bedroom. There were none; they hadn't woken her up.

Dhruv pulled his wife down the hall, where they collapsed into each other's arms.

"Holy cow," Stephanie said. "I'd heard about parental fatigue, but I had no idea how tired I could be."

"It's like being a battery that won't hold a charge," Dhruv agreed. "Even when I get a decent night's sleep, I'm beat by lunchtime." He smoothed the hair off his wife's face. "That nap was brief but powerful. I'm fine now. It's your turn to lie down."

"Thanks, sweetheart. I've set the alarm on my phone," she held up the smartphone that she always carried in her pocket, "for Amelia's next dose of antibiotics."

"Good. My mother is coming over later to bring us food for a couple of days. She said we need to focus on Amelia—we don't need to worry about meals."

"That's nice of her." Stephanie's mouth stretched into a wide yawn. "Knowing Pari, we'll have enough food to last a week. And I, for one, am profoundly grateful. Wake me up when she gets here so I can thank her."

"I'll do no such thing. You need to sleep as much as possible.

Before Amelia was born, my aunties told us to sleep when the baby slept. I thought that was ridiculous, but I now know how right they were."

"Be sure to thank her for me, then."

"Will do. Go crawl into bed and don't worry about a thing. If Amelia stirs, I'll take care of her."

Stephanie pulled back and planted a kiss on his cheek. "What are you going to do if she's quiet?"

Dhruv paused before he spoke.

"I have a few lines of code I want to test before I'm sure I've fixed the problem I've been working on. I'll attend to that and wrap up this project."

Stephanie shook her head slowly. "I hope your company appreciates how dedicated you are. Anyone else would have left the matter in their replacement's hands without a backward glance."

Dhruv looked away.

"I know you're not made that way, Dhruv," Stephanie whispered. "That's one thing I love about you. But please don't burn yourself out. We may have some rough days ahead of us with Amelia until the infection clears. I'll need to rely on you."

"I'm here for you," Dhruv replied, the depth of his conviction clear in his tone. "Now—stop talking and get some sleep."

Stephanie yawned again and headed for their bed.

DHRUV OPENED THEIR APARTMENT DOOR, his index finger raised in front of his lips.

Pari Patel nodded in recognition as she slipped quietly past him, her arms laden with canvas bags filled with sealed plastic containers.

Dhruv relieved his mother of her burden and placed the bags on the kitchen counter. "Mama," he whispered as he planted a kiss on top of her head.

"There's more," she whispered back. "A hot casserole dish of chicken shawarma is in the car."

"I'll bring it in for you," he said. "I hope we have room for all this in our fridge."

"Don't worry. You will. I'm an expert at arranging things in a refrigerator." She pulled her car keys from her pocket and handed them to him. "Leave it to me."

Dhruv exited the kitchen while his mother got to work. She opened the refrigerator and extracted a cylinder with an eye dropper cap that held Amelia's antibiotic. She knew how important the medication was and didn't want to spill any while she was rearranging the refrigerator. Placing the precious bottle on top of the refrigerator and out of harm's way, she got busy moving items between shelves to create space for the food she'd spent the day preparing. She found a spot for the medication at the back of the bottom shelf, wedged between a jug of orange juice and a large carton of Greek yogurt.

By the time Dhruv returned with the casserole, items needing refrigeration occupied every inch of counter space.

"Oh, mama," Dhruv murmured, eyeing the surrounding chaos. "Stephanie needs things to stay in their place in the fridge. You know that."

"There's just not room," Pari replied defensively. "You're home on leave now, right?"

"Well ... yes."

"Then you'll have to tell her where things are and put them back in their place once some of the food I've brought gets eaten and there's more room in here." She stacked the remaining two refrigerated items on top of other items, where they teetered precariously. "There." She stepped back and surveyed the contents of the refrigerator. "That's the best I can do."

"What about the casserole I brought in from the car?"

"It's for your dinner tonight. Set the oven to 200 degrees and stick it in there. It'll hold nicely until you're ready for them. Chicken thighs don't easily dry out."

"Will you stay to eat with us?"

She shook her head. "We're having your uncles and their wives over for dinner. It's been on the calendar for weeks." She pointed to the refrigerator. "That's why I brought so many dishes. I was already fixing all this, anyway. I simply made a bit more of each."

The baby monitor on the kitchen counter crackled. Amelia began to whimper.

"Oh, no," Dhruv said. "She's not due for either her painkiller or her antibiotic for another four hours."

"Sounds like she's hungry," she said.

"I'll wake Stephanie." Dhruv moved toward the hallway.

"I gave Amelia a bottle of breast milk from the freezer last week. Do you still have some?"

"We do."

"Let's allow Stephanie to sleep. Fix a bottle while I get Amelia before she wakes her. I'd love to give her a bottle. In fact, I'd like to rock her until I have to go home to get dinner on the table."

"That would be helpful," Dhruv said, already digging through the freezer for the milk. He had the bottle ready when his mother walked into the living room, her granddaughter held against her chest, Amelia's head nestled against Pari's neck.

"I changed her," she said, settling into the rocking chair.

Dhruv handed her the bottle.

She double-checked that the milk was the correct temperature, then offered it to Amelia.

The baby latched onto the nipple and drained the bottle in no time.

Her grandmother burped her and cradled her in her arms. Amelia drifted off to sleep without a peep.

"You make it look so easy," Dhruv said.

"She's a smart one—knows not to give her grandma any trouble." She hugged Amelia to her chest.

"Are you sure you want to stay here to rock her?"

"Positive."

Dhruv shifted from foot to foot, rubbing his hands together.

"What?" his mother asked. "You do that when something's on your mind."

"Is it all right if I head to my office for a few minutes? I need to run a test on our work computer. It'll go much faster there than on my laptop."

"I thought you were on this newfangled paternity leave."

Dhruv continued to fidget. "I am. I'm revising a project I thought I'd finished before I went on leave. It needs a few corrections before it's all done. My team is working extra hours, covering for me while I'm out. I hate to dump this on them, too. It's much simpler for me to finish this."

His mother looked at him. "You'll be back before I want to leave?"

He nodded.

"We're having company. I need to be home on time to get dinner on the table. Everything's ready, but I still have a few last-minute things to do."

"No worries. And Stephanie is here. If you have to leave, put Amelia back in her crib. She'll wake up if she cries."

Pari narrowed her eyes.

"But I'll be home."

"Then get going."

Dhruv snatched his keys from the dish by the door. "Thanks, Mom. This is so helpful. I'll be back before you know it."

CHAPTER 9

*D*hruv tore his eyes from his computer screen as he reached for his cell phone and swiped to accept the incoming call.

"Hey, Mom."

"Are you almost home?"

He didn't answer.

"Dhruv! You're still at the office, aren't you?"

Dhruv remained silent.

"You should have left for home ten minutes ago. Stephanie's still asleep and so is Amelia. I put her in her crib half an hour ago."

"You can leave." He checked his watch. "It's almost two hours before her next doses of antibiotic and painkiller. I'll be home by then."

"I certainly hope so, Dhruv," his mother huffed. "I hate the thought of Stephanie waking up, not knowing if one of us is here."

"I'll text her that I'm at the office. She'll check her phone first thing when she wakes up."

"She'll still be alone."

"Mom—Stephanie can take care of herself and Amelia on her own. You don't need to worry."

"I'm aware of how independent she is." His mother's tone was stern when she continued. "Sick babies are a lot of work. This is the first sick infant that either of you has experienced. It would be helpful for you to be here."

"I understand. And I will be. This program should finish running in another five minutes. I'm so close to being finished with this project. Ten minutes at the most."

"I'm heading home now," his mother said. "Promise me you'll send that text the minute we hang up—before you put your head back into your work. I know what you're like when you're focused on that computer. Everything else ceases to exist for you."

"I promise. And thank you for bringing us food for the entire week and for staying with Amelia."

"I'm happy to help. That little girl is my special sunshine. I'll call tomorrow to see how she's feeling."

They disconnected the call, and Dhruv sent his text to Stephanie before diving back into his work.

STEPHANIE HEARD the ping on her phone, alerting her to an incoming text message. She reached for it on the bed next to her and listened to Dhruv's text.

He assured her he would complete the revisions to the software program he was working on and be home long before Amelia needed her meds.

Stephanie dropped the phone onto the bed next to her and listened for any sounds from the baby monitor that lived on her nightstand.

Amelia was quiet.

Stephanie snuggled into her pillow and slept until the monitor crackled. She heard Amelia's low-volume whimper. "Dhruv," she called. "Dhruv," she repeated, with more volume.

Her call remained unanswered.

Biscuit rose from her bed in the corner of Stephanie's room and came to her side, resting her nose on the edge of the bed.

Stephanie tapped her watch, and it gave her the time. Amelia was due for her medication in an hour. She ran her hand along the top of her guide dog's head.

"I hear, girl. Amelia is hungry." She swung her feet to the floor and padded into Amelia's room, with Biscuit at her heels. "I'll nurse Amelia, change her diaper, and take you, Sugar, and Rocco out to do your business. Unless Dhruv gets home before I'm done and can attend to all of you. Then it'll be time for Amelia's antibiotic and painkiller."

Stephanie picked up Amelia and settled into the rocking chair in the corner of the nursery.

Amelia sucked hungrily. When she was done, Stephanie held the baby against her shoulder, rubbing and patting her back until she burped.

"That was a good one," Stephanie whispered as she pressed Amelia's forehead against her cheek. "You don't feel feverish."

She stood and moved to the changing table. "Let's get you changed, and then we'll take your doggies outside."

Stephanie reached for the baby wipes and clean diapers before she began her task. Everything was in its assigned place, and she moved through the diaper change with lightning speed.

Stephanie returned Amelia to her bed while she washed her hands, grabbed her phone, and placed Biscuit in his working harness. She reached out with her left foot for her hands-free slip-in sneakers. They weren't in their usual spot below Biscuit's harness. Stephanie swept her foot over the floor where her shoes should have been but didn't find them.

She rested her palm against the wall and fought a rising tide of irritation. *Who moved my shoes?* Dhruv's mother had just left, and his aunt had stopped by the day before. Stephanie remembered that his aunt had commented on how much baby stuff they'd had lying around. Maybe the woman had tidied up, thinking she was being helpful.

Think. Where would she have moved my shoes?

Stephanie took two steps to the left and found the door to the coat closet. She opened the space she and Dhruv rarely used and, once more, stretched her foot out to explore for her shoes. Her foot found what she was searching for. *Yes!* She stepped into her shoes, pleased she'd figured this out. She strapped on the front carrier and went to the nursery to install her daughter.

They exited the apartment. Biscuit obeyed Stephanie's command and took them to the rear door of the building. Sugar and Rocco, Dhruv's golden retriever and dachshund, trailed behind. Stephanie removed her dog's working harness and walked with her on a short leash. When Biscuit squatted, Stephanie put a plastic waste bag over her hand. She bent and ran her hand along Biscuit's back until she reached her tail.

Biscuit stood when she was done. Stephanie lowered the waste bag to the ground and easily found what she was looking for. She scooped up Biscuit's waste, tied a knot in the bag, and put Biscuit back into her working harness. She deposited the bag in the waste can by the door into the building. Dhruv would clean up after the other dogs when he got home.

They retraced their steps to the apartment, Rocco leading the way. Stephanie hung Biscuit's harness on its hook by the front door. "Let's feed you," she said as she stepped into the kitchen. She scooped kibble into each dog's bowl and set it in its assigned spot on the floor.

The trio dug into their supper with relish.

Amelia whimpered.

Stephanie took her into the living room and removed her from the front carrier. Amelia's forehead was warm to the touch. The anti-inflammatory painkiller was wearing off and her daughter's fever had returned. She consulted her watch. It was still thirty minutes before Amelia's next doses.

Amelia was now crying and tugging at her earlobe.

Stephanie stood and paced, jiggling the baby.

Amelia sobbed.

Stephanie walked into the nursery and retrieved the talking fore-head digital thermometer they'd received as a baby gift. She took Amelia's temperature and winced when the readout told her Amelia had a temperature of one hundred two and a half.

"You poor girl," she murmured in Amelia's ear. "No wonder you're crying. No one feels good with a fever." She slipped Amelia out of her onesie and continued to walk with her, holding her loosely so Stephanie's own body heat didn't make her daughter warmer.

Amelia took a deep breath before emitting a high-pitched cry.

Stephanie closed her eyes and inhaled slowly. Listening to other people's babies crying was annoying; listening to her own infant wail was torture. She resumed walking with Amelia in a futile attempt to comfort her suffering infant.

CHAPTER 10

*D*hruv checked his watch. Amelia was due for her meds in thirty minutes. He needed to head home. There wouldn't be much traffic early on a Sunday evening. The drive should only take twenty-five minutes.

He reread his email to the business unit that explained his software program modifications. He corrected two typos and broke a run-on sentence into two shorter ones. He double-checked that he'd copied Kari, his counterpart in the Denver office, and pressed send.

Dhruv stuffed his laptop and phone into his satchel, logged off his desktop, and hurried to the elevator. He stabbed at the button.

The elevator arrived, and he stepped into it. Dhruv was about to press the button for the lobby when he stepped back onto his floor.

He'd forgotten to attach the file to his email. He was certain of it. The file would load much quicker from his desktop computer than from his laptop.

Dhruv ran back to his office. He dropped his satchel to the floor, logged into the network, and opened his email. He'd been correct—he'd forgotten to include the attachment. Dhruv rectified his error with lightning speed and had logged off again when his phone began to play "You Are My Sunshine." Stephanie's ringtone.

He answered on the first ring and winced when he heard Amelia's yawling.

"Are you on the way home?" Stephanie's words were hard to hear above the baby's cries.

"I'm leaving right this instant." Dhruv thought about giving her the comforting assurance that he was on his way, but he was incapable of lying.

"DHRUV!" Stephanie's patience drained away like a flushed toilet. "You should have left long before now and you know it."

Dhruv recoiled at the rebuke.

"You're not here to help comfort her. She's clearly miserable."

"I can hear that." His voice was full of regret that she didn't notice. He picked up the satchel and ran back to the elevator. Once again, he stabbed at the button. "I'm at the elevator. I'll lose this call when I step on it and the doors close."

"You'd better not go back to do one more thing," Stephanie's voice snapped like a whip. "And don't pretend you haven't done *that* before."

"I won't," Dhruv made a guilty shake of his head. "I've got everything I need with me and I should be home in twenty minutes—twenty-five, tops."

"I need you here, Dhruv." Stephanie disconnected the call.

The elevator doors opened and Dhruv hurled himself inside, dropping his phone into his satchel as he punched the button for the lobby. He didn't notice the phone catch on the zipper and slide to the floor of the elevator.

When the elevator arrived at the first floor, Dhruv ran across the lobby and raced across the concourse to the parking garage. Leaving Stephanie alone with their child the first time she was sick was unfair to his wife. He was determined to be home in the twenty minutes he'd promised her.

CHAPTER 11

Stephanie's phone alarm announced Amelia's medication time. "Thank goodness," she muttered under her breath. "Let's get that painkiller in you first, sweetheart." She brushed a kiss against Amelia's damp and feverish forehead.

Stephanie located the bottle of infant anti-inflammatory on the kitchen counter. Dhruv had scored the plunger with a pair of scissors to mark the spot for the proper dose. She pulled out the plunger and made sure she could feel the marking. Confident she would administer the correct dose, Stephanie picked up the inconsolable infant and cradled her in the crook of her arm. Stephanie held her breath as she placed the syringe between Amelia's cheek and gum. She'd read stories about infants that spit out their medicine. Online new-mom chat groups were full of them.

Amelia quieted in her arms.

She eased the plunger to deliver the small dose of sweet-smelling liquid. Stephanie released a heavy sigh when Amelia swallowed. She felt the baby's face and wiped away a tiny, sticky drop of the medicine from the corner of her mouth.

"Look at you! You're a champ at taking medicine." Relief washed over Stephanie, and she kissed the top of her daughter's head. "You'll feel better when this medicine takes effect."

She lowered Amelia into her pack n' play. "Now you need your antibiotic. That's what will make the infection in your ear go away."

Amelia fussed.

"I know, I know. I'll be back with your antibiotic in a jiffy."

Stephanie returned to the kitchen and opened the refrigerator door. They'd placed the precious antibiotic on the front of the top shelf, on the far right side. She extended her right hand, hitting an immovable wall of plastic storage containers and ziplock bags; she found no small bottle of medicine.

Cold air from the refrigerator poured onto her bare arm. She pursed her lips and felt along the side of the interior of the box, making sure she was exploring the top shelf. She was—as she knew she would be. Her muscle memory knew each shelf of her refrigerator.

Amelia wailed.

Stephanie searched the entire width of the top shelf. Amelia's medicine wasn't along the front of the shelf. Now, the irritation she'd squelched earlier when someone moved her shoes flared. She rested her head against the refrigerator and tried to calm her racing mind.

If Dhruv's mother had packed the entire refrigerator as full as she had the top shelf, finding Amelia's antibiotic would be a formidable task.

She ran her hands across the shelves. The refrigerator was as full as if they were hosting thirty for Thanksgiving. The medicine bottle wasn't along the front of any of the shelves. She'd have to move things out of the way so she could reach into each shelf and feel every item until she found the medicine.

"Mommy's sorry, honey," she called over her shoulder. "I've got to find it, and that'll take time." *Because your grandmother and daddy were thoughtless.*

The refrigerator's fan speed increased because of the open door. Stephanie's fingers were numb. She moved a covered glass bowl to the counter behind her and reached her hand into the middle of the top shelf.

Working fast, she examined every item. As she completed one section of the shelf, she scooted items over to access the next section.

As she was rearranging items to complete her exploration of the top shelf, she heard a gurgling sound. Stephanie reached for the sound and felt a cylindrical metallic object lying on its side. Liquid poured out of it, falling to the shelves below.

An open can of soda?! Who left that in here? She cursed in a way that would have astonished her fellow third-grade teachers.

Stephanie grasped and righted the open soda can. As she pulled her hand back, she knocked a plastic container onto the floor. The lid dislodged. Noodles in a pungent sauce puddled at her feet and seeped between her toes.

Amelia's cries increased a few decibels.

Sugar entered the kitchen and began helping herself to the noodles, licking the floor until Stephanie shooed the dog away.

"Where the hell are you, Dhruv?" She tapped at her watch. He wouldn't be home for another ten minutes, at the earliest. "This is taking too long. I'm going to call your daddy and ask him to FaceTime with me. He'll be able to find your antibiotic in the refrigerator."

Stephanie placed her call. It rang and eventually went to voicemail. Dhruv didn't answer the phone when he was driving. Stephanie expected this.

She dialed again. Two consecutive calls from her signaled an emergency. He'd pull over and call her.

Stephanie waited. Dhruv didn't call.

Amelia sobbed.

Stephanie repeated the sequence of calls. Dhruv didn't respond. He wasn't available to help resolve the problem. Anger flooded her until she felt like she was drowning in it.

"I hear you, sweet girl," Stephanie raised her voice to be heard above Amelia's shrieking. "It's crucial to take your antibiotic on time and we're already late on your dose because I can't find it. I'm going to call someone who will help us. Hang in there. I'm going as fast as I can."

Stephanie opened the Be My Eyes app on her phone and requested assistance. A sighted volunteer answered her request within seconds. The app connected Stephanie and the volunteer on a live video feed through her phone's camera. They heard each other, and the volunteer saw video captured by Stephanie's phone.

Amelia's cries died down as the painkiller took effect.

"Hello. I see the inside of a refrigerator and part of a floor. If you raise your camera six inches, I'll be able to see more of the refrigerator," the volunteer said.

Stephanie explained what she was looking for.

The volunteer directed Stephanie's movement of the camera as they went through the refrigerator, shelf by shelf.

"Do you see something spilled?" Stephanie asked.

"Yes. There's a dark pool of liquid that appears to be contained within the rim of a food storage lid in the middle of the second shelf. Do you want me to direct you to clean it up?"

"No. I'll do it later. It's good to know where it is."

They continued their search.

"It has to be in here," Stephanie said, panic seeping into her voice as they worked their way along the bottom shelf. "I know …"

"I see it," the volunteer interrupted. "It's really hidden." The volunteer described the placement of the medication bottle between the jug of orange juice and a large carton of Greek yogurt at the back of the bottom shelf.

"I'm going to reach for it," Stephanie said. "Will you stay on the line with me to make sure I find it?"

"Of course. I've got children. They're older now, but I remember how important those antibiotics were when they had ear infections."

"Here," Stephanie exclaimed. "Got it." She pulled the small bottle from the refrigerator, being careful not to upend any of the items in her path.

She turned her phone toward the bottle, and the volunteer

directed her to rotate it slightly left. The volunteer read the label to Stephanie.

"That's it!" she cried.

"Do you need me to read dosage instructions for you?"

"No. I'm clear on that."

"Is there anything else I can help with?"

"No. You've been great. Thank you so much."

"Happy to help."

Stephanie tapped the end call button. She took a deep breath to steady her nerves. These last twenty minutes had been intensely stressful. And it all could have been avoided.

She'd have words with Dhruv when he got home. Right now, she needed to give Amelia her antibiotic. She dispensed it the same way she'd done the painkiller. Amelia was as accepting of this as she had been with her earlier medication.

Stephanie replaced the antibiotic in the right front corner of the top shelf and settled onto the sofa, cradling Amelia on her lap. As she waited for Dhruv, she rehearsed what she wanted to say to him.

The door opened ten minutes later, and Dhruv rushed into the living room. Rocco and Sugar bounded over to greet him, but Biscuit stayed at Stephanie's side.

Stephanie leaned against the sofa cushions, her feet tucked under her.

Amelia lay against her mother's chest, sound asleep.

"Sorry I'm so late," Dhruv said. "There was an accident on the way home, so traffic was detoured. How did she tolerate taking her medicine? It looks like everything is peaceful here …"

Stephanie held up her hand to stop him. "Amelia did fine. We are peaceful now. But I've had an awful time, and your thoughtlessness—and that of your family—is the cause."

Dhruv stopped in his tracks. "You'd better tell me—everything."

Stephanie recounted her evening, starting with her call to Dhruv that he didn't pick up.

"I didn't get your call. I would have pulled over and FaceTimed with you." Dhruv patted at his pockets. "I don't have my phone." He raked his hands through his hair. "I must have left it at my office."

"You're NOT going back tonight to get it!"

"Of course not. I wouldn't think of it." Dhruv crossed the room to the sofa and sat next to her.

Sugar and Rocco followed close on his heels, sensing that their master was in hot water.

"You're completely justified in how you're feeling. I let you down." He laid his palm against her cheek. "I'm more sorry than I can express. As you know, I'm obsessive-compulsive about my work. I will change that behavior."

"This wasn't fair to me." Stephanie stopped, allowing her words to hang between them. "Imagine how you would have felt in my shoes."

"I wouldn't have coped like you did. You're remarkable."

"This can't happen again."

"It won't—I promise.

"I'll hold you to that."

"Fair enough. I'll talk to my mother and aunts, too."

"You can't control them," Stephanie replied.

"I should have made sure Mom knew where to put the antibiotic in the refrigerator. That's on me. But my family knows they can't move things around our apartment. It's dangerous for you."

"What makes you think they'll listen to you now?"

"I'll explain that we won't allow them in our home if they don't follow this rule."

Stephanie bit her bottom lip. "That sounds harsh."

"It's necessary. I let you down tonight, and I won't allow that to happen again."

Stephanie nodded.

Dhruv got to his feet. "I'll clean up the soda spill in the fridge. Mom brought us a ton of food. Are you hungry?"

"Starved. Do I smell chicken shawarma?"

"Yep. It's staying warm in the oven."

"Let's eat. Amelia will be hungry again in another hour."

"I'll take care of her after that. Have a long soak in the tub. You've earned it."

CHAPTER 12

*G*arth

We spent a quiet Sunday at home yesterday, after our busy day at the Foundation for the Blind. Lazy Sundays, Grant calls them.

Sabrina and I moved between our beds in the various rooms so that we spent time with each human in our family. Grant could always be found on the sofa in the family room, napping in front of the television screen, where people were running around after each other and a ball.

Emily was often in the kitchen, fixing what she called comfort food.

The girls were in their rooms or the backyard. We have beds everywhere. Both Sabrina and I tried to pay attention to our people, but sometimes our eyelids closed, and we had a little snooze.

On Monday, I woke well-rested and eager to be on the go with Emily. Weekday mornings were hectic in our house. Grant and the girls left together, and Emily and I waited for our rideshare.

This morning was different. We all left together. He dropped the girls off at the house I knew was Sylvia's. The girls were ecstatic about something they called Grandmas' Culinary Institute.

Grant had an early flight to Los Angeles to check on his big project. He agreed to give us a ride to Emily's office, since he was driving right by.

"Sorry you had to leave an hour earlier than usual this morning," Grant said.

"I'll use the time to prepare for the weekly department meeting after lunch," Emily replied. "I'd have come in early this morning whether you'd have given me a ride or not. It's easiest to think through my agenda for the meeting before people arrive at the office. By eight-thirty, my phone will be ringing off the hook and people will be circling my office with questions."

Grant glanced over at his talented wife. "Admit it—you wouldn't have it any other way. You love to be needed."

Emily blushed. "I can't deny it."

"Other than that idiot Ross Wilcox, you haven't had problems with anyone at work," Grant observed. "Your blindness hasn't been a barrier."

"I count myself as very fortunate. I think Wilcox's problem with me was as much me being a woman as being blind. My team didn't know what to expect when I came back to work, but once they knew I could perform my job functions as well as I did when I was sighted, they settled down. I credit Dhruv for showing them—and me, for that matter—how capable I am."

"I'm thankful you have Dhruv," Grant said, pulling to the curb in front of her office building. "And that they fired Wilcox."

Emily opened her car door and slung her satchel over her shoulder. "You and me both." She leaned across the console toward him, and they kissed. "I hope everything is in order in LA."

"With Norman Klein on site, supervising the project, I'm sure it will be. See you tonight."

Emily opened the rear door for me, and I led her into our building and to the elevator bank. She'd even trained me to push the elevator button with my nose, and I took care of that task now.

"I'll text Dhruv to remind him he's on paternity leave and can't attend our meeting."

I sat and swished my tail against the floor.

"You agree with me, don't you, boy? Our team will step into his shoes during his leave."

She dictated her text and sent it.

The elevator arrived, and the doors opened the moment she was done.

"In," Emily commanded, and we stepped into the elevator. An object on the floor of the elevator pinged.

"What? That can't be ..." She resent her text, and the object pinged again.

The elevator doors shut.

Emily found the braille markers below the button for our floor and pushed it. She then swung her foot to the area where the small, thin rectangle lay. Her shoe tapped it. Emily bent and picked up the object.

We arrived at our floor, and I guided Emily out of the elevator. She tucked the rectangle under her arm and commanded her phone to call Dhruv.

The rectangle emitted a ringtone I recognized. A lot of those rectangle things made the same noise.

"I'll be darned," Emily exclaimed. "What in the heck is Dhruv's phone doing in the elevator?"

She was addressing me, but I didn't understand what she was saying. I recognized Dhruv's name, so I wagged my tail.

"He must have snuck in here to do some work over the weekend. Even though he's not supposed to do that!"

I sensed her energy change from focused and eager to upset and annoyed.

"He could get me into trouble with HR if they found out," she said. "I'm sure he's panicked, wondering where he's left his phone." She pursed her lips. "I ought to let him sweat it out, but then he'll come here to look for it."

She commanded me to find her office. "We'll call his home number to tell him I have his phone and will bring it to him in about an hour. I want to get ready for the weekly meeting first."

Emily unpacked her satchel, filled my water bowl that lived in the corner of her office, and placed her call.

I settled under her desk for my first morning nap. She was mad at Dhruv for some reason, but I loved being with him. I hadn't had a crunchy Cheeto since we'd visited him when Amelia came home from the hospital.

I closed my eyes, visions of those delicious orange cylinders—my favorite snack in the whole wide world—dancing through my mind.

I LOVED RETURNING to our old stomping grounds. Dhruv and Stephanie had moved into our former apartment when they knew they were having a baby. I'd had many fun times here. My buddies Biscuit, Sugar, and Rocco also lived here. It was always good to see them.

Dhruv opened the apartment door as soon as Emily knocked. He used his body to block Sugar and Rocco from escaping. "We just put Amelia down for her nap," he said in a whisper. "Stephanie's gone back to bed, too. Amelia's had an ear infection, and it's been a tough couple of days. We haven't slept." He held out his hand for his phone. "Will you give me my phone?"

"Not so fast," Emily whispered back. "I'm sorry she's sick and you've been having a hard time, but we need to talk."

"We don't want to wake anyone," he replied.

"Then step out into the hall. We're going to have a conversation." Even at low volume, Emily's tone held the force of a sword.

Dhruv joined us, with Sugar and Rocco pushing past him before he pulled his door shut.

My friends bounded over to me, but I was still working. I ignored them.

"Let's take these guys outside to the dog area to play," Emily said.

We made our way to the familiar spot, and Emily removed my working harness.

"Okay, boy. Enjoy your friends."

I said hello to my buddies but stuck close to the humans. Something important was happening, and I wanted to know what it was.

Emily retrieved Dhruv's phone from her purse. "You were at the office this weekend, weren't you?"

Dhruv hung his head and nodded.

"Words, Dhruv."

"Yes. Late yesterday afternoon and evening. Where did you find my phone?"

"In the elevator. You're lucky I came in early. You might never have gotten it back." She held the phone out to him.

"Thank you, Em. You didn't have to bring it to me. I could have run in to pick it up."

"You shouldn't be anywhere near the office, Dhruv, and you know it. You're on leave—company policy demands that you don't work while on leave."

"I know." He shifted his weight from foot to foot and sighed.

"Then why were you there?"

Dhruv explained what he'd been working on.

"I'm covering that business unit while you're out." Emily raised her shoulders and gestured with her hands. "They never said a word to me about a problem."

"All I know is that the department manager was furious about a glitch in the program I created right before I went out on leave. It's complicated code, and I figured I'd made a mistake."

"And you don't think I can handle problems with complicated code?"

"No—of course not. I know how busy the team has been while I've been out. I figured it would be faster and easier for me to correct the problem. There was no reason to get anyone else involved."

"I understand your motives were to be helpful, Dhruv." Now her tone softened. "They always are. But it wasn't appropriate for you to step in to handle this. You should have referred the business unit back to me."

Dhruv remained silent.

"Did you try that?"

"I did."

"I don't have any record of them contacting me."

Dhruv fidgeted even more. "I think the department head doesn't want to work with you."

"What? Why do you say that?"

"He told me so."

Emily exploded. "It's not his choice." She stood, arms at her side, her hands balled into fists. "Do you know why he doesn't want to work with me?"

"I think it's because you're blind, Em. He kept saying he needed someone to fix the problem, and he didn't believe you could."

"*Dhruv!* You let him get away with *that?*"

"I'm sorry, Em. I know it's ignorant. And wrong. I thought I'd made a mistake in the program and didn't want to dump it on you, plus burden you with his prejudice." Dhruv lowered his face to the ground. "I've messed everything up over this—with both you and Stephanie."

"How does Stephanie come into this?"

Dhruv told her the rest of the story from the night before.

"Holy cow, Dhruv. This couldn't have gone much worse for you if you tried."

"I know. I won't let her down again. Or you."

Emily stood, digesting what she'd heard. "Sounds like you swung and missed, Dhruv. Happens to everyone. Your heart was in the right place. I'll address the department manager's issues with me. I won't allow him to get away with this."

"Thank you. I won't answer calls from him."

"Good."

"I'd better go back to the apartment," Dhruv said. "I don't want Stephanie to look for me and find I'm not inside. She'll know where I am because the dogs aren't there, but after last night, I don't want any more trouble."

"Good thinking," Emily said. She called to me and put me back in my working harness. "I'm sorry Amelia's been sick. How's she doing?"

Dhruv accompanied us as we walked up the back steps and headed down the hall like we'd done when we'd lived here..

"I think the antibiotics have taken effect. She's much better than she was."

"I'm glad to hear it. Do you need anything?"

"As I told you, my mom gave us meals for the week. We're all set."

"Tell Stephanie to call me when she's ready to get out of the house. We'll grab coffee at that place around the corner. It's not far—she can walk home in under five minutes." Emily smiled in Dhruv's direction. "I think Amelia's mommy needs a few minutes off duty."

"I agree. I'll insist on it."

Sugar and Rocco surged ahead and stopped at their door.

"Thanks, Em. For understanding."

She extended her arm to him, and they hugged, then we headed out the door. Emily gave me the commands I knew took us to the bus stop we'd used when we'd lived here.

I'd be back in my spot under her desk in no time. I hadn't scored a crunchy Cheeto from Dhruv, but bigger issues had been at hand. There was always next time.

CHAPTER 13

Zoe popped the last bite of her cinnamon roll into her mouth and licked the icing from her fingers. "This is so good," she said around the mouthful of pastry. "Will we learn to make these?"

Sylvia glanced across her breakfast table at Martha, raising an eyebrow.

"We hadn't planned on it," Martha replied, "but we'll add it to our agenda at the end of the week." She took a sip of her coffee and trained her eyes on Sylvia.

"We've decided to teach you how to make things for breakfast, lunch, and dinner," Sylvia said. "You'll be able to pack your own lunches for school and prepare snacks, too."

"You'll learn to use the countertop kitchen appliances, how to read a recipe and plan a meal, and you'll practice knife skills. That's on deck for today," Martha said.

Zoe and Diedre snapped their heads toward each other and grinned. "We're not allowed to use the sharp knives in the knife block at home," Diedre said.

"For good reason," Sylvia said. "You can hurt yourself if you don't know how to hold and operate a knife properly."

"Like chefs on TV. I've seen them do onions." Zoe demonstrated, holding an imaginary onion with one hand and slicing through it by pumping her hand up and down.

"It takes years—and dozens of onions—to get that fast. Our aim is safety and precision, not speed. You'll learn the difference between a chop, a dice, and a mince."

"Before we start, we wanted to ask if you'd like to make the food for our family dinner this Sunday?"

Both girls leaned across the table, their eyes large and earnest, as they nodded their agreement.

"That would be so cool," Diedre said.

"You'd have to come over by noon on Sunday to prepare it," Martha said. "You'll do all the work. We'll only be here to answer questions."

"Do you have other plans on Sunday?" Sylvia asked.

The girls looked at each other again, then turned back to their grandmothers.

"We don't have anything this weekend," Diedre replied. "We could spend the night and start first thing Sunday morning."

Sylvia now looked at Martha, who nodded. "That's a great idea."

"We suggest you make baked chicken thighs, rice pilaf, and roasted broccolini."

"Is that the chicken you make sometimes?" Diedre asked.

Sylvia nodded.

"My dad loves it," Diedre said.

"We'll take you to the market to teach you how to shop for the ingredients. By Sunday, you'll know how to follow a recipe and prep everything," Martha said.

"What about an appetizer?" Zoe asked.

Martha and Sylvia turned to her. "We never have an appetizer with our Sunday night family dinners."

"But this will be our first meal to make," Zoe said. "People on TV always have appetizers."

"That's right," Diedre said, nodding her head knowledgeably. "We should have them."

"What do you have in mind?" Martha asked, suppressing a smile.

"We've been watching cooking shows ever since we knew we were doing Grandmas' Culinary Institute," Zoe said. She bit her lower lip and narrowed her eyes. "I think we need something with phyllo dough."

"Gracious—that's fancy."

"We can use frozen phyllo," Martha said. "I've got a recipe for sausage and cheese bites in phyllo that's delicious. I haven't made them in years. We could do those."

"So they'd be hot?" Zoe asked.

"Yep."

"That's very fancy. Let's do them."

"We could also make one of those board things with cheeses and grapes and crackers. I'll arrange it," Diedre added.

"You're artistic," Zoe said. "You'd make it so pretty."

"Right," Sylvia said. "We'll add sausage and cheese phyllo bites and a charcuterie board to our menu."

"What about dessert?" Diedre asked. "We have dessert on Sunday nights."

"You've already learned to bake a pie with me," Martha said, "so we thought you could bake a cake. Mixes are delicious and easy."

The girls stared blankly ahead.

"You love cake," Sylvia prodded.

"We want to make it from scratch," Zoe said. "We've seen them do it on The Great British Baking Show."

"We can do that, too," Sylvia said. "I'm glad to see that you're so interested in making Sunday night such a success."

"It's our first company meal," Zoe said. "We want it to be special."

"Let's make a ganache for the filling and have a mirror glaze on top," Diedre said.

"We'll see," Sylvia said. "That might be a bit much."

"Why don't we stick with a cream filling and buttercream frosting?" Martha suggested.

"Can we decorate it with roses and stuff?" Diedre asked. "It looks easy to do on that show."

"Hmmm …" Sylvia narrowed her eyes in thought. "I'll get out my cake decorating supplies and you can practice. It might not be as simple as you think."

"Or you could be a natural at it," Zoe chimed in. "That's what Prue said about that one woman."

"Zoe may be right." Sylvia grinned at Diedre. "We're going to find out."

"We need to spend a lot of time on our dinner," Zoe said, turning to her stepsister. "We could stay over Friday night, too, so we have the entire weekend to work on this."

"That's a great idea," Diedre agreed.

"Sylvia is going to a dance on Friday night with Doug and me," Martha said. "We won't be home. You'll have to come on Saturday morning."

The girls looked thunderstruck.

"A dance?" Diedre asked.

"More like a dance class," Sylvia said. "And I'll miss it so you girls can spend the night. I don't mind."

"You'll do no such thing, Sylvia Johnson. Doug and I have been trying to get you to come with us for months. You're going to have a ball. I know it."

"Grandma—you should go with them. Martha's right." Diedre straightened her spine and her tone was definite. "Emily says both of you need to have your own friends."

Zoe nodded in agreement. "Your whole world shouldn't revolve around us and Alex. That's what she says."

"It's settled, then. We've got a lot to cover, so we'd better get started." Martha picked up her plate and headed to the sink. "Let's clean up breakfast and begin."

CHAPTER 14

$\mathcal{M}$artha knocked on Sylvia's door. "Ready? Doug called to say he'll pick us up in ten."

Sylvia opened her door. "How do I look? Is this appropriate?" She ran her hand along her midi dress in a blush and coral print. The jersey fabric swirled around her as she executed a turn.

"That dress is gorgeous on you. Coral is your color. It's perfect." Martha lowered her gaze to Sylvia's feet. "I'd change out of those high heels, though. You won't want to dance in those the entire evening."

"But you're wearing heels." Sylvia pointed to them.

"That's because I'm bringing my dancing shoes to change into. They're low-heeled and have a strap that buckles."

Sylvia pursed her lips.

"Lots of women dance in flats. Do you have a pair you can bring?"

Sylvia nodded. "I'll change into them now." She swapped out her shoes. "Are you sure you don't mind me tagging along? I hate intruding on your date."

"Positive," Martha said. "After the week we've had with those girls, I'd have felt guilty leaving you home alone while I went out."

"A night at home doesn't sound bad to me. The girls are terrific fun, don't get me wrong. But we worked our buns off this week."

"Right? I never dreamed they'd take this business of learning to cook so seriously," Martha agreed. "We were on our feet in your kitchen from dawn until dusk every day."

"Weren't they the best students? I'm so proud of them. I think the family will be amazed."

"Watching those chef shows gave them an appreciation for how much work it takes to become an accomplished cook."

"That must be part of it. Plus—they both like to excel at anything they do."

The doorbell sounded.

"That'll be Doug," Martha said.

Sylvia grabbed her purse from her bed and followed Martha to the door.

"My gosh," Doug said, stepping inside. "Look at the two of you! I'll be the envy of every man there."

"Before we go, I want to make sure you don't mind me coming with you," Sylvia said.

"I believe it was my idea," Doug said. "These dances have more people who attend as singles than as couples. You'll feel right at home."

Doug stepped aside to let the ladies precede him out the door.

"Except I don't know how to dance," Sylvia said.

"West Coast Swing is a simple one to learn. The first hour is a lesson. The leaders spend twenty minutes teaching steps. After that, they line people up in two lines, facing each other. You partner with the person opposite you for one dance." Doug opened the car door for each of them. He resumed his explanation when he'd taken his seat behind the wheel. "When the song ends, you thank your partner for the dance. You then line up again and partner for the next song with someone else. That gives you the chance to dance with other novices and with experienced dancers."

"You'll be surprised how much you'll learn during the first lesson," Martha said. "When it's over, there's another ninety minutes of free dancing."

"What if no one asks me to dance?"

"Believe me, they will. The leaders keep their eyes peeled for anyone who is sitting on the sidelines, and the regulars make sure to ask newcomers." Doug caught Sylvia's eye in the rearview mirror. "This isn't like a junior high school dance," he assured her.

Sylvia burst out laughing. "You mean I won't feel like a wallflower?"

"Not in a million years. The people who attend these dances love to dance. Unlike the school gymnasium, gawkers don't fill the walls," Martha said.

"You'll have more offers than you know what to do with," Doug chimed in.

"If you want to take a break, there are chairs in the hallway. Grab any open seat—don't worry if you have to join a group. Everyone sits wherever," Martha said.

"One more thing," Doug added. "If you'd like to leave, let us know. We'll spend as much or as little time here as you'd like. If we're wrong and you're not enjoying yourself, say the word. We're out of there."

"I'm sure I can manage two and a half hours of West Coast Swing. Thank you for the offer, but I wouldn't dream of making you leave early."

As they were pulling into the parking lot, Martha said, "I predict you're going to love it. We'll be the ones dragging you out of there."

SYLVIA STOOD next to Martha in a group of women facing two instructors.

One instructor raised her hand to get their attention. "How many of you know the basic step and what's called the sugar push? Also called the break push."

Of the twenty-some people around Sylvia, half raised their hands.

"That's great," the instructor said. "You can practice while the others learn. Newcomers—watch your neighbors who have mastered the steps, too."

She turned her back to them and swung her head to talk over her shoulder as she demonstrated the steps. "You'll begin on your right foot. Step forward with your right, followed by your left foot. Then step in place right left. Step back on your right. Then left, right, left in place. Your right foot is now available to start again."

She showed and described the step again. "The counting is one-two-three and four-five-six. Now let's all try it."

The instructor called out the numbers, and Sylvia was following smoothly by the third repetition.

Martha gave Sylvia the thumbs-up sign.

The instructor had them practice what they'd learned to music. She and the other instructor then taught the basics of the away and toward connections, the side pass, and the whip.

Sylvia followed along. When the instructors told them it was time to line up to practice with a partner, Sylvia sank back.

Martha turned to her. "Aren't you enjoying yourself? Would you like to go?"

"I think it's really fun, but I'm not ready to dance with anyone. I've got the basic step, but none of the rest of it."

"Nonsense. I watched you—you were catching on fast."

"I might be able to do the sugar push, but not a side pass. And certainly not a whip—the beat changes on that from a six to an eight count. I've barely got the six-count down."

Martha chuckled. "That's how everyone feels at their first lesson. There are lots of experienced dancers here tonight. When you dance with someone who knows how to lead, your steps will come naturally to you."

Sylvia raised skeptical eyes to Martha. "I think these experienced dancers will be eager to get rid of me and move on to someone who knows what they're doing." She gestured with her head to the wall. "I'll wait over there and watch. I'm sure I'll learn from observing."

"Give it another twenty minutes. Line up and dance with partners. I think you'll find I'm right."

Sylvia bit her lip.

"Didn't you once tell me you loved to polka?"

"That was when I was a little girl. I'm sure I couldn't remember how to now."

"You love to dance, and you know it. Wait a few more minutes before you pull the plug."

Sylvia brought her chin up. "You're right. Let's give this a whirl." She lined up with Martha.

The instructors called for leaders to select a partner. A neatly groomed man extended his right hand to Sylvia. She put her left hand into his as she'd learned to do for the sugar push. The music started, and the dancing began.

Martha had been correct. Sylvia kept up with the moves every experienced dancer led her through. When a newbie asked her to dance, they stuck to the basic step. Either way, she wanted to keep on dancing.

Sylvia was amazed when they announced the last dance of the evening. She couldn't believe she'd danced every song and never even wanted a break.

When the last dance was over and she'd thanked her partner, she scanned the room for Martha and Doug. They were nowhere to be seen.

Sylvia stepped into the hallway to find them relaxing in chairs, their legs stretched out in front of them.

"Look who's the life of the party." Martha chuckled. "You outlasted both of us."

"OMG—I'm so sorry!" Sylvia said. "You should have told me you were ready to leave."

"Not on your life," Martha said. "You were having such a good time. We only sat out the final two dances, anyway. The buckle on my shoe broke." She pointed to her broken strap.

Sylvia sank into a chair next to them. "I had more fun than I've had in years. You were right. I'm so glad you encouraged me."

Doug grinned. "Would you like to come with us next week?"

"You're sure you don't mind me tagging along?"

"Positive," Doug said.

Martha nodded her agreement.

"I understand those granddaughters of yours will be at your place early tomorrow morning. Martha told me about your plans. Sounds like you'll be busy this weekend. I'd better get you home."

"That's a good idea," Martha said.

They rose and headed to the exit with the last of the dancers and spent the drive home chattering about the evening.

"I'm going straight to bed as soon as I get inside," Sylvia said. "Come in and stay as long as you like. There's just one thing I'd like to know before I say goodnight."

"What's that?" Doug asked.

"Will you join us for dinner on Sunday night?" Sylvia asked.

"That's just family, isn't it?" Doug asked. "I wouldn't want to intrude."

"Sylvia's right," Martha said. "The girls adore you. They're so excited about this dinner they're making. They'll love to show off in front of you." She touched his arm. "Please come."

"Please," Sylvia echoed from the back seat.

"How can I say no to both of you? Thank you. I'd love to."

"It's settled." They all got out of the car. "I'll see you on Sunday, Doug. Martha, thank you again for encouraging me. You're a wonderful friend."

CHAPTER 15

*G*arth

I heard Sabrina's paws hit the rug next to Zoe's bed, followed by Zoe's soft footsteps in the hallway.

Emily was hunched over her laptop at the kitchen table, listening to her screen reader read lines of code at a pace much faster than normal human speech.

We usually did this at the office. We'd come home after an especially boisterous family dinner at Sylvia's. A new person was there—I think his name is Doug. I'll remember his scent even if I forget his name.

Everyone oohed and aahed over the food. The girls' smiles never left their faces. I can't comment on whether it was good or not because no one snuck me so much as a morsel.

We'd all gotten ready for bed—including Emily and me. The house settled down, but Emily tossed and turned. She finally threw back the covers, found her slippers, and padded into the kitchen.

I knew the moment she pulled her laptop out of her satchel and opened it on the kitchen table that we'd be here for a while. I settled into my bed in the corner to wait. If my Emily was up, so was I.

Emily didn't notice when Sabrina stepped into the kitchen,

followed by Zoe. They stood in the entry to the dark kitchen, silhouetted by the nightlight in the hallway.

I uttered a muffled woof and thumped my tail against the side of my bed to get Emily's attention.

It worked. Emily paused her screen reader and brought her head up. "What is it, Garth?" She listened. "Is anyone there?"

"It's me, Em," Zoe said.

"Hey, sweetie. What are you doing up? You've got a big day tomorrow. It's the first day of your STEM summer camp program."

"I'm so excited about it, I can't fall asleep. I thought I heard you in the kitchen." Zoe's voice was brimming with enthusiasm. Emily opened an arm wide and beckoned to Zoe.

The girl who had become Emily's ward when her grandmother had died melted into Emily's embrace.

"Why are you up?" Zoe asked.

"I'm familiarizing myself with a project for one of Dhruv's internal clients. I've never worked with this client, and I'm nervous about it. It's kind of like the first day of school for me with these people—and I've got the jitters."

Zoe nodded against Emily's shoulder.

"I'm distracting myself by reviewing Dhruv's work." Emily pointed at her laptop. "It makes me feel confident and in control."

"The cooking Diedre and I did with Martha and Sylvia distracted me. I didn't think about tomorrow. Now that the dinner is over, I'm looking forward to camp. Not worried like before."

"I'm happy to hear that." She smoothed Zoe's hair away from the girl's face and planted a kiss on her brow. "That meal was terrific," Emily said. "The entire family will talk about it for weeks."

"That's what Sylvia said. Martha told Diedre and me she and Sylvia are going to have to 'up their game'—whatever that means—after tonight."

Emily chuckled. "It means they'll have to make better dinners in the future."

"Did you like our cake?"

"Are you kidding? That was the best part. I think it's the best cake I've ever eaten."

"I found the recipe online. It's supposed to be like the Publix Raspberry Elegance Cake. Publix is a store."

I could tell Emily was trying not to smile.

"We made the white cake from cake flour, using the reverse creaming method. It creates a tight crumb, like a bakery cake." Zoe's tone grew confident as she recited what she'd learned online. "We cooked the raspberry puree filling on the stove to make it thick."

"The whole thing was perfection," Emily said. "Was that cream cheese icing?"

Zoe nodded her head against Emily's shoulder again. "We thought about using buttercream, but the cream cheese compliments this cake beautifully. That's what the notes in the recipe said."

"Having tasted it, I agree."

"Diedre made a fancy border around the top with icing that she squeezed out of a pastry bag. Sylvia had cake decorating supplies. Diedre said it was a lot harder to do than she thought. She wasn't happy with how it turned out, but I thought it looked so fancy."

"It was delicious, that much I know."

"We brought leftover cake home with us." Zoe leaned forward. "Could we each have a slice?"

I recognized the eagerness in her voice.

She added, "I bet it'll help you feel better about tomorrow."

Emily shut her laptop. "I think that's a brilliant idea. We can't polish it off, though. That wouldn't be fair. Is there enough?"

Zoe was already pulling a plastic container out of the refrigerator. "There are four small slices. One for each of us."

"Then I think it's fine for us to eat ours whenever we want. And I'm with you—I want mine now."

"I'll get plates and forks," Zoe said, swinging into action. "Do you want a glass of milk?"

"Absolutely," Emily said. "Thank you."

They were soon enjoying the fragrant cake.

Sabrina sat at Zoe's feet, her paws on the girl's thigh. She whimpered and raked her paws across Zoe's knee, begging. I was too well-trained for such behavior, but I wanted a taste of that cake. I wanted it bad.

"Have you girls decided what you'd each like to do for vacation?"

"Yeah." Zoe sighed heavily. "That's another thing. She wants to see *Wicked* on Broadway. I'd like to tour the National Air and Space Museum in Washington, D.C. We can't go to both cities, so I'll look for something in New York City."

"Hold on," Emily said, bringing her fork to her lips to lick off the last morsel of icing. "You don't have to pick something else."

"But Broadway is in New York," Zoe said.

"And the Smithsonian is in D.C.," Emily replied. "New York City and Washington, D.C. are an easy train ride apart. Have you ever traveled by train?"

"No. I've never been on a plane, either."

"You've got a lot to look forward to. I'll talk to Grant, but I don't see any reason we can't hit both cities on this trip."

"Really?" Zoe flooded the word with happiness.

"We'll discuss it as a family this week. Right now, we'd better get to bed. Let's clean up these plates."

Zoe grasped both plates. "Can I?" she asked.

Emily hesitated, then nodded. "They stayed up late with us. I think they deserve a treat."

Zoe held out a plate to each of us and we licked our assigned plate until every molecule of cake, filling, and icing was gone.

Crunchy Cheetos were still my favorite people food, but that cake was a close second.

 *E*mily reviewed the email she'd drafted to Bruce Horton at her kitchen table the night before. It had seemed like a good idea then, but now, after a full night's sleep, she had her doubts.

It would be better to call the head of the business unit who had gone behind her back to solicit Dhruv's help while he was on paternity leave. *Emails are easily misconstrued,* she reasoned. The email's tone sounded accusatory this morning. Maybe Dhruv had been mistaken, and Bruce hadn't been avoiding her because she was blind. Or a woman. Or both. There was only one way to find out.

She was searching the company directory for his phone number when a call came in for her from Kari, Dhruv's counterpart in Denver. Like Dhruv, Kari had been instrumental in Emily's success managing both the Denver and San Francisco teams. She set aside her effort to contact Bruce and answered the call.

"Happy Monday," Emily said. "Did you have a nice weekend?"

"Fine." Kari inhaled quickly. "And yours?"

Emily knew the question was a polite formality. Kari was upset about something.

"Fine as well. What's up?"

"We've got a situation," Kari said. "Or at least, I think we do. I don't want to raise an unnecessary ruckus. And I may be imagining things ..."

"You'd better tell me what's bothering you," Emily said.

"It's probably nothing."

"Then we'll be able to figure that out. Shoot."

Kari took a deep breath. "Do you know who Bruce Horton is? He's here in the Denver office."

"I learned about him last week. Funny you should mention Bruce. I was just about to call him."

"So, you heard?"

"Heard what?"

"He's requested our team put on a two-day training with his people for the program Dhurv wrote before he went out on leave." Kari paused. "Thursday and Friday of this week."

"What!" Emily's intention to give Bruce the benefit of the doubt evaporated in an instant. "San Francisco is covering that project in Dhruv's absence. He should have come to me."

"That's what I thought," Kari said. "He just now stopped by my office to inform me he'd set up the training. He wants me to have three people available."

"You've got to be kidding me. That's completely inappropriate. Did you ask him if he'd contacted me? I'm Dhruv's backup on this project."

"I did. His answer was really odd. He danced around my questions and intimated that you'd approved it. I've seen him in action for years. I can't stand the guy. He's full of BS. I felt certain he was lying. That's why I called you."

"I'm glad you did. Don't waste time working on this. The Denver team won't handle this."

"Thank you." The relief in Kari's voice was clear. "We're happy to jump in if you need us to," she hastened to add. "It's only that we're stretched to the max here as it is. Most of us spent the weekend in the office."

"I know you are, and I won't allow you to step in. Thank you for offering. I assigned coverage of this project to San Francisco, and we'll handle the training his team needs."

"Good. I was hoping you'd say that."

"Have you told your team about his request yet?"

"No. Frankly, I was dreading adding anything else to their workload."

"Now you don't have to."

"What are you going to do?" Kari asked. "Bruce's team needs this training, and he'll raise hell if they don't get it."

"We'll take care of him," Emily said. *In more ways than he wants,* she thought to herself. "Email me the details about the training. Where, what time, and how many people will attend. Send me their names if you have them."

"Sure. I'll get the information to you this morning. His people are pleasant and hard-working. Most of them are entry-level, so they won't be as skilled as most of the people we deal with."

"That's helpful to know. I'll include quizzes and contests—with prizes. That keeps people's attention."

Kari chuckled. "Your trainings are always fun. I wish I had time to sit in. I'd like to learn from the master."

"That's nice to hear. We'll work on a training together in the future —when Dhruv is back to work, and we have time to hear ourselves think."

"I knew he was a workhorse, but now that he's on leave, I realize he ran rings around us. I shouldn't say this to my boss, but it's true."

"He's one in a million," Emily said. "But don't sell yourself short, Kari. We'd be scrambling if *you* were out of the office."

"Thanks," Kari said. "What should I tell Bruce?"

"Nothing. Leave it to me. I'll place my call to him now." *Only I'll be approaching the call way differently after talking to Kari,* Emily thought as she hung up the phone.

EMILY PLACED her call to Bruce Horton. He didn't answer, so she left him a message. She emailed him before lunch, requesting he return her call.

She hadn't heard from Bruce by mid-afternoon. She sent a new email, copying their division head, and Executive Vice President Howard Kent, telling Bruce she needed a return call by the end of the day so her team could respond to his urgent request for help.

"Emily … Bruce Horton here. What's the trouble?"

Emily nodded in satisfaction. She'd gotten his attention by copying the big brass on her email. "I don't know, Bruce. You tell me."

"What're you talking about?"

"Come on. You know why I was calling. You contacted my Denver team to train your people."

"They need help and Dhruv's not available. Any longer."

"Exactly. That's why I took over the program he was developing for you. The San Francisco team and I are up-to-speed on the entire project. We're available to help you."

"I didn't know …" he mumbled.

"You most certainly did know," Emily replied. "It was in an email I sent when Dhruv went out on leave."

"I … I didn't see that."

"I've got a message-read stamp on it from you, but I'll send another copy."

He didn't respond.

"You contacted him—you went behind my back—to get him to help you while he was on leave. You know that's against company policy. Your actions could mire the company in legal trouble, too. Why didn't you contact me, Bruce?"

"I need someone who can do the work. We don't have time to wait for you to find people to do it for you," he snapped in return.

Emily felt as if someone had doused her with gasoline and lit a match. "What are you talking about?"

"Oh, come on. This program is thousands of lines of code. It's difficult enough for sighted programmers to find errors. You can't possibly …"

"Stop. Right there." If he'd been near her, he would have felt spittle on his chin. "My blindness does not interfere with my ability to do my job. I can do anything a sighted programmer can do. Using my screen reader, I review code faster than when I was sighted. My accuracy is higher because I listen to the code, too."

Bruce harrumphed in disbelief.

Berating him for breaking the law by discriminating against her was on the tip of her tongue. She stopped herself from venting her rage over his ignorance.

"Three members of my team and I will be in Denver on Thursday to train your team, as requested."

"You'll stay through the end of the day on Friday?"

"It won't take that long, but we'll make ourselves available."

His breathing was rapid.

Emily sensed his anger.

"Let me know who you're sending for training, so I have enough copies of our handouts." She already had the list of names from Kari, but she wanted to see if Bruce would cooperate with her.

"Sure," he replied curtly.

"The training begins at ten," Emily said. "I'm coming in the night before, ahead of my team. Do you have time to meet for breakfast? It'll give us a chance to get to know each other since we'll be working with each other until Dhruv returns."

"I've got an extremely busy morning on Thursday," he said.

"Coffee, then. Let's carve out a few minutes to spend together. I want to reassure you so nothing like this happens again." She smiled. He could hardly refuse her invitation.

"All right. Coffee." He gave her the name of a coffee shop within the office complex where the regional headquarters building was located. "Seven-thirty. I have a meeting at the office at eight."

"Seven-thirty it is."

"Don't be late."

"Of course not. I'll see you Thursday morning."

CHAPTER 17

*E*mily listened to the rain pelt the window of her hotel room. Her wayfinding app told her the coffee shop where she was to meet Bruce was a mile away. Because the hotel closest to the regional headquarters was fully booked, she'd had to stay farther away than anticipated.

The mile walk had seemed welcome when she'd agreed to meet Bruce. Garth would enjoy the chance to stretch his legs before a day of being cooped up inside during the scheduled training sessions. Emily hadn't counted on the morning's pouring rain. She and Garth couldn't walk—she'd look like a drowned rat by the time she was ten feet outside the hotel.

She pulled up her rideshare app and ordered a ride. Her screen reader told her the car would be there in eight minutes.

"Okay, Garth," Emily said, placing him in his working harness and slinging her satchel over her shoulder. "We'd better head downstairs. The ride will get us to the coffee shop earlier than necessary, but better to be early than late. Bruce made a big deal about meeting at seven-thirty because he has to be in the office at eight." They exited her room and headed for the elevator. "And we don't want to ruffle

Bruce's feathers. We're in Denver to train his team, and I want to establish a good working relationship with him, too."

They rode the elevator to the lobby and stepped out of the covered entrance to the hotel. Wind whipped the rain sideways into them.

The screen reader told Emily that her rideshare was arriving. She heard a car approach and slow.

The doorman stepped forward and gave Emily the make and model of the car. "Is this the car you're expecting?"

She confirmed they matched the description of her ride.

The doorman reached for the rear car door handle.

The driver rolled down his window. "Nope. No pets allowed," he called above the din of the rain.

Emily leaned toward his voice. "Garth isn't a pet. He's a service dog."

"I don't care. No dogs."

"Service dogs have a legal right to travel in rideshares. The law— and your company's policy—require you to accept both of us."

"I'm not taking you. Order a car with pet privileges."

Emily raised her voice several decibels. "You're breaking the law. You have to take us." She swung to face the doorman, who stood motionless next to her, his hand on the door handle. "Open the door."

The rideshare driver powered his window up and pulled away.

The doorman released his grip on the handle. "I tried to open it, but the door was locked." He sighed. "I'm so sorry, ma'am. You should file a complaint with the company."

"And you know what good that will do? They'll give me a $5 credit on my account and promise to provide better training to the driver." She spat the words as she tapped at her phone to order another rideshare from a different provider. "It's a good thing I left the hotel with plenty of time for our meeting."

The new car arrived ten minutes later, but the result was the same. The driver wouldn't allow Garth to travel in his car.

"Does this happen to you often?" the doorman asked.

"All. The. Time." Emily replied in staccato fashion. "Eighty-three percent of blind people report being denied access to a rideshare when accompanied by their guide dog. It's against the law—but happens frequently."

"That's reprehensible," the doorman said. "Do you want to try again?"

Emily listened to the time on her phone. "If I leave now, I can walk to my destination and only be a few minutes late."

"But it's pouring," the doorman said. "Do you have an umbrella?"

Emily shook her head no. "I forgot to pack one. With this wind, I'm not sure an umbrella will do me much good." She pulled the hood of her jacket over her head and tightened the drawstring closure.

"You'll both get drenched," the man said. "I'd walk you there myself under an umbrella if I could."

Emily gave him a wan smile. "That's kind of you, but we'll be fine. Garth loves the rain, and I'd rather be wet than late for this meeting."

She opened her wayfinding app and listened to the directions the screen reader gave her. She commanded Garth to move forward, right, accompanied by a gentle sweep of her right hand. They stepped into the steady downpour and headed out.

CHAPTER 18

arth

We waited under the awning at the coffee shop door while a man exited. I took the opportunity to give myself a low-intensity shake. Rain scattered off my coat like shrapnel.

Emily pulled her hood off her head and tucked damp tendrils of hair behind her ears. She brushed water off her jacket onto the pavement.

I wanted to step inside the coffee shop and shake with full force, but I knew from experience that none of the humans inside would appreciate that. This meeting was important enough to Emily that we'd walked a long way in the rain. I couldn't let myself do anything to mess it up.

The man stepped past us, then turned and held the door open. We entered the shop. The aromas of coffee and baked goods mingled in a way that set my nose twitching.

Human voices—engaged in conversations, ordering beverages or pastries, and calling out names when orders were ready—set a base level of noise for the busy shop.

A man called Emily's name.

She raised her hand over her head in response.

He moved to us and stuck out his hand. "Bruce Horton," he said.

"Nice to meet you, Bruce." Emily extended her hand because she couldn't see his. "Emily Main."

He moved his hand to hers, and they shook. "You're late," he said. "I've got to leave in five minutes."

"I'm sorry," Emily replied. "I hope you got yourself a coffee while you waited."

"No. I had my eyes on the door."

She didn't see the scowl on his face, but I did. I rarely took an instant dislike to someone, but this guy was an exception to the rule. My Emily had walked a long way in the rain to see him. The least he could do was be nice.

"You told me you'd be on time, but evidently that's too much to ask."

"I promised you I'd arrive at seven-thirty and I didn't. I apologize for that. Garth and I walked thirty minutes in the rain to get here. I assure you this meeting is important to me."

"Why did you walk? Don't you know how to order a rideshare?"

Emily's grip on my harness tightened, and her breathing deepened. She was about to let him have it. I—for one—couldn't wait.

"*Of course* I know how to order a rideshare. I ordered two of them this morning—well before seven. If either of them had complied with the law, I would have been here early—and dry."

"What do you mean?"

"Neither of them would let Garth into their car. And that's against the law."

"So you gave up on the idea and walked in the rain."

"This happens all the time. Our meeting was important, so I decided to walk. The rain slowed us down more than I'd anticipated."

Bruce looked from Emily to me and back again. "You're determined, that's for sure. I've heard that about you."

"Really? Who from?"

"Ross Wilcox."

Emily groaned. "How do you know him?"

"He's a member of an organization for IT professionals. I didn't know him when he worked at our company, but we're both on the membership committee of the organization."

"Ross wasn't my biggest fan," Emily said. "I'll bet he didn't call me 'determined' in a complementary way. No wonder you weren't excited about working with me. What else did Ross say about me?"

Bruce hesitated, pursing his lips. His eyes darted along the floor.

He was going to lie. I was certain of it.

"It's been a while since we spoke. I really don't remember."

"He told you I'm not capable, didn't he?" Her tone was strident. A couple standing nearby turned to look at us.

"He advised me to stick with Dhruv," Bruce said. He lowered his voice. "Ross said Dhruv is the brains of the operation."

"I won't deny that Dhruv is a genius and a key member of my team. The entire team—including myself—is more than qualified to help you. You'll find that out when we conduct our training sessions the next two days."

"I certainly hope so."

"Will you attend any of them?"

"I hadn't planned to. I don't use the software—just my staff does."

"I'd like you to step into this morning's training for at least a few minutes. I'll be leading the initial group sessions. I want you to see me in action," Emily said. "You can decide for yourself if Ross's assessment of me is correct."

"Clear your name, so to speak?" Bruce asked.

"Yes."

"That's fair. I'll slip in the back before you break for lunch."

"Thank you," Emily replied. "What's Ross doing now? I thought he retired when he left the company."

"He's a consultant. Landed some sweet gig at a local firm." Bruce cleared his throat. "Or so he says." He looked at his watch. "I've got to get to my eight o'clock meeting. Let me give you a ride to the office."

"That's kind of you," Emily replied. "But I'm afraid you'd not only have a dog in your car, you'd have a wet one, at that."

"You haven't seen my car," Bruce said. "I have three small children. I'm sure a wet dog makes less of a mess than they do."

"It sounds like it hasn't let up out there," Emily said. "I'd appreciate a ride."

"My car is close, and I have an umbrella. How do we do this? I've never walked with a blind person."

"Since your car is close, I'll forego the umbrella and put my hood up. Walk in front of us. I'll tell Garth to follow you."

"Got it," Bruce said. He rocked from foot to foot as Emily pushed her hair into the hood of her jacket.

"Okay. Let's get you to your meeting," Emily said. "Garth, follow." She pointed to the man, but I already knew what we were doing.

We set out at a brisk pace, and I soon found myself wedged onto the floor of the messy back seat. Bruce hadn't been kidding when he'd said his kids were messy.

I was squirming to find a more comfortable position when I spotted a small mound of something orange underneath the front passenger seat. I hoovered up the stale—but still delicious—handful of Crunchy Cheetos. Bruce wasn't as bad a guy as I'd first thought. Helping him clean up some of this mess was the least I could do to thank him for giving us a ride.

CHAPTER 19

*E*mily stood at the end of the long conference table, her laptop open in front of her. Michael and Rhonda from her San Francisco team sat on either side of her. The Denver employees there to learn Dhruv's new software program filled the other seats.

Emily introduced Michael and Rhonda. "After lunch, you'll run practice drills. They'll guide you through them, and all three of us will be here to answer questions. By lunchtime tomorrow, you'll be proficient with this program. We tailored it to your department's needs, and it will save you a ton of time. You're going to love it.

"I'll present an overview of the software now." She rested her left hand on top of her laptop. "I'm blind and I work with this software as easily as you'll be able to do. I just access it through a screen reader—different tools, same result. Instead of my eyes, I use my ears."

The conference room door opened, and Bruce entered the room. He slipped into the only vacant chair at the table.

"We're going to do a fun exercise before we dig into the new program." She nodded at Rhonda and Mike.

They passed a stack of papers down each side of the table.

"Take a paper from the stack, but leave it face down on the table.

Don't turn it over until everyone has a copy." She paused until the rustling of paper stopped. "Everyone has one?"

Someone murmured yes.

"Turn it over and read the text."

She paused again.

"Would someone read it aloud?"

A woman at the far end of the table cleared her throat and read a paragraph summarizing a famous university's research demonstrating that people can accurately read words when the first and last letters are correct, regardless of the arrangement of the letters in between.

"Did you all read this correctly?"

Everyone around the table nodded.

"I can't see you, but I assume you're all nodding your heads. A fun fact is that hearing is more accurate than seeing. Our eyes fill in words or—in the case of programs—numbers or characters that aren't there. It's easier for me to find errors in programs because I listen to the code rather than see it."

A smile played at the corners of Bruce's lips.

"We've got a lot to cover, so let's get started. It's best if I take questions as we go along. Since I can't see you if you raise your hand, please call out my name. I'll finish my slide and then take your questions. Sound good?"

The group in front of her nodded.

"I'll bet you're nodding," Emily said. "Let's try this again, speaking your answer. Sound good?"

A chorus of yes filled the room.

Emily brought up her first slide and began instructing the eager learners in front of her.

Bruce observed her presentation, voicing his responses to Emily's questions with the rest of the group.

Emily didn't see the look of admiration he gave her when he quietly left the room thirty minutes later.

BRUCE ENTERED the conference room as Emily wrapped up the training session the next day. He leaned against the wall and joined in the applause as she acknowledged Rhonda and Michael for their participation.

"Thank you for your excellent questions. You've been terrific to work with. We talked at breakfast," she gestured to Rhonda and Michael, "and every one of you has demonstrated great proficiency. You've got our contact information if you have questions, but we think you've got it."

Applause rang out again.

Emily motioned for silence. "One last thing—and it may be the most important. We always end our trainings by drawing names for company swag." She pointed to a large cardboard box behind her. "We brought this stuff from the stash at corporate headquarters. Michael— are we ready?"

"Yep. I've got a donut box with scraps of paper with everyone's name on it." He held the box high. "Rhonda, would you do the honors? Let's see who's won the fleece-lined zippered hoodie with the company logo."

Rhonda pulled a slip of paper from the box and read the name.

A hand shot in the air and Michael rummaged in the large box, found the hoodie, and tossed it to the winner.

"Look at the label," the winner said. "It's a top brand—and it's my size. Thank you."

People pushed back their chairs.

"Hold on," Michael said. "There's more in this box. We'll draw names until we've given everything away. I'm not hauling this box home on the plane."

He and Rhonda repeated drawing winners until every attendee had a nice item of corporate swag in front of them.

Michael made a show of searching the large box. "That's it. I guess we're finally done."

Bruce started another round of applause.

The attendees filed out of the room, stopping to shake hands and thank their trainers.

Bruce was the last to leave. "A word, Emily?"

"Sure." She turned to Michael and Rhonda. "I'll catch up with you at Kari's office."

They left the conference room.

"So …" Emily began.

"You proved me wrong, Emily Main. You *can* do your job as well as a sighted person. I'm grateful for the help you—and Michael and Rhonda—gave my team. They've been singing your praises." He stuck out his hand. "I'm extending my hand."

Emily held out hers in response, and they shook hands.

"Do you have time for lunch before you head to the airport?"

"Our flight isn't until six," Emily replied. "I promised you we'd spend the day here in case you needed extra time with us. I'm taking the team I supervise here in Denver to lunch."

"Of course. Well … the next time you're in town, I'd love to buy you lunch."

"That'd be nice. I'll let you know when I'm headed back to Denver."

They strolled out of the conference room.

"Do you need help to find Kari's office?"

"Nope. Garth and I have it covered."

Bruce grinned. "I thought you might. Thanks again, Emily."

"One last thing," Emily said. "Will you do something for me?"

"I'd be happy to."

"The next time you see Ross Wilcox, please share your opinion of me with him. And tell him I said hello."

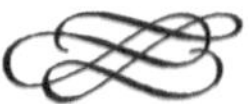

CHAPTER 20

"What do you think?" Martha stood in the open door to the dressing room, tugging at the bodice of a navy blue fit and flare dress.

"It's a nice dress," Sylvia said. She leaned against the wall of the hallway in the dressing room aisle. "Fit is good."

"That's what I thought," Martha said. "I'll change back into my clothes and get this one. We'll be on our way to lunch in ten minutes."

"Whoa." Sylvia held up a hand to stop her friend. "This is only the first dress you've tried on. You've got at least ten more in that dressing room with you."

"That you picked out for me," Martha said, reaching one hand over her shoulder to hold the back of the neck opening while her other hand grappled for the zipper pull.

"Turn around," Sylvia ordered. "I'll get that." She unzipped the dress. "I picked out the other dresses because that navy one is similar to everything else in your closet."

"You said it looks good."

"It does. And predictable. You brought me along to help you select new clothes for your trip to London with Doug. Don't you want something a little less business-y? Something flirty—sexy, even?"

Martha snickered. "At my age? Are you out of your mind?"

"What do you mean—at your age? Look in the mirror. You're beautiful. Older women can be seductive."

Martha blushed.

"That dress is perfect for church—or a hundred other ordinary occasions. You're going to tea at The Ritz with a man who's clearly smitten with you. I think you owe it to yourself to be more feminine." She fixed Martha with her gaze. "He'll love it if you wear something that you wouldn't for a night out with me or the kids—something just for him."

"You're not going to let this go, are you?"

"Nope. Not until you've tried on every dress hanging in the dressing room."

"That'll take at least another thirty minutes. You'll have to wait for lunch."

Sylvia checked her watch. "It's only 10:40. We've got loads of time." She took a step back. "There's a three-way mirror and chairs at the entrance to the dressing rooms. I'll wait for you there. Put on each dress and walk down there to show me."

"If you insist," Martha said. "I'm buying this blue one even if I find something else. I need a new church dress."

She stepped back into the dressing room while Sylvia positioned herself in a chair by the three-way mirror.

Martha walked to the mirror in a cream-colored jersey wrap dress and turned this way and that. "What do you think?"

Sylvia shook her head. "It doesn't have the pizzazz we're looking for."

"I kind of like it. I could see myself wearing this to church."

"Then get it, but we need to keep looking."

Martha retreated to the dressing room and modeled a parade of dresses, from an eggplant silk sheath to a vibrant geometric print. "The eggplant sheath is the best of the bunch," she said to Sylvia, who followed her to the dressing room after she'd modeled the final dress.

"I agree. If the fit was better, it would be just the thing," Sylvia said.

"I'm a home seamstress, remember? I'll take up the shoulders, move the darts, and shorten the hem."

"Is that all? Seems like a lot of work to me." Sylvia sighed. "I say we keep looking."

Martha held out the hanger, studying the sheath.

"Admit it," Sylvia said. "That dress doesn't make your heart sing."

"It'll be good enough when I've fixed it."

Sylvia took the hanger from her friend and placed it on the rack of garments to be returned to the floor.

"Nope. We didn't come here for 'good enough.' Let's take the navy and the cream dress to the register and keep going."

Martha made her purchase. "I'm happy with these."

Sylvia's neck swiveled like she was a bobblehead as they headed to the mall entrance of the department store.

"We don't …" Martha began.

"There!" Sylvia inhaled sharply and took off at a fast pace toward the far corner of the store.

Martha sighed and followed her friend. When she caught up with her, Sylvia was holding a dove gray embroidered cocktail sheath in one hand and a floral embellished royal blue midi dress in the other.

"These are very different from each other—and from anything in my closet."

"Exactly," Sylvia said. "It's been so long since I've shopped for a special occasion dress, I forgot this department existed. Do you like either of these? If not, there's plenty more." She gestured with her head to the racks of dresses behind her.

"They're pretty," Martha said. "Let's start with these."

Sylvia followed Martha into a large dressing room and helped her into the gray sheath.

Martha drew in a breath before Sylvia had it completely zipped. "I don't think I've ever had a more perfect off-the-rack fit."

"It's like it was custom-made. The color is gorgeous on you." She stood behind Martha and they both looked at her reflection in the mirror. "Looks like something Kate Middleton would wear."

Martha burst out laughing.

"I'm serious."

"I'm laughing because I thought the same thing." She turned to check how the dress looked from the back. "This is it. I'm getting it. We'll be on our way to lunch in a few."

"Hold on," Sylvia said. "I agree you *must* get this dress. I also want to see you in the other one."

Martha fingered the floral appliques on the midi dress. "These are lovely, and royal blue is my favorite color."

Sylvia had her out of the sheath and into the dress in a flash.

Martha stared at herself in the mirror, admiring the graceful drape of the fabric. She spun in a circle and the folds of the floral hem flared around her calves. "It twirls!" She spun again. "This would be so much fun to dance in!"

"You lit up when you put on each dress, but I think this one is your favorite."

"Maybe … but the other is more practical. I'm getting the gray."

"Martha Main! I swear. You don't need to be practical every second of every day."

Martha twirled one last time in the blue dress before stepping out of it. "I'll have bought three new dresses today. I don't call that practical." She zipped her slacks, pulled her T-shirt over her head, and picked up the gray dress. "Let's pay for this and find somewhere to eat. I'm starved."

Sylvia grabbed the blue dress and followed Martha to the register.

The salesclerk rang up Martha's purchase and turned to Sylvia. "I'm glad you found something, too." She reached for the blue dress.

"That one goes back out on the floor," Martha interjected.

"No, it doesn't," Sylvia said. "I'm buying it for you, Martha."

"What? You can't do that."

"I most certainly can. It's a 'just because' gift for my best friend."

"Aww … that's so nice." The salesclerk completed Sylvia's purchase and put it in the garment carrier with Martha's other dress.

"I can't believe you did that," Martha said as they walked into the mall and headed for the food court. "It's incredibly generous. Thank you."

"I haven't been shopping with a girlfriend since—gosh—college? I refuse to say aloud how many years that's been. Today was fun. Let's do it again."

"Actually, I think we should continue shopping after lunch."

"Sure. I've got all day. What else are you looking for?" Sylvia asked.

"Not for me. I've got what I want. You should have something new for your trip to New York City and D.C. with the kids."

"All I'll need are slacks, T-shirts, and sneakers. Plus a hoodie. I've got plenty of those."

"You made a valid point about having something new for a trip. It makes it more exciting. You deserve to feel sharp on your trip."

"I'm with Grant, Emily, and the girls. Grandma clothes will be fine."

"Nonsense. And you never know. You might meet someone on the trip."

"As if," Sylvia retorted. "You've been reading too many romance novels."

"I admit I enjoy a good love story, and they happen in real life—not just in books."

"I've got plenty of time to pick up something new if I need to."

"Doug and I leave in two weeks, and you take off in three. You don't have plenty of time. Besides, I want to be with you to help. Like you did for me."

They stepped into the queue for a popular Thai restaurant.

Sylvia looked at Martha. "You're not going to give up on this, are you?"

"I'm afraid not. It's on."

"All right. Let's eat and head to the big sporting goods store at the other end of the mall. I need new sneakers, and they have cute activewear, too."

Martha squeezed her friend's shoulder, and they moved forward in line.

CHAPTER 21

Stephanie placed the onesie on the stack of clothes she was folding and answered her phone.

"Hello, dear," Pari said. "May I stop by for a minute?"

"You just missed Dhruv. He's gone to the grocery."

"It's not Dhruv I'm coming to see," her mother-in-law said. "I was hoping to catch you alone. Can I come up? I'm in front of your building."

Stephanie inhaled slowly. She'd been hoping to take a nap as soon as she'd finished folding the load of baby clothes. This would be her first time with Pari since Dhruv's family meeting after the disastrous incident with Amelia's antibiotic. She didn't have the energy for a confrontation.

"I won't stay long," Pari continued. "I can't rest until we talk."

"Sure," Stephanie said, groaning inwardly. She couldn't refuse.

Pari was at their apartment door in an instant. She knocked softly.

"Is Amelia asleep?" Pari whispered when Stephanie opened the door.

"She just went down for her nap." She led the way to the living room. "I was folding laundry," She hesitated, then finished her sentence, "and then was going to take a nap."

"I'll help you," Pari said, "so you can get to that nap quicker." She picked a romper off the top of the mound of clean clothes and began folding it. "I'm here to apologize to you, Stephanie. Dhruv described in detail your ordeal when I didn't put Amelia's medicine back in its place. Having a sick infant is hard enough—especially as a new parent—but listening to her scream in pain while you searched for something that should have been in its designated spot? That was unnecessary and unforgivable."

"It was tough at the time, Pari, but I know it was a mistake. You didn't intend to hurt either of us."

"That's true, but regardless of my intentions, I made things awful for you both. I've been stewing about this since Dhruv came over. I finally decided I had to apologize in person and ask your forgiveness." She stopped folding clothes and faced Stephanie. "I'm so sorry."

Stephanie extended a hand toward her mother-in-law.

Pari caught it and held it in both of hers.

"I know you would never want to hurt us," Stephanie said. "I also know how much you love your granddaughter."

"I love all my grandchildren the same," Pari said, "but boys have been running in our family for two generations. I'm thrilled to at last have a girl to spoil."

Stephanie chuckled. "I've noticed that you and your sisters dote on her."

"It's not just Amelia," Pari said. "I love you, Stephanie. You're the soulmate to my Dhruv—his perfect partner. I prayed he'd find his special person, but as the years went by, I'd all but given up. And then you appeared." Pari's voice grew thick with emotion. "You're a mother's dream and I think of you like the daughter I never had."

Stephanie leaned toward her mother-in-law and opened her arms wide.

Pari stepped into the hug. "I want you to trust me, Stephanie. I promise you I understand what I need to do to keep you safe. Dhruv made everything crystal clear."

"He's never once made a mistake or overlooked something." Stephanie moved back. "I've nicknamed him the Safety Tzar."

Pari chuckled. "That suits him to a T. I can picture him around here, going through his mental checklist of items and their assigned locations. There's one thing, however, my son isn't good with."

"What's that?"

"Emotional well-being," Pari said. "He's a kind and empathic man, but he doesn't know how to deal with things that aren't quantifiable."

"Well ..."

"Many partners aren't good at talking about feelings. That's another reason I wanted to see you. How are you?"

"The baby is great. I'm learning to cope ..."

"She is, and you are. But that's not the question."

"I feel like I've lost track of myself. Amelia is our focus. I think that's natural."

"It is, but being a mom doesn't mean you give up your own interests. Are you getting time to do the things you enjoy?"

"I sleep most days during Amelia's afternoon nap," Stephanie replied.

"That's great, but napping wasn't a hobby before you had a baby, was it?"

"No. Of course not."

"Catching up on sleep doesn't count as 'me' time. What did you love to do before you had Amelia?"

Stephanie rested her hand on her hip and blew out a breath. "Let me think. I loved to take long walks with Biscuit. We'd sit on a bench, and I'd listen to an audiobook before heading home. Knitting—I love to knit. And having coffee with Emily every weekend was something I looked forward to."

"Have you done any of these since Amelia was born?"

Stephanie groaned. "That would be no." She turned back to the pile of laundry on the sofa. "Those things are from another life."

"I've got an idea. Let's move them back into your life—the one you're living now. I'd love to babysit one day a week. Stay home, go out, or a combination of the two, but you'll have no responsibilities here. We'll call it 'Stephanie Day.' "

"That's awfully generous of you."

"You'd like that?"

"Heck, yes."

"I'd love it, too."

"What about Dhruv?"

"I don't need his help with Amelia. He can explore his own interests. Maybe you'll do things together. Just don't let this devolve into a day where you're running household errands. We're calling it 'Stephanie Day' for a reason. It's your time to refill your creative well and maintain friendships. A happy and fulfilled parent is a good role model, too."

"Sold!"

"Let's start this Saturday. I'll be here at eight."

"I'm not ready to leave Amelia for an entire day yet," Stephanie replied. "This sounds wonderful for the future."

"We'll start with a half day to give you time to get used to it. You could buy yarn for a new project." Pari warmed to her subject. "You're going back to teaching full-time in the fall?"

"I am."

"Let's decide right now that the Saturday before you go back will be a full day. I'd like you to plan something really special. Why don't you and Emily book that spa day you missed when you went into labor early? You have plenty of time to contact her and make arrangements."

"You're going to make sure 'Stephanie Day' becomes a reality, aren't you?"

"Count on it."

"I wondered who Dhruv got his single-minded tenacity from. Now I know."

Pari chuckled. "I told you I'd only stay a few minutes and here we've gone on and on. Go take that nap you wanted before Amelia wakes up. I'll fold the rest of this laundry and see myself out."

"You're the best, Pari."

Pari threw her shoulders back and turned her attention to the laundry. "I'll stack everything here on the sofa—just like you've done. I promise nothing will be out of order."

CHAPTER 22

$\mathcal{G}$*arth*

I heard the squeaking noise from the backyard before Sabrina did. And I knew what was making that sound. *A cat!* There was a cat in our yard.

I shuddered as I recalled my first—and I hoped only—encounter with a cat. Katie and John—my puppy raiser family and their two children—had a cat named Liloh. That feline was a she-devil in fur. My nose still smarted from the blow she landed on me with those claws of hers.

Those were the old days. My new family sat around the kitchen table. Our other grandmother—Sylvia—was with them. Emily typed on her laptop while each of them talked in turn.

Sabrina napped in her bed on the far side of the kitchen.

"Let's recap," Grant said. "Emily ..."

"And Garth," Emily interjected.

I appreciated being included by name.

"And Garth," Grant said, "want their one-day activity to be the High Line park."

"Tuesday is the only day without the possibility of showers in the forecast, so it'll be perfect for the park. We'll start our day with break-fast at the Chelsea Market," Emily said.

"The Empire State Building is on our way back to our hotel, so we could stop there afterward if we have time," Grant said.

"That sounds neat," Diedre said. "For my day, I'd like to see *Wicked.*"

"We've already bought tickets for Wednesday evening's perfor-mance," he said.

"Can we wait at the stage door afterwards so I can get my playbill signed?" Diedre asked.

"Sure," Emily replied. "We take the train to D.C. on Thursday, but don't leave until right after lunch. We'll sleep in after our night on the town. What do you want to do during the day on Wednesday?"

"Shopping," both girls said in unison.

"Works for me," Emily said. "We'll do the Air and Space Museum on Friday for Zoe and the Dupont Circle and Embassy Row Architec-ture walking tour on Saturday for Grant. We fly home on Sunday."

"That leaves Monday wide open for your pick, Mom," Grant said. "You said you wanted to have a museum day?"

"Yes. I've decided on the Museum of Modern Art. The MOMA has an exhibition on turning points in design that I think we'll all enjoy." She cleared her throat. "Except maybe you, Emily."

"I enjoy museum exhibits. I've got a phone app that reads the label of a work of art to me and searches the internet for additional infor-mation if I direct it to." She turned toward her mother-in-law. "I read about this exhibit when I was researching what I want to do with my day. It sounds extremely interesting. I almost picked it, myself."

Sylvia leaned over to pat Emily's hand. "I'm the luckiest mother-in-law in the world."

"Let's go over logistics," Grant said. "Travel arrangements and hotel reservations."

The squeaking resumed from the backyard—louder and closer this time.

Sabrina's head shot up.

The squeaking continued. None of the humans noticed.

Sabrina hopped to her feet and raced to the back door, clawing at the glass.

Zoe got out of her chair and opened the sliding glass door.

I was comfortably stretched out in a sunny patch on the floor, but I got to my feet and ambled after Sabrina. Sometimes that dog didn't have the sense God gave geese. She had no idea how vicious cats could be. I needed to protect my little buddy.

Sabrina had already bounded to a spot in the shrubbery bordering the back patio. The scene I witnessed as I made my way to her was comical.

Something behind those bushes squeaked. Sabrina stuck her nose into the bushes, her tail wagging at warp speed, causing her short body to vibrate.

The squeak became a squawk.

Sabrina retracted her muzzle.

I arrived at her side, and she turned to me. Her nose bore no evidence of contact with a cat's claws.

The bush squeaked again, and the process repeated itself.

I didn't need to join Sabrina in her inquiry. My nose confirmed that we had a cat in our midst.

Another iteration of the entire scenario caught the attention of our family. Diedre was the first to join us, followed closely by Zoe.

Diedre got on her hands and knees and gingerly parted the bushes.

Zoe pulled Sabrina away and restrained her.

I didn't need to be told to stay away. I already knew that.

"It's a cat!" Diedre froze in place. "It's got black, brown, red, and white stripes. There's even gray."

Sylvia led the pack of adult humans. She knelt next to Diedre. "It's a tabby. Beautiful one, too."

"Will it hurt me?" Diedre asked her grandmother.

"Extend your hand slowly, but don't touch him—or her. Let the cat come to you."

Diedre followed Sylvia's advice.

The cat pushed her face forward, her nose twitching, to greet

Diedre. After a thorough olfactory introduction, the cat inched closer to Diedre and squeaked again.

Before long, Diedre held the cat in her arms. To my amazement, my humans were soon crossing the patio and entering the house.

What were they doing? We didn't want a cat in the house!

"I agree," Emily said. "We shouldn't leave it …"

"Him," Grant supplied.

"In the bushes."

"Can we keep him?" Diedre's voice was so full of hope it actually choked me up.

"He may already have a family," Grant said. "He might be lost."

"If that's the case, you'd want him to go home to his family, honey," Sylvia said. "Consider how you would feel if Sabrina or Garth were lost."

Diedre's lips puckered, but she didn't disagree.

"I'll make lost cat signs and post them in the neighborhood today," Zoe said.

"If nobody claims him, we'll take him to the vet to have him scanned for a microchip on Monday," Grant said.

"Until then, can he stay in my room?"

"What do you think, Em? Should we keep him in the garage, away from Garth?" Grant asked.

I watched Emily, eager for her reply.

"This cat isn't aggressive. And it's only for the weekend. I don't see why not."

"I've got an extra litter box, litter, and some cat food you can have to tide you through," Sylvia said. "I hope he's litterbox trained. He's awfully friendly and his fur is clean. He's not feral. I'll be surprised if someone doesn't claim him."

What was going on? We were now hosting a *cat* for the weekend?

The cat squeaked loudly, as if he could read my mind.

"I'm calling him Squeaky!" Diedre said, peppering the top of his head with kisses.

"Good name," Grant said. "But don't get too attached to him. We may not be able to keep him."

Diedre's eyes shone as she looked up at her father. "You mean, if he doesn't have a family, we can keep him?"

"We'll see," Grant said. "Nothing has been decided yet."

I looked from face to face of my family, including Sabrina. Who was he kidding? They all wanted to adopt this cat.

I snorted my indignation. No one noticed. Turning my back on them, I padded to my bed in the living room and plunked myself down. I needed a moment to process what had just happened.

CHAPTER 23

 artha rested against the oval back of a gilded Louis XVI armchair and gazed at the surrounding opulence. "The Palm Court is even more beautiful in person than it is in photographs. Breathtaking." She crossed her legs beneath the starched white linen tablecloth that fell to the floor. "I wish I could take a photo and send it to Sylvia. And the kids."

"There's something nice about the etiquette that prohibits them," Doug said. "Tourists have been snapping photos with their phones everywhere we've gone. It's relaxing—more intimate—without recording every moment of our experience with a photo."

Martha considered this as she took in the room. Paneled mirrors of beveled glass in gilt bronze frames surrounded them. "This room has been done up in this shade of apricot since The Ritz opened in 1906. After weeks of experimentation with different shades, Cesar Ritz decided the color flattered women's complexions." She lifted her gold-rimmed cup to her lips and sipped the hotel's exclusive Green Elderflower Tea Blend. "You know, I like ignoring my phone and concentrating on this experience."

"It's easy to imagine all the famous people who have sat where we're sitting and taken tea. Just like we're doing."

Martha gestured to the tiered stand filled with elegant tea sandwiches, plain and fruit scones, and tea cakes and pastries that were miniature works of art. "These are so beautiful, it's almost a shame to eat them." She smiled at him. "Almost. What would you like to try?"

"Ladies first," Doug said. "I'm planning to have one of each."

"There's a lot of food here," she replied. "But I'm going to force myself—even if I waddle out of here." She served them each a chicken sandwich with tarragon creamed mayonnaise on malt bread. "I read about this sandwich in a novel recently. It's iconic."

"Perfect place to start," Doug said. He finished the small rectangle in two bites. "That was delicious."

"You're not supposed to wolf them down," Martha teased. "Tea sandwiches are meant to be nibbled while you enjoy the music." She gestured to the grand piano, where the white-jacketed artist was playing "All I Ask of You" from *The Phantom of the Opera*. "Or talk to the person you're with."

"That song sounds familiar," he said, cocking his head to one side. "But I can't place it. I'm hopeless at *Name that Tune*."

Martha supplied the information. "It's probably playing in the West End right now. I imagine the hotel likes to promote the London theater scene."

"Have you seen it?"

"Years ago. The music is gorgeous."

"Would you like to go while we're here?"

"Gosh ... I'd love to. If we can get tickets."

"We'll ask our concierge to help with that as soon as we go back to our hotel."

She served them each a cucumber sandwich with cream cheese on granary bread. "Here's another teatime classic."

Doug took a tiny bite and set the uneaten sandwich on his plate. "Better?"

"You're getting the hang of it."

"I've got a question."

Martha cocked an eyebrow at him.

"Have you ever seen so much gold trim in your entire life? It's on all the furniture." He tapped the arm of his chair. "Embellishes the carving on the walls and covers every statue I've seen so far. And it's so shiny. Not a spec of tarnish."

"That's part of the Louis XVI style of the hotel. They have an in-house gilder on staff. It's their job to keep it all gleaming."

She continued her recitation of facts about the proud history of The Ritz as they worked their way through the remaining sandwiches —ham and mustard, egg salad, cheddar cheese with chutney, and smoked salmon—followed by scones with Cornish clotted cream and strawberry preserves.

"I'm about to burst," Martha said, "but I'm going to take at least a bite of each of these glorious pastries. "Where shall we start?"

Doug did the honors by placing on each of their plates a tiny cream puff topped with a chocolate square imprinted with the words THE RITZ in gold leaf under a flourish of meringue.

"Dig deep," he said with a smile. "I know you can do this."

She smiled and cleared her plate in three bites. "Let's try the round one that looks like a tiny cheesecake with cherry icing next."

Doug did as she requested. "How do you know so much about this place? Did you study up on it for our trip?"

"The Ritz is featured in scores of movies, television shows, and novels. I've been fascinated by it my whole life. I've always dreamed of having tea here."

"Then I'm glad I got to make that dream come true."

Martha reached across the table to squeeze his hand.

"One final question. It's kind of corny—and old-fashioned, but I'm an old-fashioned kind of guy. Will you make a dream come true for me?"

A smile played at her lips as her eyes held a question.

"I've fallen in love with you, Martha Main. Will you go steady with me?"

CHAPTER 24

Kari re-read the email she'd just written, her hand hovering over the enter button. She hated to bow out of the interview later that morning with an intern candidate. Her position on her company's intern recruitment committee was something she was proud of.

The company had initiated the committee to improve their success at attracting and retaining top talent in the competitive job market. Kari had been a member of the committee since its inception eighteen months ago and was proud of the results they'd achieved. She had kept in touch with all ten of the interns she'd met during the process, helping them integrate into their business units, and serving as a mentor during their internship. The company considered it a tremendous success that eight of these interns had accepted permanent positions.

She shook her head as she hit send. With Dhruv still out on paternity leave and Emily on vacation, she couldn't spare the hour for the interview. She'd worked the entire weekend and would be lucky if she got home before midnight tonight.

She picked up her coffee cup and headed to the break room for a refill. By the time she returned to her desk, a reply to her email awaited her.

She groaned and rested her forehead in one hand as she read the response. The other three members of the committee had pulled out of the interview. The business manager assured her he would continue without her—he'd been interviewing interns for years and didn't need help.

Kari didn't know him personally, but the guy had a reputation for being a pompous know-it-all. Someone from their committee should be present during the interview to make sure the company didn't come off in a poor light. There was nothing for it—she had to make time for this.

She threw her shoulders back and typed a terse reply, telling him she'd be there, then dug into the long list of projects on her plate.

THE BUSINESS UNIT manager and Kari sat together on one side of a small conference table, waiting for the receptionist to show the internship candidate into the room.

"Did you see his résumé?" The manager tapped the document lying on the table.

"I didn't have time to review it," Kari said. "We're swamped."

He slid it to her. "Take a look while we wait. He's got everything we're looking for. Top-notch school and stellar grades. If his references check out, he's a perfect fit. To be honest, I'd hire him without even interviewing him."

Kari ran her eyes down the résumé. "I see what you mean. I'm sure he'll have a lot of offers. We need to make sure we sell him on the benefits of working for us."

"Our salaries are the highest in our industry," the manager said.

"That's a great selling point," Kari said, "but—as they say—money isn't everything. Corporate culture; job satisfaction; opportunity for advancement—they're all extremely important to today's recruits."

The manager harrumphed as the conference room door opened.

The receptionist stepped inside, followed by the recruit. He swung a white cane in front of him, tapping to the right as he stepped with his left foot and to the left when he moved his right.

"A conference table is six feet straight in front of you," she said. "Your interviewers are on the other side of the table and there are chairs on casters on your side of the table. Would you like me to pull one out for you?"

The recruit had already made his way to the table and found the chairs. "Thank you," he said. "I've got this."

The receptionist left the room.

Kari leapt to her feet, motioning for the manager to do the same. "Hello, Anthony. I'm Kari," she said. "I'm extending my hand." She and Anthony Cordoba shook hands.

The business manager followed her lead. He stood, staring at Anthony.

"Let's take our seats and get started," Kari said, taking charge of the meeting.

Anthony took his seat and folded his cane, setting it on the table in front of him.

"Before you joined us, we were talking about what a terrific résumé you have. Your skills align perfectly with our open position. Let's go over what's involved. Are you familiar with …"

"How do you find the bathroom?" the manager interrupted.

"With my cane. It's easy." Anthony's tone was cordial. "I made preliminary inquiries about the job. I'd like to know more."

"But how do you know if it's a men's or women's bathroom?"

"There will be braille markers by the doors." Anthony's voice remained even. "I'm proficient with the JAWS screen reader. I'm confident I can access any of your software using JAWS."

"You're correct," Kari interjected. "My boss is visually impaired, and she uses it all day long."

"That's helpful to know," Anthony said. "As long as software is accessible, I can …"

"What about stairs?" The manager leaned across the table.

"I'm proficient at climbing and descending stairs."

"Let's focus on the job requirements," Kari said tersely.

"Getting around this huge regional headquarters is part of the job," the manager said. "Regular interns frequently get lost."

"You're more than qualified for our internship position," Kari said, ignoring the manager. "I'd like to tell you more about our company and open the discussion up for your questions."

"We had one who couldn't find his way back from the cafeteria on his first day," the manager said.

"I function in the world just fine as a blind person," Anthony said. "Stairs, bathrooms, and cafeterias pose no problem. I have the skills and experience you're looking for. I was terribly excited to come in for this interview today. Having a career at your company has been a dream of mine."

"I'm happy to hear that," Kari said, relief clear in her voice. "We'd love to bring you onboard."

The manager swung his head to hers. "The opening is in my unit, not yours."

She held up a hand to silence him.

"I have a question before you tell me more, if I may," Anthony said.

"Sure," Kari said.

"Who would I be working for?"

"The internship is in my department," the business unit manager said.

"Then I'm not interested."

The room was silent for a beat.

"What? You don't want a job with this company?" The manager was indignant.

"I very much wanted a job with this company." Anthony's voice was level and professional. "I've mastered the tools and will soon earn a degree that will allow me to contribute to your company's success in significant ways. But only if you allow me to do so. This interview shows me you will never see me as capable. You won't give me the opportunities I deserve."

He reached for his cane. "I entered this room excited about what you offer and proud of what I can do. I'm leaving feeling ashamed and discouraged. What started as a hopeful day has now become a dark one. You see my disability instead of my talents."

Kari fixed the manager with a look that caused him to recoil. "I'll give you the internship," the manager said.

"I don't want only an internship," Anthony said. "I want a career. You'd put up with me for eighteen months and wouldn't offer me a permanent job because you won't give me anything to work on during the internship to prove my worth. I'm not going to put myself through that."

He pushed his chair back and extended his cane. "I'll see myself out."

CHAPTER 25

"That exhibit was so interesting, Grandma," Diedre said. "I didn't know that stuff about Post-It notes."

"I'm going to write what I learned in the journal I bought in the gift shop," Zoe said.

"That was nice of Martha to give both of you spending money for your vacation," Grant said.

"I'll write in my journal every night and show it to her when we see her next time."

"I'm sure she'll be happy to hear all about it."

Diedre said, "I'm saving my Martha money for the *Wicked* gift shop. I know I'll want a T-shirt and a poster."

"It's almost dinnertime," Emily said. "Let's get pizza at one of those little storefront pizzerias. They have the best slices in this city. We'll wander through Times Square while we eat."

"Yeah!" the girls cried.

"I'm game," Grant said.

"I'm jet-lagged and worn out from the day at the MOMA. Go enjoy yourselves. I'm heading back to the hotel. My room has a lovely bathtub, and I intend to have a long soak." Sylvia reached for Zoe's bag from the museum. "I'll take that back to the hotel for you, if you'd like."

"Thank you."

"Would you like us to bring you some pizza?" Grant asked.

Sylvia shook her head. "I'll order something from room service. I'm in for the night."

"We'll walk you back to the hotel," Grant said.

"You'll do no such thing. I can navigate six blocks on my own."

They parted ways under the marquee of Radio City Music Hall.

Sylvia went to her hotel room, kicked off her shoes, and lay back on the bed. She'd intended to rest for a few minutes, but when she opened her eyes, an hour had passed. By this time, she was ravenous.

Sylvia walked to the small desk in the corner of the room where she'd spread out her makeup. Containers of foundation, powder, and blush buried the room service menu. When she got to it, she flipped through the pages and decided she couldn't go wrong with a Cobb salad. She rang the number on the menu, only to learn that her order wouldn't arrive for another ninety minutes.

"That's a long wait for a Cobb salad," she said.

"I'm sorry. We're short-staffed tonight. Our café on the second floor will serve you much faster. They offer everything on our room service menu."

"Thanks for the tip," Sylvia said. "I'll head to the café."

Her leisurely soak in the tub would have to wait. She slipped into her shoes, headed to the elevator, and pushed the down button to summon it.

FRANK BLAKE COMMANDED LONNY FORWARD, into the elevator. Lonny was his fourth guide dog. They'd only worked together for a few weeks, but he had high hopes for his new guide. Lonny was smart, responsive, determined—and loved to work. They already knew each other's habits and routines.

The elevator doors closed.

Frank could hear that they were the only ones in the elevator. "Find buttons," he commanded Lonny.

The obedient guide took him to a display panel to the right of the elevator door opening.

Frank felt the smooth class of the display panel. It must be a touch-screen, he thought. Those were great—unless you couldn't see the screen.

He ran his hand along the wall below the touch screen, to a row of old-fashioned buttons. The law required those to be supplemented with braille markings.

The braille markings were missing. A button labeled "Lobby" should have been there. He cursed under his breath.

The elevator remained in place. He needed to get to the ground floor. If he wasn't on his way soon, he'd be late.

He pulled his cell phone from his pocket and tried to place a call. "No service," he muttered to the dog, who sat at his side and waited for his handler's next command.

The bellman had accompanied him to the lobby when he'd arrived. They'd ridden the elevator to the lobby because it wasn't on the ground floor. The ride had taken a long time. The bellman hadn't mentioned where the lobby was located, but Frank felt certain it wasn't on a lower floor.

Frank considered the keypad. It consisted of twelve rows, each containing three buttons. The hotel had thirty floors, so some of these buttons accessed other floors or features.

Pushing elevator buttons in random fashion wouldn't help him find where he wanted to go. His best bet was to get off the elevator before it moved from his floor. He could return to his room and place an irate call to the front desk to complain about the inaccessible elevator and ask for assistance.

The lack of markings on the elevator buttons prevented him from finding the one that opened the doors.

Frank was trapped in the elevator. A trickle of sweat ran down the back of his neck into his shirt collar.

Lonny sensed his handler's distress and rested his muzzle on Frank's thigh.

Frank understood he wouldn't be in the elevator forever. It would eventually move, and someone, somehow, would help him. He'd be late for his appointment. What angered him was that he was perfectly capable of getting where he needed to go—independently—if only the hotel had complied with the law and assured its elevators were accessible. He set his jaw in a thin line and waited.

The door opened. A woman stepped into the elevator and joined the tall, attractive man with hair that was graying at the temples and a sour expression. A black lab, wearing a guide dog harness, sat at his side.

"Good evening." Her tone was pleasant. "I'm reaching in front of you to push the elevator button."

He shuffled back to give her room.

She tapped at the touch screen, and the elevator moved. "Heavens," she said. "There aren't any braille markings in this elevator. How ... where ... are you headed?"

"I'm trying to get to the ground floor," he said. "I got stuck on my floor because I can't access any of the buttons."

"That's horrible! This is an expensive hotel, for Pete's sake. The website says it's newly renovated. I can't believe this."

"Evidently, nobody checked for accessibility when they redid the elevators," Frank said.

"That's reprehensible." Her voice resembled a gathering storm. "The lobby is on the twentieth floor. Isn't that crazy? I was headed for the café on two, but now I'll take you to the ground floor."

"That's kind of you. With any luck, I'll make it to my appointment on time. I'm sorry to inconvenience you."

"Not at all," Sylvia said. "After I see you off, I'm going straight to the lobby. The manager of this place is going to get a piece of my mind."

"Again, that's kind of you. Not many people will step in to help."

"My daughter-in-law is blind and uses a guide dog," Sylvia said. "As a matter of fact, Garth bears an uncanny resemblance to this guy."

"Lonny," Frank said, extending his hand to her. "I'm Frank Blake."

She took his hand in hers. "Sylvia Johnson," she replied.

Their elevator arrived at the ground floor, and Sylvia walked with him to the doorman.

The doorman hailed Frank a cab.

Frank turned to her. "Thank you, Sylvia, for being my knight in shining armor."

Sylvia chuckled. "Have a nice evening. I hope you have nothing but good luck the rest of your stay."

FRANK AND LONNY entered the hotel lobby after midnight.

Lonny guided him to the reception desk, almost as if he had been expecting the command.

The night clerk looked up from his computer screen and smiled at them. "Good evening, sir. Are you Mr. Blake?"

"I am. How did you know?"

"We were told to be on the lookout for you."

"Really?"

"An urgent alert went out about what happened to you in our elevator. We want to apologize to you and assure you that the company is working on a temporary fix until the new panels are installed."

"That's good to hear. All you need to do is attach braille labels next to each button. If I had my braille labeler with me, I could make them myself."

"Our corporate office is sending them to us tomorrow. Until then, I'll call a bellman to take you to your room—which the hotel has comped for the duration of your stay."

"That's very nice," Frank said. "I'm grateful for your fast action."

"The guest who reported the problem was …," he paused, choosing his words, "quite persuasive. My manager said she recounted your experience with great passion. He instructed us to correct our short-comings."

"Was that guest Sylvia Johnson?"

"I'm not at liberty to disclose that information."

Frank pursed his lips as he thought. "If there were a Sylvia Johnson staying in the hotel, would you help me order flowers for her—from me? I'd like to do that unless she's scheduled to check out before she could receive them."

The clerk tapped on his keyboard. "I can assist with that. The hotel recommends a florist on the next block. They supply the flowers for our public areas."

"I'd like it to be a big, happy bouquet," Frank said. "It needs to convey my thanks."

"Certainly, sir. Would you like to include a card with it? I'm ready to take down your message."

"Your armor is shinier than I realized. Thank you. Frank + Lonny."

The clerk typed as Frank spoke.

"I'd like it delivered as early in the morning as possible."

"We receive the hotel's weekly flower delivery from them by six tomorrow morning. I'll make sure your bouquet is with it. Unless she leaves her room unusually early, she'll have it before she starts her day."

"That's ideal. Please charge it to my credit card on file."

"Absolutely," the clerk replied.

"I appreciate your help." He stifled a yawn. "And now, I'd like to get to my room. Would you please call the bellman for me?"

The clerk did as requested, and Frank and Lonny were soon on their way to their room. Frank smiled to himself as they stepped into the elevator. He hoped the flowers would adequately express his gratitude to the kind woman named Sylvia Johnson.

CHAPTER 26

*G**arth*
I liked this park. It was different than other parks we'd been to. We climbed stairs to get to it, for one thing. It was long and skinny. Grass, shrubs, and trees lined the path.

I heard Grant tell the girls that it used to be an elevated freight rail line, built in the 1930s. The train had run along the street at 10th Avenue and there were so many deadly accidents that they had elevated the trains to run above the street. When trucks replaced trains, the rail line fell into disrepair. People called Friends of the High Line made it into a park.

These friends did a good job. We walked along at a slower pace than I preferred in order to look at the buildings rising on either side of us. When we paused to admire a tall red and pink tree sitting on a square black base, Emily gave me permission to lie down.

Even I knew this wasn't a real tree. Zoe took lots of pictures. "It's called 'Old Tree' by Pamela Rosenkranz," she said, leaning in to read a placard. "It represents the tree of life, symbolizing the connection between heaven and earth. Want me to describe it to you, Emily?"

"Of course. It sounds interesting."

"It's big—like four times as tall as me. It's got a large center trunk with lots of big branches and tiny ones coming out of it. There aren't any leaves on it. I think it's a tree that loses its leaves."

"Deciduous." Emily supplied the correct term.

"Yeah—deciduous. The whole thing is the prettiest bright red and pink."

"Sounds beautiful," Emily said.

"The roots show, too," Diedre chimed in. "They're also red and pink. I'd like to have this in our backyard."

"Me too," Zoe said.

Sylvia chuckled. "It'd be an enormous souvenir to take home. You girls have nice taste in art. The colors give it warmth and energy."

Emily's phone vibrated in her pocket. She ignored it.

I got to my feet, and we continued our stroll.

The phone vibrated two more times in rapid succession.

"I'd better check on this," she said as she pulled her phone out of her pocket. The screen reader read three texts from Kari, sent in rapid succession. She apologized for interrupting Emily's vacation, but a situation had come up in the Denver office that Kari wasn't sure how to handle. It didn't involve any of the projects they were working on. Kari said it was more of an HR thing and asked Emily to call her when she could.

"Do you want to call her back?" Grant asked. "It sounds urgent."

"Kari wouldn't call if it wasn't." She bit her lower lip. "We agreed not to allow work to intrude on our family time," Emily said. "I don't want to break our promise."

"I understand," Grant said, "but things happen."

"I listened to Kari's texts, too," Sylvia said. "I think you should call her. You'll worry about whatever's going on for the rest of the day. It's better to know. We're almost at the 10th Avenue Overlook. I'd like to sit on the stadium seats and watch traffic go by on 10th Avenue below us for a while. My feet haven't recovered from all the walking we did at the museum yesterday."

"I'll call her while you take a break."

We followed the girls as they walked in front of us.

A young man passed us going the other direction. He held four leashes with one hand, each attached to a miniature schnauzer. Three were gray and black, but one was white, like Sabrina. That was where the similarity ended. This white schnauzer walked at a dignified pace with the others as an orderly pack. My friend would have tangled her leash with the others, creating a mess like a knot in a ball of yarn.

I missed my little buddy. I wished she could have come on vacation with us.

"Grandma," Diedre cried. She pointed to a cart ahead of us. Colorful tote bags hung from racks surrounding the cart. "That one looks like the flowers in your bouquet."

We followed Diedre as she ran to the cart. "The red one with the yellow flowers."

"Sunflowers," Sylvia said. She stopped next to Diedre.

"Those are the happiest flowers I've ever seen," she said. "And that was the prettiest bouquet."

Sylvia grinned. "I have to agree with you, honey." She pulled the tote down to examine it.

"It was nice of him to thank you for helping about the elevator," Zoe said.

"I'd say you made quite an impression on this guy, Mom," Grant commented.

"Frank Blake—his name is Frank Blake." The name rolled off her tongue. Sylvia tested the strap of the bag on her shoulder.

"I think he's smitten with you," Grant continued.

Sylvia cuffed her son's arm. "Don't be ridiculous. We only met for a few minutes." The back of her neck turned crimson.

"You should buy this bag to remind you of the flowers after we go home," Diedre said.

"That's a great idea! This will be the perfect souvenir from our trip," Zoe said.

"Oh … I don't know. I probably wouldn't use this bag." Sylvia removed the bag from her shoulder and replaced it on its hook. Her hand lingered on the vibrant fabric.

Emily chimed in, "It doesn't matter if you'll use it or not. It'll remind you of the helpful thing you did for the kind man who sent you flowers."

"Zoe and I talked, Grandma. We think you're a hero."

Sylvia's cheeks turned the same color as the background of the bag.

Grant pulled the bag from its hook. "We're buying it for you."

Diedre clapped her hands in approval.

"For heaven's sake," Sylvia sputtered. "You don't need to do that."

"I want to do it, Mom. You spoiled me for years—now it's my turn." He handed the vendor his credit card and completed the transaction.

We stepped away from the cart.

Grant narrated for Emily. "The overlook is thirty feet ahead, on our right. There are rows of wooden stadium-style bench seats that step down to a wall of glass overlooking 10th Avenue below."

"Is it busy?"

"Nope."

"Can I sit at the back and call Kari without disturbing anyone?"

"Absolutely," he said.

"Is it okay if Diedre and I go down to the glass window and sit there?" Zoe asked.

"Only if you're not out of our sight," Emily said.

"We won't be. It's safe."

"I'll go with the girls," Sylvia said. "There aren't too many steps for me to manage."

"I'll wait with you and Garth," Grant said.

"Nonsense," Emily replied. "Join the family. We'll park ourselves in a sunny spot on the back row. If I finish my call before you're ready to leave, I'll do like Garth and tilt my face to the sun. A few moments of solitude in the fresh air will do me good."

Our family moved off, descending the stairs to the glass wall. I was relieved we weren't joining them. From my vantage point at the top, the wall of traffic on the street below the glass wall wasn't appealing. I didn't need a better view.

Emily tapped the screen of her phone and told it to call Kari.

The woman who loved to give me treats—but always asked permission first—answered on the first ring. Emily held the phone to her ear, but I didn't have any trouble hearing both sides of the conversation.

Kari told her about a disastrous job interview with an applicant for an internship. The person was very much like my Emily.

"I should have done—could have said—more. During the interview." Kari's voice was full of anguish. "I should have shut up that bozo manager."

Emily's shoulders stiffened. "It sounds like you tried, Kari. This wasn't your position to fill. The manager outranked you. It's difficult to take on someone like that. Especially in front of a person from outside the company."

"The disappointment in Anthony's voice was awful, Em. He came in full of confidence and left heartbroken. I'm not exaggerating." Her voice cracked.

Emily remained silent, collecting her thoughts. "I hate that our company did this to him. We're better than that."

"Not this time." Kari forced herself to continue. "I need to report the manager to HR. He broke all kinds of company policies and protocols."

"That's what the company handbook says to do," Emily replied, recalling the applicable provisions from memory. "Someone has to report him."

"I'm the one who witnessed everything. I'll do it," Kari said. "You needed to know before I call HR—in case the 'you-know-what' hits the fan."

"You said he works for Bruce Horton? Bruce should report his own employee and write him up."

Kari snorted. "Do you think Bruce will do it? I'm afraid he'll sweep it under the rug."

"You may be right, but I'd like to talk to Bruce before we go to HR. He and I developed a rapport when I was in town for our training sessions recently. It may be wishful thinking on my part, but I believe he'll do the right thing."

"And if he doesn't? We won't correct the wrong we did to Anthony."

"If he doesn't, then you'll make your report. I'll contact Bruce as soon as we hang up. If he does what he's supposed to do, HR should contact you in the next day or two. Keep me posted. If they don't, you'll move forward."

"Okay. That makes sense. Thanks, Emily."

"One more thing," Emily said. "Do you have Anthony's contact information?"

"I have a copy of his résumé."

"Good. Let's recruit him for our Denver unit."

"But we don't have an open internship position."

"Not now, we don't, but I intend to get one approved." Emily smiled the smile I knew meant business.

"Really?"

"Our workload is increasing—even without factoring in Dhruv's absence. We need assistance. An intern would be hugely helpful."

"I can attest to that," Kari said. "I'm on the internship committee and approval is a slow process. Requests to add an intern to a business unit have to be submitted at least six months in advance. It's harder to get approved than a new hire."

"I know someone who will cut red tape for us."

"Howard Kent! I forgot that you're in his good books."

"I feel certain Howard will expedite my request. For now, please contact Anthony and smooth things over. We shouldn't poach him from Bruce's unit if Anthony will reconsider accepting that position."

"Got it."

"Fill me in after you've talked to Anthony. We'll figure out the next steps when we know the lay of the land."

"Perfect. I feel so much better after talking to you. Again, I'm sorry I disturbed you on vacation."

"You were right to call me. I'm glad I could help." Emily's posture relaxed as they said goodbye.

I listened as she placed her call to Bruce. Emily's body language told me this was a friendly call. I settled down in a sunny patch and rested my muzzle on my paws.

The next thing I knew, Zoe and Diedre had gathered around Emily, jabbering a mile a minute.

"The ice cream place near here also has pup cups," Zoe said.

I was suddenly alert.

"Then—by all means—we'd better get going. I'd love a cone with a triple scoop. And I'm certain Garth needs a pup cup."

Was there a more perfect human? I didn't think so.

We left the overlook area and strode out with purpose.

CHAPTER 27

$\mathcal{M}$artha and Doug stood, arm in arm, gazing up at the façade of His Majesty's Theatre.

"My gosh—it's grand," Martha said. "Look at the ornate carvings, Corinthian columns, and decorative moldings over the arched windows."

"The light-colored stone is beautiful. It was only recently renamed 'His' after the coronation of King Charles III," Doug replied. "This looks like the sort of theater where one should see this play."

"I can picture kings and queens stepping out onto the curved balcony above the entrance." She sighed, resting her hand on her chest. "Do you ever wonder what's behind those windows on the top floors?" She pointed to the upper façade. "Most of them are dark, but there's a light in a couple of them. Maybe a cozy dressing room with a lumpy old sofa and a hot plate for making tea?"

"I'll bet they're dusty storage rooms full of discarded costumes and broken set pieces."

"I like my imagined vision better." She smiled at him. "Let's take a selfie to send to the kids." Martha turned her back to the theater and Doug leaned in close to her. She fidgeted with her phone, holding it at arm's length as she struggled to include both of them, the marquis showing the name *Phantom of the Opera*, and part of the ornate building in the photo. "There," she said, a note of triumph in her voice.

Another theatergoer on the bustling sidewalk brushed her elbow as she snapped the photo.

Martha groaned and studied the photo. "Nope," she said, holding her phone out to Doug to look at the blurry image.

"Both our heads are cut off," he said. "Let's try again."

"The doors are about to open. This sidewalk is packed. I think we've lost our chance."

"Excuse me. I couldn't help overhearing." A middle-aged man with a refined British accent smiled at them both. "May I be of assistance?"

"Would you? We'd love a photo of ourselves in front of this glorious theatre," Martha said.

"Rightly so," the man said. "It's a jewel." He extended his hand.

Martha laid her phone on his palm.

"First time at the theatre?"

"Yes," Doug said. "First time in London."

"Then you must have a photo," he said, waiting for a cluster of theatergoers to pass behind him. As soon as an opening appeared, he stepped back and framed the photo. "This will be grand. Say cheese!" He snapped several photos in rapid succession.

"Better check them," he said, handing the phone back to Martha.

She scrolled through the photos as Doug hovered over her shoulder.

"These are fabulous!" Martha grinned at him. "I'm going to frame one when I get home."

"The gentleman's black suit and your white dress printed with a red rose in the corner are the perfect costumes for this photo," the man commented.

"Are you a professional photographer?" Doug asked.

The man shrugged. "Once upon a time."

The four sets of double theater doors opened in unison and the crowd milling around on the sidewalk surged forward.

"Thank you," Martha called to the man as the crowd swept him away with the other theatergoers.

"We'd better find our seats," Doug said.

"Wait a sec," Martha replied. "I don't know if we'll have service inside the theater and I want to text this photo to Sylvia and the kids. She and Grant's family will board their train to Washington, D.C. any minute."

"Good idea," Doug said. "Send it to Gina and Craig, too."

"I've already included them."

"They'll be amazed that we're out on the town, in London, after dark."

"Isn't that the truth?" Martha chuckled as she pressed send. "They think we're old fogies who put on our pajamas right after dinner. Although that's true for me—most nights."

"Me too." Doug placed her hand in the crook of his elbow. "But that photo is proof that we still know how to dress up and paint the town red."

She squeezed his arm, and they swept past the iconic blue poster of the Phantom's white mask with a single red rose and into the theater.

MARTHA AND DOUG STOOD, clapping with the audience until their hands stung. They followed the crowd through the double glass doors onto Haymarket.

"That was fabulous." Martha smiled at Doug. "How did you get such terrific seats? Second row center—those must have cost you a fortune."

"Worth every penny," Doug said. "To be honest, this is the first musical I've seen in person."

"You're kidding."

Doug shrugged. "I've had the wrong idea about them all along." He took her hand in his and brought it to his lips for a kiss. "What would you like to do now? Should we be fashionable and have an after-theater dinner?"

"We ate before we came here," she replied. "I don't want to eat two dinners in one day. I'm already dreading stepping on the scale when we get home."

"How about dessert, then?" He brought up his other hand to cover a yawn.

"I'm afraid I'm in the same boat you are," Martha said. "I'm beat. Do you mind if we take a cab back to the hotel?"

"Honestly—I was hoping you'd say that." Doug hailed a London taxi, and they settled into the roomy back seat. He gave the driver the name of their hotel.

"I'd love to see the other musicals running in the West End. And plays," Doug said. "Maybe we should extend our stay in London to see more of them."

Martha caressed his cheek and kissed him. "That's one of the best ideas I've ever heard, but I can't."

"Something with the girls? I'm sure Grant and Emily could make other arrangements. They'd understand."

"I'm sure they would. It's not that." Martha pulled back to look at him. "There's something I haven't told you. I haven't mentioned it to anyone."

His lighthearted cheerfulness faded to serious concern. "Is anything wrong?"

"No. At least I hope not." She patted his arm. "I signed up to be a guide dog puppy raiser weeks ago. They completed my home inspection, and I understood it might be six months—or more—before I received a puppy. The week before we left for London, they notified me I'd been assigned a puppy. I'm scheduled to pick her up from the puppy truck the week after we get home."

"You never said." Doug's expression was shrouded in shadow, but his tone was warm and encouraging.

"I don't know why I kept my decision a secret. I guess I didn't want anyone to try to talk me out of it."

"Why would they do that?"

"I'm not an experienced dog trainer," Martha said. "I've learned more about dogs in the short time I've known Garth and Sabrina than in my entire life up to this point."

"Do you need to know how to train dogs to be a puppy raiser?"

"No. I'll be part of a puppy raiser club that holds weekly meetings. I've already attended orientation sessions run by the club for new puppy raisers."

"That's encouraging. Sounds like you'll have lots of support."

"Absolutely. My club has two leaders who have each raised dozens of puppies. They work closely with Guide Dog Center staff. And other members of the club—there are about thirty raisers—help each other. Some of them are newbies, like me, but others have been at this a long time. The puppies are at every level of development."

Doug tightened his arm around her shoulder. "This is an extremely selfless thing you're doing."

"After seeing what Garth has done for Emily, I had to volunteer. There's a two-year waiting period for a guide dog because there aren't enough puppy raisers."

"That's tragic," he said. "How long will you have your dog?"

"They said about a year."

He whistled softly. "That'll be tough to let her go."

"Not when I think about how much she'll help someone else, like Emily."

"Would you like me to come with you to pick up your puppy? I'd be happy to drive."

"You don't have to do that. The truck is stopping in a church parking lot that's two hours from my house. It'll take the best part of a day."

"Nothing I'd rather do than spend a day with you."

"Then I'd love for you to come with me. The other newbies in my puppy club—a mother and daughter team—are also getting their dog." She smiled at Doug. "Who knows—maybe you'll decide to become a puppy raiser, too."

CHAPTER 28

As they boarded the Northeast Regional Amtrak train, Grant said, "Let's snag the seats in the third row in front of us." He pointed to the comfortable, high-backed seats as his family proceeded down the aisle, rolling their suitcases behind them.

Zoe raced ahead to secure their claim to the four chairs that sat, two on each side, facing each other across a small table.

Diedre staked their claim to one of the seats in the identical configuration across the aisle. "There's five of us, so we can talk to the fifth person even if we can't sit on the same side."

"I'll lift your suitcases into the storage bin above the seats," Grant said, hefting them into place.

"You'll want window seats," Sylvia told the girls. "It's fun to watch the world go by from a train window."

"One of us will ride backwards," Zoe said. "Which do you want, Diedre?"

"Let's take turns," Diedre said.

"I like the sound of that, girls," Emily said.

Zoe and Diedre took their positions by the window.

Sylvia settled into the seat across the aisle.

Emily commanded Garth to go down and under the table in front of her.

"Would you like to be with Emily and the girls?" Grant asked his mother. "I can sit over here."

Sylvia shook her head. "I'm fine." She reached into her oversize purse and pulled out a plastic shopping bag imprinted with the logo of a popular gift shop from the train station. "I bought snacks for the trip."

"We just ate lunch," he chided.

"I know, but it's fun to have snacks for the journey. It's a three-and-a-half-hour trip from Penn Station to Union Station, so we'll be glad to have them." She handed the bag across to her son and withdrew her arm quickly as passengers moved down the aisle, searching for seats.

Two men and one woman took the other three seats in her quad. The woman pulled out a stack of papers from her satchel and began marking them with a red pen. One man buried his head in his newspaper, while the other crossed his arms over his chest and closed his eyes for a nap.

Sylvia sank back into her seat and watched the people making their way down the aisle. A tall man with graying hair at his temples caught her attention. She sat up straight and strained to get a better view of him.

The black lab guide dog at his side confirmed what she already knew. The man from the elevator—Frank Blake, and his guide dog Lonny—were on their train.

She'd sent him a thank-you note for the flowers through the hotel, but now she could thank him in person.

Frank and Lonny were abreast of her.

Sylvia called Frank's name at the same time as the man walking ahead of Frank turned to address him.

"We're going through to the next car to find seats together," the man said.

Lonny led Frank behind his companion, oblivious to Sylvia's attempt to get Frank's attention.

She turned to watch him go, but the rush of people claiming their seats quickly obscured him.

Her phone pinged, notifying her of an incoming text. She pulled it out of her bag and opened the message from Martha. She and Doug, dressed to the nines, stood in front of an impressive theatre marquee. The backdrop looked like something from a movie. The smiles on their faces confirmed what Sylvia already knew: these two were in love.

She read the caption:

> Having the time of our lives!!!!!!

Sylvia brought her phone to her chest. They most certainly were. And she was thrilled for them—even if she felt a bit envious.

The train began to move, and they soon exited the dim station into the bright sunshine of a perfect summer afternoon.

Sylvia leaned across the aisle. "Did you notice the man with the guide dog?" She asked Grant.

"I was too busy opening that bag of trail mix you bought," he replied.

"I thought you'd just had lunch and didn't need snacks?" Sylvia chided.

"You know me," Grant said. "I'm always hungry."

"I swear," Emily chimed in. "That son of yours could eat all day long and never put on a pound."

"Both my boys are blessed with their father's fast metabolism," Sylvia said. "Anyway, Frank Blake and his guide dog just walked by us."

"The man that you met in the elevator at the hotel?" Emily asked.

Diedre turned away from the window. "The one who sent you flowers?"

"Yes. I'm sure it was him."

"That's quite a coincidence," Grant said.

"Or fate," Zoe entered the conversation. "Where is he?" She turned in her seat and sprung to her knees, trying to see around Emily into the train car.

"He's in another car," Sylvia said.

"Do you want to go see him?" Diedre asked.

"I tried to thank him for the flowers as he walked by, but he didn't hear me."

"You need to find him and tell him," Zoe said. "I read online that passengers are allowed to move between train cars. You can go to the café car for snacks or use the restroom in another car. The thing connecting a train car is called a vestibule."

Sylvia smiled at her encyclopedic granddaughter. "I don't know." She shrugged. "I already sent him a note."

"Zoe's right, grandma. This is fate," Diedre said.

"I agree," Emily interjected. "And if you don't at least try to find him, you'll kick yourself later."

Grant said, "There are more than ten stops before we get to D.C., and he could detrain at any of them. No time like the present!"

Sylvia looked at the four eager faces turned to her.

"You think so?"

Her family nodded in unison.

"Okay," Sylvia said, getting out of her seat. "Here goes. I'm sure I'll be back shortly."

SYLVIA WALKED through the next train car and into the one beyond that, searching for Frank. She spotted a head of gray hair ahead of her in an aisle seat on the left. The presence of a large black lab at the man's feet under the table in front of him confirmed that she'd found him.

Frank was leaning forward, chatting with the man seated across the table from him.

Sylvia halted in the aisle next to them.

Frank's traveling companion looked at her.

"I'm sorry to interrupt," she said. "I wanted to thank Frank for his thoughtfulness."

A smile spread across Frank's face like butter on toast as soon as she spoke. "Is that Sylvia Johnson?"

"It is." It was Sylvia's turn to grin.

Frank's traveling companion got out of his seat. "I'm going to the café car to get something to eat."

Sylvia swayed as the train navigated a curve.

"Take my seat while I'm gone," the man said.

"I don't mean to intrude," Sylvia mumbled.

"Please," Frank said, gesturing to the now vacant seat.

The train lurched again, and Sylvia lowered herself into the seat. "I don't know if you received the thank-you note I sent through the hotel, but I'm happy to be able to say it in person."

"They delivered the note," he replied. "I'm glad you liked the flowers. I don't know what you said—or to whom—after the incident, but I wish I'd have been a fly on the wall. You got results. By the following evening, they had outfitted the elevators with Braille labels. I could get around the hotel without anyone's help. Except Lonny's—of course."

"We noticed the labels. I'm so glad they made the elevators accessible."

They fell silent.

"I'd better vacate this seat before your friend gets back."

"Stay. Please." Frank's voice was warm and inviting. "I've been wondering about you since we met. I know you're kind and have a daughter-in-law with a guide dog who looks like Lonny."

"Good memory," Sylvia said. "As a matter of fact, she's on this train, a few cars back. I'm on vacation with my son and his family. Our trip began in New York, and we're traveling to D.C."

He asked about her family, and she told him about her granddaughters and the fun they'd had in the city.

"What brought you to New York?" Sylvia asked. "You mentioned a meeting on the night we met. Did you have business in the city?"

"You could say so," he replied. "I play accordion in a polka band. I've been filling in for a colleague who's been out for medical reasons."

"Is the man you're traveling with part of the band?"

"He is."

"So you do this professionally?"

"We do."

"You must be very good if you're playing out-of-town gigs. Do you live in D.C.?"

"The rest of the band does. I'm from San Francisco."

"You're kidding! That's where I live. Both my sons are there, too."

"Is your husband on the trip with you?" Frank leaned closer.

"I'm a widow," Sylvia said. "Have been for many years."

"We have that in common. I'm a widower."

"I'm sorry to hear that."

"It's been a long time for me, too. Music has been a great healer for me."

"I must say, I'm terribly impressed that a band on the East Coast recruited you to come all the way across the country to play with them."

Frank shrugged. "I've been a musician for years. The singer with this band has been a friend for decades. I'm retired, and he guessed I'd be available on short notice."

"I suspect you're being modest. I'm sure there were other accordion players they could have hired to fill the vacancy."

Frank's cheeks turned pink.

"Are you playing in D.C.?"

"We're doing a wedding reception Saturday night. Three hundred guests."

"My goodness. That's a huge wedding."

"It's being held at a fancy hotel in Crystal City. I can only imagine how much this wedding is costing the bride's family."

Sylvia took a sharp breath. "Which hotel?"

Frank told her.

"You're not going to believe this. We're staying at that hotel while we're in D.C."

"No way! The same hotel in each city? Especially when New York and D.C. each have hundreds of hotels. Plus, we are on the same train."

"What a coincidence," Sylvia said.

"It's more than that. I believe the universe wants us to connect," he said, voicing what she was already thinking.

Her family would agree.

"Have you ever seen a polka band in person?" he asked.

"When I was a child," Sylvia said. "I danced with my cousins. It was a lot of fun."

"No one can remain unhappy while doing the polka."

Sylvia chuckled. "I wouldn't dispute that."

"Are you busy Saturday night?"

"We're doing an architectural walking tour on Saturday and flying home early on Sunday. I'm sure we'll turn in early."

"Perfect! Care to watch us play a few songs before you go to sleep?"

"Are you asking me to be a wedding crasher? I can't do that."

"I'm not suggesting you pretend to be a guest and eat dinner or anything like that. With three hundred-plus attendees, no one will notice someone slip in with the band. They'll assume you're with us—and, in fact, you will be."

Sylvia sucked air through her teeth. "I'd love to see you play. I might not have another opportunity to see a live polka band."

"There you go," Frank said. "Carpe diem. It's settled. We go on at eight-thirty."

"I'll only stay for a few minutes. We check out of the hotel at five-thirty the next morning."

"You can vanish like Cinderella at nine o'clock. Or close the place down and sleep on the way home. Whatever you choose."

"I must be out of my mind," Sylvia said. "But—yes. Thank you for the invitation."

"Let's exchange phone numbers." Frank pulled out his phone. "I'll text you where and when to meet me. I think you'll have a wonderful time."

"It'll certainly be a memorable way to end my vacation," Sylvia said. "I've got a request."

"What?"

"I'd like a selfie with the band—to send to my best friend." Martha wouldn't be the only one with an interesting vacation photo.

"Consider it done," Frank said.

They didn't notice Frank's companion step past them in the aisle and take a seat in the next row.

"I'd like to hear more about your life in San Francisco," Frank said. "After all this, I wouldn't be surprised if we were neighbors."

Sylvia laughed and the two continued chatting like old friends. They were both amazed when the automated public address system announced their arrival at Union Station.

Sylvia leapt out of her seat. "I'd better go. My family must be wondering what happened to me."

"I'll see you Saturday night, Sylvia," Frank said, holding his hand out to her.

She gave it a warm squeeze and was gone.

CHAPTER 29

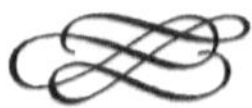

"Anthony! Thanks for returning my call. I was beginning to think I wouldn't hear from you." Kari's tone conveyed her relief.

"I needed time to think about it," he replied evenly.

"That's fair enough. As I said in my voicemail, I apologize for some of the questions you were asked by my colleague. I shouldn't have allowed them."

"I remember that you tried to steer the conversation back to the requirements of the job opening."

"I'm glad to hear that. I wish I'd done more to stop him. Please accept my apology for letting him continue."

"I appreciate that," Anthony said. "What did you do after I left?"

"Our company has procedures for this type of situation. I reported him to my manager, and she took it from there. I don't have any details, but I understand he's been disciplined."

"I'm not sure that'll do any good."

Kari groaned. "I can't speak to that."

"At least you're honest."

"I also want to follow up on our internship opening." Kari proceeded as Emily had directed. "I've confirmed with the department head that the position is yours, if you want it. Would you like to know more?"

"Definitely not. It's a hard no for me."

"Okay. I expected you'd say that. I still want you to consider a career with us. We're one of the largest corporations in the world, so there are plenty of opportunities in other areas of our business. This is a wonderful place to start—and advance—a career. Would you consider an internship in another department?"

Anthony didn't respond.

"I believe I mentioned that my boss—Emily Main—is blind?"

"You did."

"She has an internship available in my unit, here in Denver."

"I didn't see that one when I was applying."

"It's only recently become available."

"Can you tell me about it?"

"Emily would like to do that in person. I'll fill you in on what our business unit does." She explained their function.

"My experience is better suited to the first internship," Anthony said. "So ..."

"Don't worry about that," Kari cut him off. "Nobody we hire has all the experience we require. We train everyone who joins us."

"I see."

"I love my job," Kari continued. "It's fast-paced and I'm constantly challenged. The work is never dull. Emily is the best department head I've ever worked for. She builds strong, collaborative teams. We support and learn from each other."

"That sounds intriguing."

"If you give this company another chance, you won't be sorry," Kari said. "Or have you already found something else?"

"No. Not yet."

"Emily is on vacation this week, or she would have called you herself. She asked me to reach out to you. Are you available to come back next week to speak with Emily?"

"Who does this internship position report to?"

"Me," Kari said.

"Then—yes—I'd like to learn more."

"Terrific!" Kari's enthusiasm was palpable. "I'll let her know and we'll get back to you on Monday to set up a meeting. She's in our San Francisco office, so I'm not sure when she'll be able to fly to Denver after being out on vacation, but she assured me she'll make it happen next week."

"I'm open," Anthony said. "Even the week after is fine."

"Emily told me meeting with you is a top priority, so it'll be next week."

"I'm looking forward to learning more about her experience with the company."

"She's a straight shooter, Anthony. You'll get an honest overview from her."

"I'm glad you called, Kari." His voice held a tinge of optimism.

"Me too. Have a nice weekend."

"You too."

"See you soon." She hesitated before continuing. "You won't leave the company ashamed and discouraged next week. I promise you that."

CHAPTER 30

Sylvia and Grant snaked along the wall of the large hallway flanking the hotel's ballrooms.

Servers carrying trays of canapés and glasses of champagne weaved through the throng of men in suits and women in wedding-guest finery. Fragments of cheerful conversation reached their ears as they passed by.

"Look at the full skirts on most of the women." Sylvia leaned into her son to be heard above the din. "This is sure to be a crowd that loves to dance."

"I hadn't noticed," he said. "I've been on the hunt for Ballroom A." He looked at the placard affixed to the wall by a set of double doors. "Ballroom D. The letters are going down. We're headed in the right direction."

"You didn't have to walk me down here, you know," Sylvia chided her son. "It's only eight o'clock. This is a nice hotel. I'd have been fine finding it on my own."

"You're probably right. But I'm certain you're safe with me. I wasn't doing anything in our hotel room, anyway. We're packed up and ready to go. The girls are already in bed, reading. Besides, I'd like to meet this man who's taken a shine to my mother."

Sylvia cuffed his shoulder. "He's done no such thing. Frank is simply a kind man who's interested in sharing his hobby."

"Ahh … Then why are you blushing?"

"I'm flushed with exertion," Sylvia replied. "Keeping up with those long legs of yours. You forget I'm a foot shorter than you."

"I don't think that's it." Grant slowed his pace. "Here's Ballroom A."

"Frank said to take a left at the end of the hallway and walk around the corner to the last door on the left. The band will be set up along the far wall of the ballroom. That door will take me to their staging area."

They proceeded down the deserted corridor, the joyful sounds from the wedding guests trailing away. The last door on the left was slightly ajar.

Grant held the door open for his mother and they stepped into the room.

"Thank you, sweetheart," she said. "I've got it from here."

"Not so fast," he said. "I'm going to make sure we're in the right place."

Sylvia pointed to a black lab in a guide dog harness lying on a mat along the rear wall of the ballroom. "That's Lonny. Frank's guide dog. This is the right place."

Eight people were scattered across a ground-level stage. A sturdy-looking man was testing a microphone while others were warming up their instruments. In addition to the singer, the band included drums, a clarinet, a trumpet, two guitars, and two accordions.

"Which one is Frank?" Grant asked.

Sylvia pointed to him. "I'll let him know I'm here and ask where I should stand." She looked up at her son. "You can go."

"No way. I'm meeting this guy." He motioned for her to lead on.

They approached Frank as he was turning away from the other accordion player.

"Hello, Frank," Sylvia said.

"Sylvia! You're right on time. Thank you for coming."

"I've been looking forward to this since the train," she said. "I'd like to introduce you to my son."

"I'm extending my hand," Grant said. "Grant Johnson."

"Frank Blake." He put his hand out and Grant grasped it. "Nice to meet you." Frank motioned to his right. "There's a small table on the other side of the room for you to sit," he continued. "We've got water, sodas, and snacks for the band. Take anything you'd like. Please make yourselves comfortable. The doors are supposed to open in ten minutes, and we'll play a special entrance for the bride and groom."

"He's not staying." Sylvia fixed Grant with a stern gaze.

"You're more than welcome," Frank replied.

"That's kind of you," Grant said, "but I should get back to my family. I just wanted to make sure Mom got here safely."

"Rightly so," Frank said. "I assure you I'll see her back to her room —no matter how long she plans to stay."

"You'll be busy playing in the band," Sylvia said. "As I told Grant earlier, I'm perfectly fine returning to my room on my own."

"It's already arranged," Frank said. "There are two accordions, so I can step away for a song or two to walk you to your room. The elevators in this hotel are accessible, so I've got no problems here. Lonny will want a break, too." He smiled at Sylvia. "Whenever you're ready to go, text me and we'll be on our way."

"I'll wait until you've finished a set," Sylvia said. "You won't need to stop playing."

"You can always call me to come back to get you," Grant said.

"For crying out loud," Sylvia huffed. "Stop fussing over me—the both of you. I've been competent to find my own way my entire adult life."

"It's not a question of competence." Frank's voice was calm but firm. "It's a matter of respect. I'm an old-fashioned kind of guy. My mother, God rest her soul, would have reprimanded me if I didn't see you to your door. It sounds like you've raised your son the same way."

"You're exactly right," Grant said. He gave Frank an admiring glance. "I'm glad we agree. I'll leave this in your hands, but if plans change, have Mom text me."

"I'll do it." Frank extended his hand again, and Grant shook it.

"Nice to meet you, Frank. Have a fun night, the two of you."

Sylvia rose on tiptoes to kiss Grant's cheek. "Text me in the morning when you're heading downstairs."

"Will do," Grant said. "Emily figures we need to leave the hotel at four forty-five."

"I'll be ready and waiting," Sylvia said.

～

SYLVIA TOOK a chair facing the stage, grabbed a water bottle, and settled in to watch the wedding guests file into the room. People were still locating their assigned tables when spotlights went up on the middle set of double doors leading into the room.

The band's singer went to the microphone. "Ladies and gentlemen, are you ready to get this party started?"

Applause erupted.

"Let's welcome the wedding party with the Grand March! If you don't know how this works, the maid of honor and best man will lead the bride and groom into the room, followed by the parents of the bride and groom, and the wedding party. They'll circle the room and when they pass your table, you're invited to join in. We want everyone out of their seats and on the floor! The newlyweds and wedding party will form a bridge for you to pass under. After you pass under the bridge, line up in a circle and the bride and groom will have their first dance. And after that, dinner will be served."

The guests cheered.

"We'll be playing them in with the 'Double Eagle Polka.' And a one and a two and …"

The band played. The double doors on the other side of the room flew open, and the maid of honor and best man led the procession, stepping in time to the lively music.

Sequins on the bride's gown sparkled under the light.

The guests got to their feet and clapped in time to the music.

The groom removed his white cowboy hat and waved it at the crowd.

People cheered and whistled.

The wedding party danced their way across the room, with members of the audience joining their ranks at the end of the line. When they reached the stage, they separated into a line of women peeling off in one direction while the men went in the other.

The two lines circled the large dance floor and rejoined in the center, with the bride and groom joining hands and raising them above their heads to form the bridge. The parents of the bride were the first ones to pass underneath and join the bridge on the other side.

The band played the springy rhythm over and over as all but a handful of guests joined in the dancing. Those who remained at their tables captured the merriment on their phones.

Sylvia tapped her toes and bounced in her chair. The circle of guests blocked her view of the dance floor, so she focused on the band. Their smiles told her they were enjoying the music as much as their audience was. Frank, in particular, played with complete abandon. The fingers of his right hand flew across the keys so fast they were a blur, while those on his left hand pressed the buttons.

Lonny lay on his mat, his paws stretched out in front of him, with his head held high. Sylvia swore his tail swished from side to side in time to the music.

The wedding guests joined hands in a swaying human circle at the edge of the dance floor. The groom pulled the bride into the center, twirling her under his arm. They completed a series of flawless polka moves and completed their dance with another flourish and a kiss.

The people lining the dance floor applauded their approval.

"Nice job, ladies and gentlemen. I can see you're a fine dancing group. We've got a night of fun ahead of us, but first, it's time for speeches, toasts, and dinner."

The band put their instruments down, and the dance floor cleared.

Sylvia sat, mesmerized by the happy interactions of guests as they returned to their seats. A tap on the shoulder startled her.

She turned to see Lonny and Frank at her side.

"My gosh … I didn't see you on your way to the table."

"I'm sorry. I guess it's pretty chaotic in here."

"Delightfully so. The band is fabulous. And you, Frank, are the best one. I've never understood how anyone masters the coordination to play piano keys sideways, press buttons, and work the bellows of an accordion—all simultaneously. You're a remarkable musician."

"I don't know about that, but the band is top-notch. I'm glad you've enjoyed seeing us." He held out his hand to her. "Do you want to go back to your room? I know you have an early start in the morning."

"I'd like to stay longer if that's okay. I'm enjoying myself. This brings back memories of my childhood."

"You're welcome to stay as long as you like. I'm going to take Lonny out for a comfort break. Care to stretch your legs?"

"I'd love to." Sylvia rose from her chair. "It was all I could do to force myself to stay in my seat during the Grand March. I never learned the fancy steps, but I think I still remember the basic polka my grandfather taught me."

"It's like riding a bike. You might be rusty, but you never forget." He directed Lonny to take them out the door and along the corridor to an exterior exit. "I scoped this out earlier. The dog relief area is outside, on the left."

They stepped into the warm summer night. "I have to tell you—I think Lonny loves polka music as much as you do. He could have been directing the band with his tail," Sylvia said.

Frank laughed. "Other band members have said that."

"His love of polka music makes him even more perfect for you," Sylvia said.

"Tell me about this polka-ing grandfather of yours," Frank said.

Sylvia smiled and warmed to her topic, recounting happy times from her childhood. "What about you? When did you begin playing the accordion?"

Frank filled in his backstory until a buzzer on his watch sounded. "We're about to go back on stage," he said. "That break went fast. Are you sure you want to stay longer?"

"Positive," Sylvia said. It was late, they'd walked all over Washington, D.C. that afternoon, and she would leave the hotel in a little over six hours. But the only thing she wanted to do was stay right there and listen to polka music.

CHAPTER 31

Frank and Sylvia spent the band's final break in a jovial conversation about the best bakeries in the Bay Area. He and Lonny escorted Sylvia to her spot at the table. "I'm going to check out the one you insist has the best loaf of sourdough in the city," he said. "I'm skeptical, but I'll keep an open mind."

Sylvia chuckled. "I hope you'll let me know what you think."

"I'll do that." He turned to her. "You're sure you want to stay for the last set?"

"Positive," Sylvia said. "As I said earlier, I'm having the time of my life. I'll sleep on the plane." She didn't mention that she'd never fallen asleep on a plane and would probably spend the day miserably tired. But happy, she thought.

Frank directed Lonny to *Go to Bed*. Lonny understood the command and went to his mat. Frank returned to the stage.

The band struck up "The Pennsylvania Polka." The wedding guests on the dance floor had thinned out, but Sylvia estimated there were still over a hundred dedicated dancers. Women in full skirts twirled by her, their bright colors mimicking a kaleidoscope.

She plunked herself down into her chair, her feet moving in the familiar basic steps from her seated position.

The band took up the energetic "Tic Toc Polka." As if propelled by the vibrant music, Sylvia sprang to her feet. She stood behind her chair and moved to the music in a tight rectangle, keeping her eyes on the dance floor. No one noticed her, so she allowed her arms and shoulders to join her feet as she danced in place.

Sylvia gave herself over to the joy of dancing and didn't notice the other accordion player lean over and speak into Frank's ear.

Frank nodded his agreement to whatever the man said. He moved to the back of the band and placed his accordion on a chair. He pulled his folding cane out of his pocket and navigated to the spot where he knew Sylvia would be.

Once more, he caught her unawares when he tapped on her shoulder from behind.

Sylvia spun around.

"May I have this dance?" he asked, folding his cane and replacing it in his pocket.

She hesitated, then stepped into his arms. "I thought someone was coming to tell me to sit down. I'm a wedding crasher, after all."

"And doing a very poor job of it, I understand. What wedding crasher worth their salt doesn't soak up the free food and booze? The other band members have reported you've consumed two water bottles and one bag of chips. That's it."

"Well ..."

"And until the last dance, you've remained in your seat. The other accordion player told me to get out here and take that beautiful woman I've been spending my breaks with for a spin on the dance floor."

"That was nice of him."

"This is our second-to-the-last song. Will you take us onto the dance floor?"

"Sure. You know how to polka?"

He snorted. "I was born polkaing!"

Sylvia led them to the outskirts of the swirling mix of dancers.

Frank was, indeed, an expert dancer. He was soon leading her through the basic steps with ease.

Sylvia relaxed as they moved together. She giggled when he twirled her under his arm, and they finished the number with a flourish.

"Thank you, sir," Sylvia said, slightly out of breath. "That was wonderful!"

Frank beamed.

"You're a fabulous dancer."

"I'm glad you enjoyed it. There's one more song to close out the dancing at this reception. I'd love nothing more than to stay with you, but I'm afraid I need to get back up there to play."

"Of course," Sylvia said. "I'll take you to the stage. Put your hand on my elbow."

Frank resumed his spot in the band. The singer announced the final song of the evening and led the crowd in that singalong favorite "The Happy Wanderer." Couples on the dance floor swayed and sang, arms around each other, as the band repeated the last verse twice. When the music stopped, the audience gave the band a rousing round of applause.

The singer directed everyone to gather in the hallway outside the ballroom to say goodbye to the bride and groom.

Sylvia settled into her chair and, for the third time that night, Frank and Lonny surprised her.

"I think it's time I took Cinderella home," Frank said. "It's already after midnight."

Sylvia laughed. "Where's your accordion?"

"I'll come back to get it," he said. "You've got to get up in a few hours."

"I stayed knowing that. I'll wait while you get your stuff," she said. "I insist."

"Thank you. Be right back."

Frank was true to his word and he and Lonny were at her side in moments, a heavy nylon backpack in place.

They exited the ballroom and made their way through the dwindling group of wedding guests to the elevators.

They were at Sylvia's door in record time.

"Thank you for such a lovely evening, Frank."

"You really enjoyed yourself?"

"I can't tell you how much."

They stood in silence.

"Have a good trip home," he said.

"You too. When do you get back?"

"A week from today. I'm headed to Florida tomorrow afternoon to visit my brother."

"Sounds nice. After seeing how physical playing an accordion is, I think you've earned a vacation." She paused, searching for something to say. "Be sure to let me know what you think of my sourdough recommendation."

He reached for her arm and ran his hand down her sleeve until he found her hand. "I've got a better idea. Why don't we embark on a citywide tour of bakeries together? We can hit our own favorites and include a few new ones that are getting a lot of buzz."

"Update our familiarity with the local bakery scene? I love that idea, Frank." She stepped closer to him. "San Francisco has so many bakeries, that'll require several outings."

"I thought of that."

"And once I eat all that bread, in the name of scientific research, I'll need to go dancing to wear off the extra calories," she said.

"Obviously," he said, leaning closer to her. "I can arrange that."

"We've got a plan," Sylvia said.

"I'll call you as soon as I get back to town," Frank said.

She felt his breath on her face. "I've got one last question before you go," Sylvia said. "May I kiss you goodnight?"

CHAPTER 32

*G*arth

We got home from the airport, and everyone was moving fast. Grant and the girls were bringing suitcases into the house. Emily had gone to the kitchen to fill my water bowl. Sylvia was waiting in the car for Grant to drop her at her house as soon as they had unloaded our stuff.

I'd taken a nap on the long flight and was ready to stretch my legs. I stood over my water bowl for a long time, lapping up cool, delicious water.

When I was done, I searched for Emily. I passed by the front door on my way to our bedroom. My working harness hung on its peg by the door. I gave it a wistful glance, wishing Emily and I would soon be enjoying a long walk.

I found Grant hoisting a large suitcase onto the bed. Emily was digging through the other suitcase, already open on the bed.

"I'll pull out our dirty clothes and start a load of laundry," she told him. "Did you put your dirties in the appropriately marked mesh bags?"

"Yep. I separated the whites and colors."

"Perfect."

146

I settled into my bed in the corner. We weren't going on a walk anytime soon.

"Everything's in from the car. I'm going to take Mom home. The girls want to go with me. To pick up Sabrina. And Squeaky."

My head rocketed up from my paws like it'd been shot from a cannon. I'd forgotten about that ridiculous cat the girls had found in our yard right before we'd left for vacation.

Emily sighed and collapsed onto the bed. "I'm nervous about having a cat," she said. "I don't need another tripping hazard around the house."

"We're going to stop by a pet store to pick up a bell for his collar before we come home," Grant said.

"That's fine, but I can't keep track of him every second of the day."

"If you have issues with him, we'll find a new home for Squeaky."

"Maybe he'll naturally get out of my way. Zoe researched and found that some cats are good at avoiding people. She also learned that blind people put mats or rugs down in their cat's common hangout areas. I'll feel the different texture underfoot and know he might be lurking."

Grant sat next to her and put his hands on her upper arms. "I won't allow our home to be hazardous for you. The minute you say the word, that cat is gone."

"Great. Then I become the bad guy who makes Diedre give up her cat."

"Hmm … I hadn't thought of that. Would you rather I not bring Squeaky home with Sabrina? It would be easier to say 'no' now."

I nodded my head in agreement. Best to nip this cat idea in the bud.

"No. I've agreed to give Squeaky a try. I'll keep my word."

Grant and the girls left. Emily and I were home alone—a rare occurrence I usually enjoyed.

Instead of settling my head back on my paws, I followed Emily as she moved through the house, dealing with laundry and unpacking their bags.

I heard the garage door opener engage as Grant's car turned onto the driveway. I went to the door that led into the house from the garage and waited.

Sabrina was the first one through the door. She ran directly to me and rose on her hind legs, her paws resting on my shoulders. We placed our open mouths on each other in greeting. Sabrina brought her front paws to the floor, and we gave each other an intimate sniff.

I was about to lead us on a romp through the house when Diedre stepped inside, carrying the large striped feline in her arms.

Squeaky emitted a high-pitched sound worthy of his name.

"I'm taking him to my room," Diedre said. "So he can get used to it. He'll sleep with me." She moved off with the cat.

Emily joined us in the hallway. "I'd like you girls to unpack your own bags. You're old enough. Put your dirty clothes in the hampers in the laundry room."

"Will do," Zoe said, trailing after Diedre and Squeaky. "Come on, Sabrina."

My buddy followed her girl.

"I'd like to stretch my legs," Emily said to Grant. "Do you mind if I take Garth for a short walk?"

My ears twitched at the sound of one of my favorite words.

"Of course not. I'll head to the grocery, so we have milk, bread, and eggs for breakfast."

"Will you pick up a couple of rotisserie chickens and sides from the deli department for dinner?"

"Great idea," he said. "I'll let the girls know I'm leaving, and that you and Garth will be in the neighborhood."

After finding the girls, Grant headed to the garage while Emily slipped my working harness over my head. We stepped out into a cloudless midsummer day. I kept going at a good clip. I knew by Emily's pace that she was enjoying our walk. I was pretty sure our short walk had turned into a long one.

We returned home to find Grant and the girls in the kitchen. Zoe was putting groceries away while Diedre set the table. Grant was removing lids from the side dishes and placing serving spoons into them. He'd already dissected the rotisserie chickens and placed fragrant pieces on a plate.

I went in search of Sabrina. And I didn't like what I found. I had to blink twice to make sure I wasn't seeing things.

Sabrina was lying on her back in the oversize dog bed in the living room, her paws poking into the air and her eyes shut tight. This was normal for her.

What wasn't normal was what—or rather who—was next to her.

Squeaky lay against Sabrina, his back nestled into her side. The cat's eyes were firmly shut, and his nose twitched. It looked like their bodies were Velcroed together.

This cat—this intruding, usurping feline—was in my spot. And Sabrina was obviously fine with it.

I stared in disbelief.

Sabrina stirred and opened her eyes. She looked at me, then shifted to the side, making a space between her and the interloper.

As a guide dog, I knew my manners needed to prevail over instinct, so I padded over and gingerly inserted myself into the opening, nestling myself into the thick memory foam of our bed. I brought my muzzle to my paws.

Squeaky stretched and yawned before attaching herself to my side.

I grew warm and cozy, drifting off to sleep with the pleasant memory of being back with my littermates.

Kari tapped on the doorframe of her coworker's office. "I hate to interrupt, but Emily and I have an interview to conduct in a few minutes."

Emily swiveled to face the door. "We've been comparing notes about our summer vacations," she said. She turned back to her employee. "If there's anything else you'd like to discuss, I'll come back after the interview."

"I'm good," the man said. "I appreciate you took time to chat with me."

"I plan to do one-on-ones with each person on the Denver team every time I'm in town," Emily said. "I like getting to know you better, and it's helpful to hear directly from you about your career goals and your challenges." She rose from her chair and grasped Garth's working harness. "I'm committed to your success," she said as she left his office.

"Thanks for flying in last night so you could meet with everyone this morning. None of our other managers have talked to us individually," Kari said. "We're still working lots of overtime, but morale is super high. That's due to the fact that we know someone recognizes our contributions and wants each of us to get ahead."

"I'm glad it helps," Emily replied. "Flying out on Thursday evening after we just got home from vacation on Sunday wasn't ideal, but the next two weeks are packed with Back-to-School Night and Meet-the-Teacher for my girls, plus the actual start of school. Grant and I promised each other we'd both be in town for all of it. Besides, I want to fill this new internship position that Howard Kent approved for me."

"I realize the intern will require training, but I believe they'll be able to assist with our backlog before too long."

Emily smiled. "Relief is right around the corner. If we can convince Anthony to accept the job."

They entered the same small conference room where Anthony had been interviewed previously.

"Did you review his résumé?" Kari and Emily took seats.

"On the plane home from D.C. All I can say is 'Wow.' I can't imagine finding anyone more qualified."

"Right?" Kari's phone buzzed. "The receptionist is bringing him back."

This interview progressed much differently than the prior one. Anthony presented his credentials and Emily and Kari asked pertinent questions.

Emily discussed the company, her department's responsibilities, and its place within the corporate hierarchy.

Kari described the specific projects her unit handled and the tasks that would be assigned to the intern.

"You're experienced using the JAWS screen reader?" Emily asked.

"Very," Anthony replied.

"All of our software is accessible. You'll be fully functional in no time. I have no doubt that you'd be a terrific addition to our team." Emily leaned toward him. "Kari filled me in on the less-than-favorable experience you had with our company last time you were here."

"Well … that's accurate," Anthony said. "Kari assured me it was an anomaly—and that working with you would be different."

"With all due respect to Kari, my answer to that is yes … and no." She scooted to the edge of her chair. "Working on my team will be different. Of that, I can assure you. And not only because I'm the boss, but because I've worked with every member of my team and know firsthand how they treat a blind person. Your only limit will be your talent, not your diagnosis. But this is a huge company and people are fallible. We have policies in place to address the behavior you were subjected to, but it would be misleading if I said you wouldn't face the same misconceptions again."

"Your honesty is refreshing."

"I can assure you that the company will address all breaches of our code of conduct. We strive—every day—to be the best place to work on the planet."

Emily sank against the back of her chair.

"Do you have any other questions for us?" Kari asked.

"No. I came in with a long list, but you've answered all of them."

Emily slid a sheet of paper across the table toward Kari.

Kari scanned the terms set forth on the page and offered the internship to Anthony. "We understand you'll need time to think about this. I'll email the offer to you."

"I accept," Anthony said. "It's a fabulous opportunity and I'd love to work with you."

"That's wonderful! We're delighted you're joining us," Emily replied.

"My team will be very excited to hear this," Kari said.

"Can you start a week from Monday? Kari is on vacation next week or I'd ask you to come in this Monday." Emily chuckled. "We're serious when we say we need your help."

"If you'd like more time than that, we're flexible," Kari hastened to add.

"I'm surprised it's all happening so quickly," Anthony said. "I can't wait to get started. A week from Monday is fine."

"What a way to end our week!" Emily's enthusiasm was palpable.

"I'm so happy to hear this, Anthony," Kari said. "I can't wait, either."

"Kari will send the offer letter this afternoon." Emily swung to Kari. "Please copy me and Dhruv on that email so Anthony has our contact information."

"That's right—he returns from paternity leave on Monday," Kari said.

Emily addressed Anthony. "Because Kari is out of the office next week, contact me with any questions. Dhruv Patel, Kari's counterpart in our San Francisco office, will also be on the email. If I'm unavailable, you can reach out to him. My San Francisco and Denver teams work closely together. Our HR department will email paperwork and forms for you to fill out next week."

They all stood.

An alarm on Emily's phone sounded. "That tells me I need to head to the airport for my flight home."

"Thank you both for the opportunity," Anthony said.

"I'm going to dash," Emily said.

"If you have the time, I'd love to introduce you to your new coworkers," Kari said.

"Great idea. Have a wonderful vacation, Kari." Emily gathered up her satchel and purse and grasped Garth's harness. "Congratulations, again, Anthony. And welcome aboard."

CHAPTER 34

"What's all this?" Doug asked, taking the picnic basket Martha handed him and stowing it in the back seat.

"Snacks for the trip, plus I packed our lunch. We can't take my puppy into a restaurant until she's fully vaccinated. And she's not ready for that much stimulation yet, anyway. So, our only option will be a fast-food drive-through or bring our own."

"I'd rather eat your cooking any day. What've we got?" He pulled out of her driveway. "I bet it'll be delicious."

"I'm so excited to meet my new girl," Martha said, "that I woke up at three and couldn't get back to sleep. I got up and baked brownies. Then I turned to chocolate chip cookies. By the time I had to stop to shower and get ready, I'd made a peach pie, too. Baking is my stress reliever."

"That's what we're having for lunch? Brownies, cookies, and pie? I approve."

"No, silly. I made sliced chicken breast sandwiches with brie and cranberry aioli. The basket also contains two different kinds of chips, a bag of homemade granola, a wedge of white Vermont cheddar, and sea salt crackers. Plus, there's iced tea in an insulated cooler."

"We could go on a road trip with that spread," Doug chided. He glanced at her. "You amaze me. I hope you know that."

"I admit I may have gone overboard. I'm nervous and was distracting myself."

"What are you worried about?"

"Guide dogs are a precious resource. I don't want to mess up a puppy that could grow up to help someone like Emily."

Doug reached across the console to squeeze her hand. "You'll be the star puppy raiser of this club."

Martha chuckled. "My club has two leaders and they've each raised over thirty puppies. They're the stars."

"That's impressive," he replied. "You said they'll help you learn what to do with your puppy?"

"Yes. Our club meets twice a month. We do a training exercise and sometimes we go on an outing. The leaders demonstrate training techniques, answer questions, and help newbies—like me—learn. There are also a dozen members who have raised multiple puppies that have become guides. There's always someone willing to take calls from us newbies."

"I know you're taking this responsibility very seriously. With your commitment and the help available, you'll be fine."

"That's what I keep telling myself. Puppy raisers also get instructional emails and videos from the Guide Dog Center. The support they offer is unbelievable. When I think about it, I know I can't fail."

"What have they sent you so far?"

The miles sailed by as Martha filled him in on the vaccination schedule for her puppy, the arrangements for veterinary care provided by the Guide Dog Center, and the center's training philosophy. "I got an email yesterday telling me I'm getting a Golden Retriever, and her name begins with a 'p.'"

"That's fun! There's nothing cuter than a Golden Retriever puppy. Why didn't they tell you her name?"

"There's a tradition where the raiser solves riddles to guess their puppy's name when they pick them up."

"Huh ..."

Martha shrugged. "We'll both find out soon enough." She pointed to his dashboard. "The GPS says we get off the highway at the next exit. The church is less than a mile off the highway."

Doug pulled into the church parking lot ten minutes later.

A caravan of cars, vans, and SUVs was lined up in the middle of the lot. Each of them had their trunks or doors open. Children, teens, and adults mingled, engaged in excited conversation. Puppies and dogs frolicked together and danced around their humans.

"My gosh," Doug said. "It looks like a tailgate party." He pulled to the edge of the group and parked his car.

They got out together and were approaching the hubbub of activity when someone called Martha's name.

She turned to see one of the club leaders walking toward her. "The puppy truck is thirty minutes out," the leader said. "You've got time to grab coffee and something to eat before it arrives." The woman gestured to the spreads laid out in the surrounding vehicles.

"Are all these people receiving puppies from the truck?"

"No. Only four are getting dropped off here. You and one other person from our club are getting puppies. We made this drop-off into one of our club outings. Most of the people here are from our club." She smiled at Martha and introduced herself to Doug.

"This will be the perfect time to meet other club members," the woman said. "I'll email you our roster when I get home tonight, so you've got everyone's contact information."

"That's really nice," Martha said.

"Don't be shy," the woman said. "There are no strangers in a puppy club. You'll find we're like a big, supportive family. Minus any drama or dysfunction."

Doug and Martha both laughed, and the club leader moved off.

"I guess my manic, middle-of-the-night baking had a purpose," Martha said to Doug. "Do you mind if we offer our treats to the group?"

"I was going to suggest it."

They opened the trunk and displayed Martha's baked goods. Doug pocketed a cookie and a brownie. "These are my favorites," he said when she raised an eyebrow. "I'm not risking none being left after we make our rounds."

Martha tapped her temple with her finger, and they set out to meet the others gathered for the happy occasion, helping themselves to coffee from one vehicle and donuts from another. Everyone welcomed them like old friends they hadn't seen for far too long.

The air buzzed with excited conversation that transformed into a cheer when a long truck painted with the words Guide Dog Center in large black letters on a white background turned into the parking lot and drove toward them. Below the name were photos of puppies— white labs, black labs, Golden Retrievers, and mixes of the two breeds —all wearing red or green collars and looking adorable. The truck stopped at the edge of the assemblage and the crowd clapped.

Doug took Martha's hand, and they lined up near the truck as they waited for her life to take on a new purpose.

CHAPTER 35

$\mathcal{A}$ woman got out of the signature white and orange puppy truck. She opened the door in the center of the long truck and she and the driver went inside.

The crowd gathered around.

The driver stepped outside, waving a sheaf of papers over her head. She held a microphone to her mouth and called out a name. A man came to the truck. They went through the naming sequence. The other woman handed him his puppy, and they posed for photos before moving away.

Martha glanced up at Doug and gave him a thin smile before returning her attention to the puppy truck. The next names were the mother-daughter team from her club. The new raisers correctly guessed their puppy's name. This time, the second club leader raced forward and presented the new raisers with a banner containing their names, their puppy's name, and the name of the club. "We got advance notice of the names coming to our club," she said into the microphone. She helped the daughter slip the banner over her head, while the mother put her arm around her daughter's shoulders. Both club leaders joined them for a photo as the club cheered their newest members.

Martha sucked in a breath and pushed it out.

"It's hard to wait, isn't it?" Doug leaned down and whispered in her ear.

Martha nodded as yet another person was called to the truck.

"You said there were only four puppies for this location. The next will be yours."

Martha stood straighter and squared her shoulders. The next name called was Martha.

Doug patted her on the back, and she moved forward.

The driver announced the name of Martha's puppy club affiliation. The crowd whistled and cheered. "This is Martha's very first puppy." She leaned toward Martha. "Thank you for joining in this life-saving work."

Martha nodded as the crowd clapped.

"Did you read your email from us last night?"

Martha nodded again.

"So you know you're taking home a female Golden Retriever. She's eight weeks old, and her name begins with a 'p.' Now comes the part where you guess her name. You've heard how this works?"

"I've watched videos online."

"Good. Here's your clue: This is a popular place to hold your keys or a tissue. In fact, I'll bet you've got one on you."

"Pocket!" Martha exclaimed. "Is her name Pocket?"

"It sure is. Right on the first try."

The other woman stepped off the truck and handed Martha a squirming bundle of canine fluff.

Martha clutched Pocket to her chest and turned her face from one side to the other as the puppy swabbed her chin and neck with sloppy kisses. "Yes—I'm happy to meet you, too." Martha tried to keep her lips closed in an unsuccessful attempt to prevent the excited pup from licking her in the mouth.

The club leaders helped her into the club banner.

Doug and several members of the club snapped photos as they posed for pictures. As with the other new puppy raisers, no one had to tell Martha to smile for the camera.

When they were done, she and Doug moved to the periphery.

"Two more things," the woman said into the microphone. "We're delivering one more dog today. Dash isn't a puppy—he's a retired guide dog. He served his handler faithfully for ten years. That's a long time for a working guide. He's earned his retirement. His handler couldn't keep both him and his new guide dog, so Dash is returning to his puppy raisers. Randy and Melanie, please come forward. Dash is coming home to you."

The crowd erupted in applause as a black lab with white around his eyes and a salt-and-pepper muzzle stepped slowly out of the truck and onto the pavement. He lifted his brown eyes, opaque with cataracts, to scan the sea of faces turned to him.

Melanie held out her arms, and Randy knelt on one knee.

Dash needed no encouragement—no reminder of who these people were. Years had passed since he last saw them, yet he instantly recognized them. His tail whipped back and forth as he bounded to the beloved humans he hadn't forgotten.

Randy lay back as Dash wrestled him to the ground. Melanie threw her arms around Dash, enveloping her husband and the aging dog, who now acted like a puppy.

A host of onlookers pulled out tissues to dab their eyes as they watched the touching scene.

The driver cleared her throat before speaking into the microphone again. "And the last thing. New puppy raisers—please gather at the back of the truck. We're sending you home with toys, collars, leashes, enough food for a few days, your veterinary access card, and other essential information." She waved at the crowd. "You've been great. Thanks for being puppy raisers and coming out to support our vital work. This has been fun, but we've got two more stops today and six more puppies to place with their eagerly awaiting raisers."

Martha glanced up at Doug, who was wiping away moisture from under his eyes. "That last one got to you, didn't it?"

"You'd have to have ice water in your veins if it didn't."

Martha sniffled. "I agree. I had my hands full so I couldn't blow my nose."

"Speaking of which, would you like me to hold Pocket, or would you prefer I pick up your supplies from the back of the truck?"

"I'm not ready to hand her over yet," Martha said. "Supplies, please."

"You've got it."

"I see other members of my club are relieving their dogs over there." Martha gestured with her head. "I'll give Pocket a chance to go, and then we'll hit the road for home."

Martha and Pocket joined Doug at the car as he was closing the trunk. "Her luggage is safely stowed." He held the car door open for them.

Martha slid into her seat. "She pottied right away. I can already tell—Pocket is a very smart girl." Her voice took on a sing-song tone as Martha nuzzled the top of her puppy's head with her chin.

"You're holding her on the drive home, right?" Doug looked at them. "I guess that was a silly question."

"Will you reach into the back seat for that towel I brought with us? I'll put it on my lap—just in case we have an accident on the way home. Pocket's only eight weeks old."

Doug helped situate the towel. "Let's forget the highway and take the back roads home. That way, we can pull over quicker if she needs a break."

"Are you sure you don't mind? That'll take longer."

"So what? We're both retired, aren't we?"

"Thank you," Martha said. "Let's start driving. We'll eat lunch at our first stop."

"Sounds good. It's a beautiful day for a drive through the country."

CHAPTER 36

S ylvia's phone vibrated on her nightstand. Her drooping eyelids fluttered wide. She moved her book, lying open on her chest, to the mattress next to her. She reached for her phone, and smiled at the sight of the incoming caller ID.

She and Frank had texted every day since they'd parted at the hotel in Washington, D.C. He'd sent pictures from his brother's gorgeous waterfront property in Florida and recounted the meals he'd eaten, declaring that his system wasn't adjusting well to the spicy Cuban cuisine his brother favored.

She'd assured Frank he'd be fine once he got some San Francisco sourdough bread into his system. Sylvia pushed herself up onto her pillows and answered the phone.

"I hope I'm not calling too late," Frank said. "Are you in bed?"

"Of course not," Sylvia fibbed. "It's only nine-thirty. I was reading." That she was in bed—and had nodded off—didn't mean she'd intended to turn in. He was asking if she'd gone to bed for the night and the answer to that was definitely no. "I didn't expect to hear from you tonight."

"My flight got in thirty minutes early. We're in the rideshare on the way home from the airport."

"I love when a flight is early," Sylvia said. "We were an hour late getting back to San Francisco last week because of weather delays. I was so antsy to get home."

"That's the worst."

"What's on your agenda for tomorrow?" she asked. "Will you sleep in?"

"I've never been good at that—or naps. I plan to eat as much sourdough as I can lay my hands on," he said. "For my farewell dinner, my brother took me to a trendy restaurant. He ordered *vaca frita*, *rabo encendido*, and *ajiaco* for us. It was delicious, but I've been paying for it ever since."

"I believe that bread will be a cure for you."

"I hope so. That's why I'm calling. Would you like to start our comprehensive exploration of the San Francisco bread scene tomorrow?"

"Don't you need to settle in? You've been away from home for almost a month."

"I'll settle in later. I want to see you."

Sylvia stretched her toes toward the end of the bed. "Then I'd love to."

"I've been giving this a lot of thought." He gave her the name and address of a boulangerie. "I haven't tried this one, but it gets rave reviews on its breads, pastries, and lunch items. Have you been?"

"Nope. It'll be neutral ground for both of us. That's a good place to start. Can I pick you up?"

"It's not far from my house. Lonny and I will walk."

"I'll have my car, so I'll drive us to our next stop."

"You won't mind having Lonny in your car?"

"Certainly not," Sylvia said. "I occasionally give rides to Emily and Garth."

"Great. Shall we meet at 11:00?"

"That's perfect. And if you change your mind about a ride, give me a call. You know how fickle San Francisco weather is."

Frank chuckled. "Wasn't it Mark Twain who said, 'The coldest winter I ever spent was a summer in San Francisco'?"

"I read an article about that in the paper. History buffs and scholars say he never said that, but it's witty and sounds like something he would have uttered—or at least written."

"I hadn't heard that. I choose to ignore the naysayers and attribute it to him," Frank said.

"I'll follow your lead," Sylvia replied. "See you tomorrow. I'm glad we can get together so soon."

"Have a nice rest of your night," Frank said.

Sylvia threw her legs over the side of the bed and stuffed her feet into her slippers.

Tibs rolled onto his stomach and extended one paw and then the other, kneading his claws into the duvet cover.

"I'm sorry to disturb you, Your Highness," Sylvia said, giving her cat a quick pat. "I've got a date tomorrow."

Tibs meowed.

"You heard that right. I'm going on a date. And I need to find something cute to wear. I certainly don't have time to go shopping." She padded into her closet.

Tibs leapt off the bed and followed her.

Sylvia slid hangers along a rod until she came to the linen blend shirt in a shade of periwinkle that made her eyes pop. "I told Martha I'd never wear this." She pulled the hanger off the rod and moved to the full-length mirror in her bedroom. She held it in front of her, considering it. "It's perfect. And to think I considered returning this. Thank goodness Martha insisted I buy it."

The cat meeped at her feet.

"You agree, don't you, Tibs?"

"Let's pick out a pair of jeans and a lightweight sweater I can wear under the shirt. I'll take my trench coat in case it's the kind of day Mr. Twain was talking about."

The cat stretched and returned to the bed. He yawned his largest cat yawn.

"You're deserting me, aren't you?"

Tibs yawned again.

"I can take the hint. I know I'm keeping you up." She rubbed behind his ears. "I'll decide on the rest of my outfit for tomorrow and come right back to bed." She inhaled and shook her head. "Although I don't know how I'm ever going to fall asleep. My mind is racing. Turns out that looking forward to a date at my age is the same as it was when I was a teenager."

A wistful smile played at Sylvia's lips as she returned to her closet.

SYLVIA PARKED on the street opposite the boulangerie. Two large display windows bearing the name of the shop in gold flourishy script flanked the glass double door. Wooden molding painted a robin's egg blue surrounded the windows and door. The butterscotch-colored awning about the storefront contained the word BOULANGERIE in white letters. Rectangular planters on either side of the door each contained three double-pom topiaries. A wooden swing in the window to the right of the door featured brown-paper sleeves holding baguettes.

Sylvia checked her watch. It was ten fifty-five. She got out of her car and turned up the collar of her trench coat against the fog that showed no signs of dissipating. She crossed the street and opened the shop's door. A tinkling bell announced her arrival. She stepped onto the terracotta tile floor and closed the door on the fog that had rolled in with her.

A familiar voice called her name.

She turned to face the back of the shop. "Hello, Frank." She crossed the short distance to him. "May I give you a hug?"

"The answer to that is always yes."

Sylvia put her arms lightly around his shoulders and they embraced. "How did you know it was me?"

"I didn't. I got here fifteen minutes ago and there's only been one other customer here during that time. Since it was almost eleven, I made the lucky guess it was you."

"I can't believe they're not busy on a Sunday morning," Sylvia said. "This shop is beyond charming."

"It smells amazing, too."

"I think Lonny agrees," Sylvia said. "His nose is twitching non-stop, but he's not surfing the floor for crumbs or begging."

"A professional guide dog would never," Frank said. "Lonny's such a good boy. I've only had him a few months, but he's always ready to work and he knows what's expected of him. They told me he was a serious student and a quick learner at the Guide Dog Center."

"It's so interesting that dogs have distinct personalities and learning styles, just like people."

"That it is," Frank replied. "Are you ready to proceed with our mission?"

"Yes. Do you still need to eat bread as an antidote to Cuban food?"

"I'm out of the woods on that front," Frank said.

"Shall we buy a loaf and break off a chunk of bread at each shop? We can sample it without butter. Our tests should be on plain, naked bread."

"I agree."

"I'll write the name of the shop on each bag, so if we need to taste another sample, we won't mix up where it came from."

"Good idea. I'm beginning to think you've done this before." Frank teased.

They moved to the front of the old-fashioned wooden bakery case. Danish, muffins, turnovers, and croissants ran in rows from the front to the back of the right side of the case. "These look incredibly appealing," Sylvia said. She read aloud the neatly printed white cards positioned along the window at the front of each row, describing the baked goods. "Gooey apple filling is seeping out of the turnovers, the streusel topping on the muffins is a quarter-inch thick, and the puff pastry around the Danish is flaky and golden brown."

"Those sound amazing. To heck with the bread, maybe we should buy one of each of those."

Sylvia laughed. "The thought crossed my mind, too. We came in here, however, to sample sourdough."

"I didn't hear you mention any bread. Do they sell it here?"

"Yes. The other half of the case has more than a dozen kinds of bread." She read the names of the bread offerings, saving sourdough for last.

"Shall we get a loaf of sourdough and something else? Cherry cheese Danish is my favorite."

"Mine too! Yes—let's buy bread and Danish."

She motioned to a clerk seated on a stool at the far end of the display case. The young man folded his newspaper and approached them.

"Have you decided?"

Frank gave him their order.

The man bagged their selections and took Frank's credit card for payment. "You've bought two of our ten best-selling items," he said. "I hope you enjoy them."

"I'm sure we will," Sylvia said. "I'm starved and can't wait to tear into that Danish."

"Is there somewhere nearby to buy coffee?" Frank asked the clerk.

"We've got a small café at the back of the shop. People walk here from the surrounding neighborhoods, and it's usually packed. The lousy weather has kept everyone at home." As if on cue, thunder rumbled, and the skies opened.

"We don't want to go out in this," Sylvia said. "Let's get coffee, sample bread, and eat Danish while we wait out the storm."

"I'm in favor of that." Frank asked the clerk to direct them to the café.

The man showed them to seats in front of a small fireplace in a corner of the deserted room.

Frank directed Lonny to take his position down and under the table.

The clerk took their coffee orders. "May I bring water for your dog? We have a bowl outside the shop during good weather, but I picked it up when it started raining."

"That would be very thoughtful," Frank said. "Thank you."

The clerk told them he'd be right back.

"This is even more charming!" Sylvia pulled out her phone and snapped a few photos. "I want to show Emily and her mom. I think I told you Martha is my best friend."

The coffee and Lonny's water bowl arrived. Frank gave his dog permission to drink, and Lonny lapped up plenty before settling down for a snooze. Sylvia and Frank tore off chunks of sourdough bread. Both agreed it would be a genuine contender for Best-in-City. They finished their Danish. The rain pelted the window on the other side of the room and the fire flickered behind the hearth. Lonny's faint snore rumbled up from under the table.

The clerk refilled their coffee. "Can I get you anything else?"

"I should be full after the bread and Danish, but I'm still hungry," Frank said. "How about you, Sylvia?"

"My stomach is rumbling."

"Do you offer food?" Frank asked.

"I saw a chalkboard menu as we entered the room," Sylvia said. "I'll go look." She pushed her chair back.

"No need to get up, madam. I'll tell you what's on our menu," the man said. "I can also recommend the best thing for today."

"What's that?" Sylvia asked.

"Croque Monsieur," the man said. "We use our sourdough bread, the meltiest gruyere cheese you've ever seen, the best ham, homemade béchamel, and a smear of Dijon. Add a poached egg and you'll have Croque Madame."

Sylvia moaned. "This weather requires melted cheese. I'll have it—without the egg."

"I've never had it Madame style," Frank said. "Throw an egg on mine."

Their sandwiches came. Sylvia sliced off the end of her sandwich, the runny cheese dripping in ropes into the pool of béchamel on her plate. She bit into it with a satisfying crunch.

"Well?" Frank asked.

"This is a little slice of heaven. Do you need any help navigating yours?"

Frank tapped his fork on top of his sandwich. "It sounds messy. If I end up with cheese or sauce on my face, will you please tell me?"

"There's no 'if' about it. You will. I already have. Eating this sandwich will definitely be a messy affair. I intend to enjoy every bite. I'll make sure we're both cleaned up before we leave."

"Fair enough." They worked their way through their delicious meals as they described their childhoods and the hopes and dreams of their young lives.

A young man entered the café and settled himself at a round table. He pulled out a laptop and set to work, drinking coffee and tapping at the keyboard. The occasional tinkle of the bell at the front door announced a handful of customers.

Frank and Sylvia were deep in conversation about their college years when the man approached their table to tell them they'd be closing in ten minutes.

"What?" Frank pulled out his phone, which told him it was almost six o'clock. "I had no idea."

"I think the two of you had a very good day," the man said, smiling from Frank to Sylvia.

"We had a remarkable day," Sylvia said. "Did business pick up for you?"

The man shook his head.

"I know you're closing, but I'd love to take two bags of pastries and several loaves of bread to each of my two sons and their families." She pulled her credit card out of her purse. "Could you put that order together for me while I visit the ladies' room?"

"Thank you. It'd be my pleasure."

The man handed Sylvia her purchases as she, Frank, and Lonny headed out of the shop onto the deserted street.

The rain had stopped, and the cloud cover promised a spectacular sunset.

Frank allowed Lonny to relieve himself.

"That was nice of you to purchase all that," Frank said.

"It must be very discouraging to know you're going to lose money because of the weather." She sighed and shook her head before continuing. "My car is across the street. I'll drop these off at Craig's and Grant's after I give you a ride home."

Frank commanded Lonny to follow Sylvia.

She stashed the baked goods in her trunk and was soon pulling up in front of a mid-century modern building containing condominiums.

"This is nice," Sylvia said.

"Thanks," Frank said. "It's comfortable for us and convenient to everything." He swiveled to face her. "We didn't get far on our list today," he said. "One bakery?"

"I know. At this rate, it'll take us months to get to all of them," she replied.

"And I, for one, am perfectly fine with that."

"Me too."

"I had a wonderful time with you today, Sylvia. I could talk to you for hours." He chuckled. "In fact, that's what we did." He brought his hand up and extended it toward her.

Sylvia placed her cheek into his open palm.

"Until next time." He brought her mouth to his and kissed her.

CHAPTER 37

$\mathcal{P}$ari stood near the door, bouncing Amelia on her hip. "Honestly, you two. I've been here for twenty minutes. Are you ever going to leave?"

"I want to make sure you have everything you need," Dhruv said, typing on his laptop on the kitchen counter. "I'm almost done. These instructions will help." He tapped a key with a thwack and the printer in the next room rumbled to life.

"Your mother does not need instructions, Dhruv," Stephanie said. She and Biscuit stood by the door with Pari. "This isn't her first rodeo with a baby."

"I know that, but better to be safe than sorry." He raced to the printer and returned with a sheaf of papers. "It'll only take a minute to go through these."

"Dhruv!" Stephanie exclaimed.

Pari grabbed the papers from her son's hands. "I'll review these after you leave. I'm here so you can go out as a couple before Dhruv returns to work tomorrow. Get out of here and make the most of it."

Dhruv leaned toward Amelia.

"And don't make a big deal out of the fact that you're leaving her with her grandmother for an afternoon and evening. That'll only make it harder on her." Pari was firm. "It's raining cats and dogs. Stephanie and Biscuit are prepared." She addressed her son. "Get your raincoat from the closet and walk out that door."

"She's right, Dhruv."

He did as he was told.

Pari opened the door for them.

They stepped into the hallway, and she leaned out after them. "One word of advice: don't talk about Amelia. I understand she's the center of your world, but you need to focus on yourselves and your relationship. The world won't end if you don't discuss her for a few hours."

"Sound advice," Stephanie called over her shoulder.

Dhruv nodded his agreement.

They walked out the door of their building into the rain.

"Our car is at the curb, three cars down," Dhruv said. They hurried to the spot. Biscuit gave herself a mighty shake before hopping into the back seat.

"What a day," Dhruv exclaimed. "We won't be going on a walk in the park after all." He turned to his wife. "What would you like to do instead? Our dinner reservation isn't for another three hours."

"I've been thinking about that," she said. "You start back to work tomorrow, and I go back the week after that. I'd love to go into my classroom. The substitute teacher who took over my class while I was on maternity leave hasn't answered my emails about what she left in the classroom."

"I'm sure the tables and chairs are still there," Dhruv said.

"Of course." Stephanie reached over the console and put her hand on his arm. "I'd like to know if my bulletin boards are still there. And my library corner. Plus, I need to inventory my supply cabinet. I had my room nicely decorated. Parents commented on how colorful and engaging the room was. I'd like to make sure it's all still there."

"Can we get in?"

Stephanie patted her purse. "I've got my keys. Would you mind stopping by for a few minutes?"

"No. I'm happy to. Before I knew you, it never occurred to me that teachers are the ones who put all that stuff up in their classrooms."

"We are," Stephanie said. "And our own money buys and pays for most of it."

Dhruv put the car into gear. "Let's go see your room."

Once inside the classroom, Stephanie commanded Biscuit, "Go to bed."

Biscuit shifted her weight from paw to paw as she searched for her bed that wasn't there.

"Do you see Biscuit's bed?" Stephanie asked Dhruv.

He circled the room and opened the door to the supply cabinet. "It's not here," he said.

"What?" Stephanie licked her lips. "Is my giant bulletin board on the back wall?"

"Nope."

"Is it anywhere?" Stephanie's voice rose an octave.

"Not that I can tell."

Stephanie drew a deep breath and released it before continuing. "Describe the room to me, please. What do you see? And don't leave out any details."

Dhruv retraced his steps to the door of the room. "Your desk is on the right—where it was last year. There's nothing on it. The desks and chairs are clustered in the center of the room and the two rectangular worktables are on the far side. Six chairs have been placed upside down on top of each table. The chalkboards on the front and back walls are still there." He stopped talking.

Stephanie spun on him. "What else is on the walls?"

"Nothing."

"No colorful paper border around the room? What about the posters of the solar system, or the ones with whales in the Pacific?"

"None of that."

"I can't believe it! Why did someone take my stuff down?"

"The room looks freshly painted," Dhruv said.

"That must be it. I thought my room was on the schedule for next year."

"There are plastic totes stacked in your supply closet. Are those yours?"

"No. Maybe they packed my stuff in the totes." She commanded Biscuit to take her to the closet.

Dhruv helped her open the totes. Together, she and Dhruv determined that the items she'd so proudly displayed in her room were still there.

"At least I've got my stuff," Stephanie said, releasing a sigh of relief.

"Some of this stuff is pretty beat up. We can replace it."

"I know I said I only wanted to spend a few minutes in my room, but do you mind if we take the time to go through everything, so I know what I need to buy?"

"Sure," Dhruv said. "It'll be fun. I never really paid attention to your room." He brought a tote to one of the worktables and placed it in the middle. "You've got some cool stuff in here. We'll make a list and order things as soon as we get home."

Stephanie and Biscuit followed him. "The first thing we need is a new bed for Biscuit."

"Absolutely," Dhruv said.

They began their task and didn't notice when the rain let up and the afternoon gave way to evening.

"We've got our list," Dhruv said, holding up his phone. "It's on my notes app."

"You are the best husband," Stephanie said.

Dhruv noticed the time on his phone. "We've got to leave, or we'll be late for our dinner reservation. Maybe Mom will babysit one evening this week so we can come back when I get home from work to rehang all this."

Stephanie shrugged into her raincoat and put Biscuit into his working harness. "I appreciate your willingness to do that, but I have another idea."

They left the classroom and headed for Dhruv's car.

"Zoe and Diedre are done with their summer programs and have next week off before their school starts back up. Emily told me they're staying home alone for the first time. I bet they'd love to help me put my room in order. I'll pay them, of course."

"That's a brilliant idea!" Dhruv said. "They'll be good at it, too. Better than me."

"I wouldn't say that."

"Oh, come on. We both know decor isn't my thing."

"Everyone isn't good at everything," Stephanie acknowledged.

Dhruv held her car door open, and she slipped into the seat.

"I don't know where we're going to dinner," she said.

"It's a surprise," he replied.

"I just hope it has ice cream. I'm suddenly craving ice cream."

Dhruv dashed around the front of the car and dropped into the driver's seat. He reached for the starter and stopped. "You don't want hot sauce with that, do you?"

"I loved that when I was pregnant, didn't I?"

Dhruv sat motionless.

"You're not worried about me being pregnant again, are you? It was a miracle I conceived the first time, with my gynecological issues. Plus, I'm breast-feeding. Women don't get pregnant when they're doing that."

Dhruv started the car.

"I just really need a big bowl of ice cream. That's all there is to it."

CHAPTER 38

*G*arth

I liked it when we stopped at the coffee shop in the lobby of our office building. It always smelled wonderful. And sometimes Emily bought me one of the special dog treats they sourced from a local bakery. I'd heard Emily talk to the salesclerk about the ingredients. She'd evidently approved of them because we'd gone home with two cellophane bags tied with red ribbons. Inside were the most delicious bone-shaped treats. There was one for me and one for Sabrina, Emily had told me.

I held my breath as she placed her order for a dozen assorted muffins.

"Anything else?" the clerk asked.

"Do you have any of those dog treats?"

"We sure do," he answered.

"I'll take one of those, too." She ran her hand across the top of my head. "You can have yours when we go to the break room to celebrate Dhruv's return from paternity leave. Don't tell Sabrina."

I swished my tail along the floor. My lips were sealed.

Emily took our box of muffins, and we proceeded to our floor. Our first stop was the break room, where she placed the box on the far corner of the counter. "Rhonda is bringing her famous egg strata, and Mike is supplying fruit and orange juice. We'll gather for breakfast when Dhruv gets here. He's supposed to work from nine to five, now that he has a baby at home. No more coming in before the rest of us."

I rolled my eyes up to look at her. Did she not know that Dhruv was already in the office? Humans really didn't have the sense of smell that dogs had.

Emily was stashing her purse in her bottom desk drawer when I heard the footsteps of one of my favorite people. My tail wagged of its own volition.

Dhruv knocked on Emily's doorframe a few seconds later. "Hey, Em."

She spun around to face him. "Dhruv! It's not even eight. What're you doing here?"

"I wanted to tackle my inbox before we got busy. Kari's out this week, so I'll have a lot to juggle."

"I talked to Stephanie last week. You promised her you'd be home to help with Amelia."

"I did. And I will. She agreed I would work normal hours next week when she goes back to teaching. Our nanny starts this morning. Stephanie told me I could spend more time here this week while I'm covering for Kari."

"All right. But I'm warning you—if I find out that you're coming in early or staying late next week—or after, I'm going to rat you out for that desk drawer of junk food you keep in your office."

"You wouldn't!"

"Try me," Emily said. "I'll make sure Stephanie knows you're not following the healthy diet you both agreed to."

"You're playing hardball with me."

"Whatever gets the job done." Emily plopped into her chair. "So—how is it being back?"

"I miss her. Amelia." Dhruv shifted his weight from foot to foot, like he did when he was agitated. "I need to work—and I love what I do—but I didn't expect to miss her this much."

"I'm sure it's difficult."

"Very few men have paternity leave. I've had so much time with her and know how lucky I've been." He swayed. "I'm always thinking of Amelia."

"You've got Saturday to look forward to," Emily said. "Stephanie and I are doing a girls' day before she goes back to teaching on Monday. "You'll have Amelia to yourself."

"Unless my mother comes over. She said she'll stop by—in case I need help."

"That's kindly meant, I'm sure, but if you want uninterrupted time with Amelia, tell your mom that."

"I don't want to hurt her feelings."

"She'll understand, Dhruv."

"Oh—I almost forgot. Stephanie wanted me to ask you if Zoe and Diedre can help her set up her classroom this week." He filled her in on their discovery the day before.

"Thank goodness you went by the school. I'm sure the girls would jump at the chance."

"We'll pay them."

"You don't have to do that! They were whining about being bored before Grant and I left the house this morning. They adore Stephanie and the three of them will have a blast." She chuckled. "I should be paying you."

"It's a plan. Stephanie will be relieved I'm not the one helping her decorate."

"Both girls know how to use my braille labeler, too. They'll bring it with them. What day does Stephanie have in mind?"

"Tomorrow. If that works for them."

"Perfect."

"I'll text Stephanie. She'll be so relieved."

"We want her relaxed for our girls' day on Saturday," Emily said.

"Have you decided what you're going to do? Stephanie said she's leaving it in your hands."

"She's been housebound since the baby came and wants something active. A spa day is sedentary, so that's out. I've hired a driver and we're going to do whatever we feel like. Live in the moment. Let the winds take us where they may."

"That sounds very spontaneous. What have you done with the Emily Main we know and love? The one who makes lists and adores plans."

"She's turning a new leaf. At least for this Saturday. I think both Stephanie and I need an adventure."

"Just like I need a day at home with my baby."

"Exactly."

I watched as Rhonda hovered in Emily's doorway. "We're ready in the break room," she said. "Welcome back, Dhruv." She slid her arms around her coworker and pulled him in for a hug. Dhruv stiffened but accepted the embrace.

Emily rose from her chair. "I know emails are flooding our inboxes, but everyone wants to welcome you back and hear about Amelia. Let's celebrate the dream team being back together before we tackle the week."

I got to my feet and led the way. I didn't know about the rest of it, but I looked forward to the crunch of that fancy dog treat between my teeth.

CHAPTER 39

"The sign says the church hall is this way," Martha said to Pocket as she pointed to her right.

The puppy looked up at her mistress and wagged her tail.

"Come on," Martha said, moving toward their destination. Pocket followed her and Martha gave the puppy a small piece of kibble from a treat pouch cinched around her waist.

Pocket fell into step next to Martha, her gaze fastened on the pouch.

Martha continued to feed treats until they got to the hall. "Good girl," Martha praised as she pulled open the door and they entered the room.

"Welcome to puppy kindergarten." The woman who greeted her was one of the club leaders. A mother-daughter team who had received a puppy when Martha picked up Pocket was also there with their puppy. The only other person in the room was a man Martha recognized as one of the experienced members of the club. He had an older puppy with him.

Pocket lunged for the other young puppy, pulling the leash from Martha's grasp and bounding across the room to the puppy. They sniffed each other in the intimate way dogs do, then fell to the floor in a puppy wrestling match.

"It's time to break these two up," the leader said.

Pocket was on top of the other puppy, nipping at the dog's ears until the black ball of fluff jumped to his feet and turned the tables on Pocket.

"Do your pups know their names?"

Martha and the mother and daughter said yes.

"Great. You've made a good start. I'd like you to call their names."

The puppy raisers complied.

Both puppies abandoned their game and looked at their puppy raisers.

"Terrific," the leader said. "I'm assuming neither of them know the come command?"

Martha and the other raisers shook their heads no.

"Go pick up their leashes and bring them back to you. Puppies need to play, but now it's time for them to work."

Pocket and her classmate were soon sitting by their puppy raisers.

"I'm glad you came," the leader said. "We'll meet once a week for eight weeks to make sure you master the basics. I understand that none of our three new club members has raised a guide dog puppy before."

Martha and the mother and daughter nodded their agreement.

"Have any of you trained other dogs—pet dogs?"

Again, the three shook their heads no.

"That's great."

Martha and the mother exchanged a glance.

"It may sound surprising, but lack of experience is a good thing. There are several philosophies of dog training. The Guide Dog Center relies on positive reinforcement. The breeds we use for our guide dogs—labs, goldens, and crosses between the two—are extremely food motivated. That supports our positive training methods. We reinforce the actions we want by giving treats. Usually, it's simply small pieces of their regular kibble. We'll teach you how to do this so that by the time you graduate from kindergarten, it'll be second nature to you. Since none of you have to unlearn other training techniques, you'll catch on fast."

The other puppy glanced at Pocket and uttered a short woof.

Pocket shifted her gaze to her puppy pal but remained silent.

Martha reached down and patted her.

"Nice job, Martha," the leader said. "Petting is positive reinforcement, too. Don't forget to praise your puppy when they've done something right. Whether we're a dog or a human, we love being told we've done a good job. The rule is to only praise the behavior you want. It doesn't matter if your puppy has mastered a difficult skill or reliably performs an easier task, praise it."

The leader motioned for the man with the older puppy to join her. "Josh and Fenton will be with us every week to demonstrate the skills we'll be working on together. How many puppies have you raised, Josh?"

"Fenton is number twenty-nine."

"That's amazing," the leader said. "Josh is willing to help other club members, too. Like agreeing to spend eight mornings with us. Thank you."

"I'm happy to do it." He looked from Martha to the mother and daughter. "I'm always available to answer questions. My contact information is on the roster you got at puppy pick-up. Don't hesitate to call me if you want to discuss something."

"Josh is a terrific resource," the leader said. "And you know to call me or the other leader if you're having issues with your puppy or are unclear about anything. You're not in this alone." Her smile lit the room. "Before long, this club will feel like family."

Josh nodded his agreement.

"First—I want to take stock of where you are with your puppies." She looked at the new puppy raisers. "How's your crate training going? Martha?"

"She sleeps in her kennel next to my bed. I get up to take her out once a night and she goes right back inside when we return to my bedroom. I also have a kennel in my family room. She goes to that whenever I ask her to."

"Do you entice her into her kennel with a treat?"

"Yep. I leave her kennel door open, and she's also gone in on her own a couple of times to nap."

"That means she's comfortable with it and associates positive things with her kennel. It's her safe place. Pocket is ready to move on. The next time you tell her to go to her kennel, don't give her kibble until she's entered it. When she's inside and quiet, give her a treat while you're praising her. After she's mastered that, discontinue the treats while continuing to praise her."

"I'll work on that this week," Martha said.

"How about you?" The leader turned to the mother and daughter.

"We lure him into the kennel with treats, and then he immediately starts whining. We give him more treats, so he feels happy about being in his kennel, but he keeps whining."

"You're giving him treats every time he whines?"

"Yes," the mother said. "So he feels happy and doesn't want to whine."

"I understand why you think that will help, but what you're actually doing is training your puppy that he gets treats when he whines. Remember our rule—only reward the behavior you want to encourage."

"We've been doing it wrong this whole time." The mother and daughter looked at each other, then back at the leader.

"There's a simple fix. Lure him in with a treat and do not treat him if he whines or leaves the kennel. Stay close to the kennel so that you can give him a treat when he's inside and is quiet. Catch him being good—even if only for a few seconds. These dogs are super smart— you'll be amazed at how quickly they learn new behaviors."

"We'll work on it when we get home," the daughter said.

"Remember, carefully choose the times to work with your puppy. They shouldn't be hungry, thirsty, or tired. Humans don't learn well in those circumstances and neither do puppies. End each training session with a success—don't continue if you or your puppy are frustrated. Several sessions a day, working on a variety of skills, is the way to go."

"Got it," said the mom.

Pocket yawned and got to her feet. She moved toward the black fur ball until she reached the end of her leash. The other puppy followed suit and was also restrained by her leash. Thwarted in their efforts to reunite, the puppies returned to their raisers.

"Kennel acceptance is foundational for our guide dogs—and for most pets, too. Another crucial skill for guide dogs and pets in general is the ability to tolerate being touched and handled. All dogs need to be examined by the vet—ears looked at, abdomens palpated, heart and lungs listened to, and temperatures taken. Dogs can't get mouthy when someone touches them. Same thing with nail trimming or teeth brushing. You need to do things to your dog without being worried about a struggle."

The leader pointed to Josh. He led Fenton to the center of the room and knelt next to him. Josh looked into both ears, lifted the dog's tail, pulled up his gums to check his teeth, and picked up each paw and palpated each toe. Fenton stood still, unfazed by all of it.

"That's your goal," the leader said.

"Martha, please let Josh take Pocket. He'll demonstrate the bucket game, which is how we teach this skill."

Josh put Fenton into a down stay at the side of the room. He returned to the center and sat on the floor with his legs stretched out in a V in front of him.

The leader placed a small plastic bucket of treats next to Josh.

Martha handed Pocket's leash to him.

Josh positioned Pocket between his legs, with her head pointed away from him.

Pocket wriggled and squirmed.

Josh spoke to her in a calm voice and placed his hands on either side of her chest, below her neck.

She stopped moving and rested her bottom on the floor.

With razor speed, Josh plucked a treat from the bucket and fed it to the puppy, coming in low to the ground. She crunched her kibble and strained to reach the bucket for more.

"Nope. That's not how you get a treat from the bucket." Josh continued to hold the squirming puppy until she settled again. Josh fed her another piece of kibble.

Pocket focused on the treat bucket and didn't squirm.

This time, Josh stroked from her head to the middle of her back with one hand while holding her with the other.

Pocket was calm, and Josh rewarded her with a treat. They continued the game, with Josh stroking from her head to her tail without protest before giving the kibble.

"Good girl," Josh said with enthusiasm.

The other puppy escaped from his raisers and ran for the treat bucket. He snagged a treat before Josh snatched the bucket and held it out of the disappointed puppy's reach.

Everyone laughed.

"Fair is fair," the leader said. "This guy wants a turn."

Josh ran through the training exercise with the other puppy.

"I think that's the perfect place to end," the leader said. "Both these puppies are learning that allowing humans to touch them is just fine. Thank you, Josh."

He stood and returned the puppy to his raisers.

"Your homework for next week is to continue kennel training and to introduce the bucket game. By the time you're done, you'll be able to touch every part of your dog. You'll do it from a standing and a sitting position, and you'll roll them from side to side too. Don't worry if it takes you more than a week to accomplish this. You've got plenty of time. Every dog learns at their own pace. What's easy for one dog might be hard for another."

"This has been so helpful," Martha said. "Seeing it in person is much better than watching a video online."

"Absolutely," the mother in the other team agreed.

"One more thing before you go," the leader said. "We'll introduce pawpad at our next regular club meeting on Saturday. It teaches another foundational skill. Dogs love this game." She handed them each a flyer. "You'll need to bring your own pawpad. They're easy to make. You'll have the necessary materials on hand. This shows you how."

"I've got a couple of extras that I'll bring on Saturday," Josh said. "You can use them at the meeting if you don't have time to make one by then."

Martha glanced at the flyer, then folded it and put it in her purse. She already knew who she'd ask for help.

Pocket and the other puppy resumed rassling while their humans said goodbye.

CHAPTER 40

$\mathcal{S}$tephanie and Biscuit waited on the lawn outside their apartment building.

Grant pulled up at the agreed time.

Zoe and Diedre rushed out of the car. "Stephanie!" they cried in unison.

Stephanie opened her free arm, and the girls nestled in for a group hug.

"We haven't seen you since right after Amelia was born," Zoe said.

"It's been forever. Will we get to see her?" Diedre asked.

"Maybe later. She's down for her morning nap and I didn't want your arrival to wake her. It's our nanny's second day—and her first alone with Amelia. I want things to go well." Stephanie ran her hand along Zoe's back. "My goodness—I think you've grown over the summer. You're as tall as me, aren't you?"

"Yep," Zoe said. "I'm going to be tall."

"I'm still shorter than you, Stephanie," Diedre said. "I want to be tall."

"You'll be whatever your maker wants you to be," Stephanie said. "And it'll be perfect."

"Amen," Grant agreed. He had been hanging back, watching the happy reunion. "I need to get to the office. Are you ready to go?"

"We'll walk to school," Stephanie said. "It's a beautiful morning, and that's how Biscuit and I get there every day. I don't want to hold you up."

"I hope you have a pleasant walk, then. It's a nice day for it."

"Thank you for bringing me the two best helpers on the planet."

"I'll pick you up this afternoon," Grant said. "I can leave the office any time after two. Text me when you're ready."

"Will do, Dad," Diedre said. "We may have to stay late. Setting up a classroom is a lot of work."

"That's fine. Do what Stephanie tells you to."

"We know," the girls chorused.

"Don't worry about these two," Stephanie said. "They're always a joy to be around."

Grant retraced his steps to his car and Stephanie commanded Biscuit to move forward.

"Do you think she knows where we're going?" Zoe asked.

"I wouldn't be surprised. She's such a smart girl."

They made the fifteen-minute walk to the elementary school engrossed in conversation about the girls' upcoming move to fifth grade—and middle school.

"You handled the transition to a new school last year without a hitch. This will be much easier. Plus, you already know most of your classmates from last year."

"That's exactly what Emily told me," Zoe said.

"You see—great minds think alike."

They entered the school campus. Diedre reported that the parking lot was half full.

"Other teachers are getting their rooms ready. We have teacher in-service days next Monday and Tuesday, with meet-the-teacher on Tuesday night. Students return to class on Wednesday."

Biscuit took them onto a sidewalk.

"Find classroom," Stephanie commanded.

"Yep. She knows where she's going," Zoe said. "Biscuit is as smart as Garth."

Biscuit took Stephanie to her door. Stephanie unlocked it and they stepped inside. "The rooms in this wing were painted over the summer and they took everything off the walls."

"There's some stuff up," Diedre said.

"What do you mean?"

"The cursive alphabet is on a border along the ceiling, and there are six phonics posters," Diedre said. "Those are the same we had in my third-grade room when I went here."

"They weren't up on Sunday—" A knock on the door to the connecting classroom interrupted Stephanie.

"Hi Steph," Rebecca said. "I thought I heard you over here. Can you believe they painted our rooms and never told us?" The teacher from the adjoining classroom crossed to her friend and gave her a hug. "I want to see pictures of Amelia and hear all about everything, but it'll have to wait. Today is my only day to set up my classroom. I've got doctor and dental appointments the rest of this week."

"It's a daunting task, for sure."

"My husband came with me this morning to carry in supplies I bought over the summer. When we saw what had happened to my room, he called his office to let them know he'd be a little late to work. He hung the cursive alphabet border and phonics posters in both of our rooms. They're exactly where they were last year."

"That's so nice! Please thank him for me."

"Will do. I'm glad to see you've got helpers."

"Me too. If you need a hand with anything, let us know."

"I'll be fine. I just need to get back at it. Let's grab lunch to catch up after the school year starts."

"It's a plan," Stephanie said.

Rebecca returned to her classroom.

"Those were the things that were hung high on the walls. We won't need a ladder for anything else," Stephanie said. "I've got a step stool in my supply cabinet."

"I'm tall, remember? We won't need it."

Stephanie chuckled. "Good point. You're in charge of hanging things."

"Diedre should be responsible for design. She's great at making things pretty. Her bedroom is beautiful."

"I'm glad to hear that. Do I have six bulletin boards?"

"Yes," the girls said in unison. "And a smart board, two whiteboards, and a magnetic board," Zoe added.

"Excellent. That's what I need. I have boards dedicated to math, reading, spelling, our daily and weekly class schedule, a calm center board with posters about naming and managing our emotions, and a final board for what I call our library nook. Do you see a bookcase?"

"It's behind your desk," Diedre said. "There aren't any books on it. What goes on the magnetic board?"

"I have science-related stuff there: posters about the solar system, clouds, aquatic life, and the redwood forests." Stephanie drew a deep breath. "Let's start by moving the desks and chairs into pods of six, with the fronts of the desks pushed together. I'm going to have thirty students in my class, so how many pods will that be?"

"Five," the girls said in unison.

"Right! Good work remembering your math skills." Stephanie slipped into teacher mode. "My desk is in the right spot. Will the two of you be able to slide the empty bookcase to the wall in front of my desk?"

"We can do that."

"Once that's done, we'll pull out the bins and replace things on the bulletin boards."

"I'll make lists of what's on each one for you to access on your laptop," Zoe said.

"Let's put the important stuff up first so Zoe can make the lists," Diedre suggested. "While she's doing that, I'll install the decorative borders and make everything look pretty."

"Dhruv said a bunch of what I had—particularly the science posters—were too dog-eared to reuse. We ordered new ones. Tell me if anything else is worn. You girls are wonderful at finding things online. I remember how you helped me find my wedding dress. Please order replacements of anything we can't use."

"Sure!" Diedre's enthusiasm was palpable.

They swung into action. The furniture was soon in place and the bins from the storage closet emptied.

"Everything we think you can use is in place," Diedre said. "None of the borders survived being taken down. Someone had stapled them in place, and there are big tears in them."

"That's not good," Stephanie agreed. "It'll look tacky. Let's order new ones."

Diedre was already scrolling through an online retailer's website. "I think your color palette should be green, blue, and yellow. Not pastel, but calming, cheerful hues."

Stephanie stifled a smile. Diedre sounded like a professional interior designer.

Diedre looked at the teacher. "They're colors that look good on you, too. You wear them a lot."

"That sounds ideal," Stephanie said. "Have you found something that would work?"

"Yes. And everything's in stock. It says if you order in the next two hours and twenty minutes, you'll get your order tomorrow." She gave Stephanie the total.

"Then let's do it!"

Diedre placed the order.

"Excellent! The only things we can still do today are put my personal collection of books on the bookcase in the library nook and position supplies on my desk." Stephanie tapped her watch and listened to the time. "If we work fast, we'll have time to stop for ice cream on the way home, then text your dad to pick you up at my apartment."

"Yay! We'll be quick," Zoe said. She and Diedre began placing books onto the bookcase.

"When do you get the posters you ordered?" Diedre asked as she walked slowly with a tall stack of books balanced precariously in her arms.

"Tomorrow."

"Can we come back Thursday to help put them and the stuff we just ordered in position?"

"Are you sure you want to spend one of the last days of summer break doing that?"

"Positive," Zoe said. "When you undertake a job, you see it through."

Stephanie couldn't hold back a chuckle. She knew who had taught the girls that valuable lesson. She'd heard Emily say that on more than one occasion.

"I'd be very grateful to you. Check with your parents to make sure it's okay."

"It will be," Zoe stated.

"If not, Dhruv promised to help me."

Stephanie didn't see the girls look at each other and roll their eyes.

"It shouldn't take long on Thursday," Stephanie said. "When we're done here, could we go back to my apartment and go through my clothes?"

"That'd be fun!" Diedre said.

"I don't know what looks good on me anymore. Stuff fits differently once you've had a baby. I ask Dhruv and he always says I look beautiful."

"We'll help you pick out the perfect outfit for meet-the-teacher night," Zoe said.

Stephanie raised both arms over her head and stretched. "What would I do without you? I hope Amelia grows up to be as smart, kind, and resourceful as both of you."

CHAPTER 41

Emily and Stephanie followed Garth and Biscuit to the car waiting at the curb. Morning fog hung heavily around them.

"I can't believe you hired a driver for the day," Stephanie said. "That's *way* extravagant."

"This is instead of a spa day, remember? I'm getting off cheap." They reached the car, and the driver held the door so the women and their constant furry companions could settle into the back seat. "You said you want an adventure, and we both decided to be spontaneous. Having our own driver gives us that luxury."

"Where to, ladies?" the driver said from the front seat.

"We haven't decided yet," Emily said. "Would you take us to a drive-through for coffee while we discuss our options?"

"Of course. Do you have a preference?"

Emily gave him the name of the nearby coffee shop that she and Stephanie often frequented.

The driver pulled into traffic.

"I have two ideas for us to consider," Emily said. "Both of them will take us away from this fog and into sunshine. If neither one sounds good, we'll come up with something else."

"What're you thinking?" Stephanie asked.

"First—how about a day at the beach? I know how much you and Dhruv loved your honeymoon at the Hotel del Coronado. We could pick up a picnic from a local market and spend the day walking on the sand."

"Oh, Em." Stephanie inhaled a quick breath. "That's kind of you to offer, but I know beaches aren't your favorite place. You lost your eyesight on your honeymoon in a riding accident on the beach. This doesn't sound like it'll be a fun day for you."

"I can't live my whole life avoiding the beach," Emily said. "I'll be fine. Besides, this day is for you."

"You said you have another suggestion. Let's hear it."

"Zoe and Diedre came up with this one. They found it online and told me about it last night."

"OMG—those two. If they don't own a wildly successful event-planning business when they grow up, I'll eat my hat."

"Right? Anyway—they found an organic flower farm outside the city. It's family owned and operated. They offer classes in baking, canning, flower and herb gardening, and soap making."

"That sounds different—and interesting."

"Cold press soap making is on the schedule today. We can go to the farm and poke around without taking a class, too."

The driver pulled up to the drive-through window.

Emily recited both of their coffee orders by heart. "Please get yourself something to drink, if you'd like," she told the driver.

"That class sounds fabulous," said Stephanie. "Something new and tactile. I can't think of anything else I'd rather do."

"The website says there are trails through the flower gardens and an adjacent woods. We can walk the dogs after the class."

"Even more perfect! Are there still openings?"

Emily paused. "I signed us up last night. I hoped you'd pick this."

"Oh, Em. You're the best. Why did you even suggest a beach day?"

"As I said, today is focused on what you want."

"I'm all in on soap making and wandering through flowers."

The driver handed the coffees to them through the opening in the console. "I take it you've made a decision."

Emily supplied the address. She and Stephanie relaxed into their seats, sipping their coffee drinks, as the car headed into the countryside.

THE DRIVER TURNED onto a gravel road leading to a low stone wall. An ornamental iron archway spanned their path. A sign bearing the name Sweet Briar Farm hung from the top of the arch.

"We're here," the driver said. "It's beautiful. There are flowers as far as the eye can see. I've been to tulip fields in springtime. This farm is smaller, but just as pretty."

"Do you mind if we roll down the windows?" Emily asked.

The driver did it for her.

"I smell the flowers!" Stephanie cried. "Are there roses?" she asked the driver.

"On both sides of the road," he replied. "Want me to tell you what else I see?" He continued to drive, leaving the roses behind.

"In a minute," Emily said. "What about lavender?"

"Right again," the driver said. "There's a long, low adobe building up ahead, with a small parking area in front of it. My GPS tells me this is our destination. The gravel road keeps going through the flower fields. Do you want me to stop or keep driving?"

Emily tapped her phone and listened to the time. "Our class is about to start. We'll explore the flower fields later."

The driver parked and Emily, Garth, Stephanie, and Biscuit piled out of the car.

The dogs lifted their noses, nostrils twitching, as they savored the fragrant air.

"We'll be in our class for quite a while. Feel free to leave for a bit if you've got something you want to do," Emily said.

"I always bring a book with me," the driver said. "There's a bench overlooking the lavender field. I'll park myself there and read."

"You're sure?"

"This'll be the most relaxing afternoon I've spent in months. Text me when you finish your class and I'll be back at the car in an instant. Shall I take you to the building?"

"Sure," Emily said. "But first, we need to let our dogs relieve themselves. Let's find a good spot for that."

"There are a million of them—you're on a farm, after all." He began to walk. "Over here."

Emily and Stephanie directed their guides to follow the driver. After Garth and Biscuit took care of business, the driver led them across a deep veranda and into the structure.

A sturdy-looking, middle-aged woman stood in the center of an open room. Her graying brown hair was piled on top of her head and secured by a colorful scarf. She wore denim overalls over a long-sleeved white T-shirt. A large beige canvas apron, bearing the name and logo of Sweet Briar Farm, was tied around her waist.

She was surrounded by six other women, each wearing protective goggles and the canvas apron.

"Stephanie and Emily?" the woman asked.

"Yes," Emily replied.

"Welcome. I'm your instructor. Everyone's here." She picked up goggles and aprons and handed one to each of them. "You have to wear these. We use lye in our soap, so you'll need protection. Lye also heats up when mixed with distilled water. That chemical reaction releases fumes, so we have class outside. Follow me."

The small group of would-be soap makers crossed another veranda and made their way to a series of rectangular tables set up in an orchard.

The instructor led Stephanie and Emily to a table at one end. "Please do not touch any of the items on the table in front of you yet. Also, I don't want your guide dogs to be exposed to any of our caustic materials. Can they wait in the grassy area fifteen feet behind you?"

"Absolutely," Emily said.

"They'll be fine there," Stephanie added.

They escorted Garth and Biscuit to the dappled shade of a mature persimmon tree and commanded them to lie down and stay. Both dogs stretched out in the lush grass, muzzles on their outstretched paws.

The instructor began with a comprehensive overview of the history of soap and the soap making process. Several attendees asked detailed questions.

The dogs had each rolled onto their sides and were fast asleep.

Emily leaned toward Stephanie. "Do you get the impression some of these folks plan to sell handmade soap?" she whispered.

"I was wondering the same thing. It's fascinating, but I want to start making soap," Stephanie whispered back.

As if she'd heard them, the instructor said, "Put on the gloves we've provided for you at your workstation, and be sure to leave your goggles on. We'll follow a cold process recipe. The first step is to make the lye solution. We use one part lye to two parts distilled water. Your ingredients have been premeasured for you. The heat-resistant bowl with distilled water is directly in front of each of you—about ten inches in from the edge of the table. The beaker of lye is four inches to the left of that. A silicone spatula is at the front of the table, parallel to the edge."

The instructor moved to stand in front of Stephanie and Emily's table. "Slowly add the lye to the water, stirring gently. Remember—you're initiating a chemical reaction that will produce heat and fumes. Don't get close to the mixture." She leaned toward Emily and Stephanie. "I'll help, if you'd like."

"We both cook at home," Emily said. "I think we'll be fine."

"But watch us, just in case," Stephanie added.

Emily picked up the spatula with her right hand and slid it forward until she touched the bowl with the distilled water. She then located the beaker with lye. She brought the spout at the lip of the beaker to the edge of the bowl and drizzled the contents into the bowl while she stirred. The chemical reaction began.

"That's perfect," the instructor said. "You could have demonstrated that for me."

Stephanie had waited for Emily to finish and now accomplished the task with the same precision.

"Star students. Both of you," the instructor said.

She stepped back so everyone could see her. "As the lye mixture cools, we'll melt coconut oil and shea butter before adding olive oil. The oils need to cool to the same temperature as the lye mixture before we combine them with an immersion blender. While we wait, select essential oils and other add-ins to personalize your soaps. Today, we have lavender, peppermint, and tea tree oils. For add-ins, you've got your choice of oatmeal, dried rose petals, or lavender."

Emily chose lavender and peppermint, while Stephanie selected tea tree and rose petals. They were both as skillful with the immersion blender as they had been with combining the distilled water and lye.

The instructor hovered while they poured their soaps into the silicone molds.

"We've marked each mold with your names," the instructor said. "We cover the molds for forty-eight hours to allow the soap to harden, then turn it out of the molds and cut it into bars. The bars spend six weeks curing in a dry, well-ventilated space. That makes the soap harder and milder. We'll then mail your finished bars of soap to you." She thanked everyone for coming and the attendees disbanded.

"That was so much fun," Stephanie said. "I can't wait to get our soaps. If they turn out nice, I'll give a bar to Dhruv's mom."

"I was thinking the same for Martha and Sylvia," Emily said.

They called their dogs to them.

"What do you want to do now?" Emily asked.

Stephanie stepped out from under the canopy of trees, into the sunshine. Birds called to each other as they swooped overhead. Insects buzzed.

Biscuit snapped at a fly zooming close to her nose.

"I think these guys deserve a nice, long walk. Let's ask the instructor to lead us to the trails."

"The farm's website has an app that guides us along the way," Emily said. "Are you hungry? We worked through lunch."

"I am," Stephanie said. "Is there a café on the farm?"

"It closed fifteen minutes ago. We'll have to find somewhere to eat on the way back. The only thing available here, now, is ice cream."

Stephanie's head snapped up. "I'd definitely go for eating ice cream for lunch."

Emily chuckled. "Are you kidding?"

"Not really. I'd love it, but I'm sure you'd like proper food."

"I adore ice cream," Emily said. "Now that you mention it, I've been craving some."

"This will be the third time this week I've had it," Stephanie said. "You'd think I was pregnant again."

Emily came up short. "Are you?"

"Naw. Amelia was our miracle baby. It won't happen again."

"You never know with pregnancies," Emily said, a tinge of sadness in her voice.

"Any luck on that score?" Stephanie asked.

"Not yet," Emily replied. "Let's get going on this walk. Now that you've brought up ice cream, I suddenly can't think of anything else."

CHAPTER 42

$\mathcal{D}$hruv sat at his kitchen table. His laptop was open in front of him, and he was surrounded by scraps of paper. His phone pinged, and he checked his messages. Pari was at his front door.

He got up and crossed to the open the door, Sugar and Rocco close on his heels.

Pari smiled at her son as she stepped across the threshold, a large casserole dish clutched in her hands. "Is she sleeping?" she whispered.

Dhruv nodded.

Pari proceeded to the kitchen and motioned to the refrigerator with her head.

Dhruv opened the door, and Pari placed the dish on the left side of the bottom shelf. "In the dedicated grandma spot," she said, sounding pleased with herself. "Nothing else in the fridge has been disturbed. I won't make that mistake again." She smiled at her son. "That's for your Sunday night dinner tomorrow so you don't have to cook. I want you to have a relaxing evening before Stephanie goes back to teaching."

"That's very kind of you, Mom. I can't believe how fast time has flown and we're now both back to work."

Pari pointed to the papers strewn on the kitchen table. "Aren't you putting in enough hours Monday through Friday? You should do something you enjoy while Amelia naps."

"That's not office stuff," Dhruv said. "I'm inputting data into my spreadsheets that catalogue her feedings, weight, height, and sleep schedule."

Pari took a step back. "You're doing what?"

Dhruv repeated himself. He picked up a scrap of paper that bore a date and time, the number of minutes that Amelia nursed, and her weight. "This is important information for nursing mothers."

"Oh, honey." She paused, searching for words. "I'm sure it is—for preemies or babies who aren't gaining weight. Did your pediatrician tell you to keep track of this?"

He shook his head. "I read about it online. It's my job as her father to assure her safety."

"And you're doing a wonderful job. Your dad and I are both extremely proud of the wonderful father you are." She paused before continuing. "But these spreadsheets aren't necessary."

"What do you mean?"

"Wasn't Amelia in the eightieth percentile for height and weight at her last checkup?"

"She was."

"Well … then … that means she's thriving." She put her hand on his elbow and looked into his eyes. "You don't need to do all this."

Dhruv shrugged and looked away.

"This," she pointed to the table, "is part of what you do. Data collection and precise analysis are in your DNA. It's who you are, and how you take care of your family. But being a relaxed, happy parent is important, too. Enjoy these moments. Before you know it, Amelia will be grown and you'll be standing in her kitchen, whispering while your grandchild sleeps in the next room."

Dhruv smiled ruefully.

"Have you eaten?"

"No. I got started on this as soon as I put Amelia down."

"I haven't had lunch, either. Clear away all that," she pointed to the table, "and I'll make us each a sandwich."

Dhruv shut his laptop and gathered up the scraps of paper. He looked at his mother, who was busy cutting a tomato into thick slices.

She looked pointedly at the kitchen recycle bin.

Dhruv hesitated, then threw away the papers.

Pari put two ham and cheese sandwiches onto plates and headed toward the living room with them. "The sun has burned through the fog. Let's take these to the chairs by the window. I want to enjoy the nice weather."

Dhruv followed his mother. He sat and stretched his long legs in front of him, crossing his feet at the ankles.

They ate their sandwiches in companionable silence. Pari gazed out the window while Dhruv was deep in thought.

"I've decided what I'm going to do this afternoon to relax and have fun." He pulled his legs under himself and sprang to his feet.

"That's wonderful, sweetheart," Pari said. "What're you thinking about?"

"It's sunny." He pointed to the window. "This weather won't last. We need to be outside."

Pari nodded, encouraging him to continue.

"When Amelia wakes up, I'll give her a bottle and change her diaper. If her onesie gets dirty, I'll change her. I'll check the temperature outside and decide if she needs a jacket or not. And if her booties are warm enough."

Pari stood and put her hand on Dhruv's shoulder. "That's fine, Dhruv. I assumed that. What's the relaxing, fun part?"

"I'll put Amelia in the front carrier and take her and the dogs for a walk. In the sunshine. And fresh air."

Pari's face broke into a relieved smile. "That's absolutely perfect, son. All four of you will enjoy that. As Amelia grows older, she'll remember the time you spend with her—not the time you're working on your laptop."

"Do you want to come with us?"

"I wish I could, but I've got other plans. Besides, today is a father and daughter day, and I won't intrude on that. I only stopped to drop off the casserole." She headed for the door.

Dhruv followed her. "Thanks for everything you do for us. And for giving me advice. I guess I still need my mother."

Pari drew him to her for a tight hug. "There's nothing I'd rather hear," she said. "Give my sweet granddaughter a kiss from me and enjoy the simple pleasure of a walk in the sunshine."

CHAPTER 43

"Hello, Pocket!" Doug bent to pat the puppy squirming at his feet. He lowered himself to one knee and allowed her to wash his chin with doggie kisses. "How'd she do at puppy club this morning?"

"We worked on pawpad, and she caught on real fast. The club leaders both commented on it. They said Pocket wants to learn," Martha said. "It's obvious when she walks in the door."

"You're a star student, aren't you?" Doug ruffled the fur by her ears. "We knew you would be. I was happy to make the pawpad. Did it work okay?"

"It was great! One of the other raisers asked if you're a woodworker. She wants to buy one from you."

Doug guffawed. "It's two eight by ten by one-inch pieces of wood fastened together to make a two-inch platform, with a section of yoga mat glued on top to provide traction for their paws. The only thing I did was sand the wood and glue things together. I got the mat at a thrift shop. If anyone in your club wants a pawpad, I'm happy to make them one for free."

"I figured you'd say that. It's very nice of you."

"That's the least I can do to support anyone who's kind enough to be a puppy raiser." He gave Pocket one more pat and got to his feet. "So she's mastered it?"

"I wouldn't say that. In fact, we're supposed to work on it once a day. It helps them learn to focus." She looked at Pocket who sat quietly, gazing up at them. "Want us to show you? She's calm and attentive. It's a good time to work with her."

"Sure! Our dinner reservations aren't for another forty-five minutes. We've got plenty of time."

Martha retrieved the training-treat pouch from the kitchen counter.

Pocket's chin came up as she heard the canvas pouch snap open.

Martha walked to the pawpad, a treat in her right hand.

Pocket raced ahead of her and placed her right front paw on the pawpad.

Martha beamed at Doug. "I didn't even have to lure her onto the pawpad with a treat." She gave Pocket a training treat. "First you lure them into putting one paw on the pawpad with a treat. Then you get them to put the other paw on the pawpad."

Pocket placed her left front paw on the elevated platform.

"She did it!" Doug cried. "She knows."

Martha gave Pocket several treats, then encouraged her to step off the pad. Martha took a step back and pointed to the pawpad.

Pocket placed both paws on the elevated surface.

Martha fed her treats. "Good girl," she cooed. "Nice job."

Martha dropped a treat onto the floor in front of her.

Pocket abandoned her perch and lunged for the treat.

Martha grabbed it before Pocket scarfed it up.

Pocket scrambled back into position with both front paws without being asked.

Martha gave the puppy more treats. "Such a good girl!"

Pocket remained with both paws in position, and Martha gave her treats at varying intervals. "Pawpad is used to teach puppies to focus and disregard distractions. Like ignoring other dogs, not eating food from the floor, or staying calm in the face of something scary. They demonstrated this using an older puppy and a mylar balloon at the club meeting. Pocket's not ready to ignore food on the floor. I moved into that exercise too fast." Martha gave Pocket another treat. "For now, I'll have her stand on the pawpad while I stretch out the time between treats. She'll learn that staying on the pawpad means she gets treats."

Martha and Doug continued to chat while Pocket stood on the pawpad, her eyes glued to Martha's hand by the treat pouch. By the time Doug announced they needed to leave for dinner, Pocket waited patiently for fifteen seconds at a time between treats.

"Go to your kennel," Martha instructed Pocket.

The puppy bounded to her kennel and turned around inside it, looking at them and wagging her tail. Her expression asked if she'd done it right.

Martha fed her a handful of treats and shut the kennel door.

Pocket dropped to her belly and settled her muzzle on her front paws, her large brown eyes focused on them.

Martha and Doug stood looking at her.

"Will she be okay if we leave her?" Doug asked.

"Of course. Puppies need to learn to stay home alone. They're safer —and feel more secure—if they're in their kennels."

They continued to look at the silent puppy.

Pocket's eyes moved from one to the other, her eyebrows undulating like shafts of wheat in a breeze.

"This is her first week with you," Doug said. "It wouldn't hurt if we stayed in with her—only until she's adjusted. I'll call the restaurant and cancel our reservation. We'll have our meal delivered."

"You wouldn't mind?" Martha asked, then brought a hand to her head. "This is silly—we should go," she said, but didn't make a move to leave.

"It's not silly. In fact, it feels like leaving a newborn with a babysitter for the first time."

"That's exactly it." Martha sighed. "We all learned to do that, and everything was fine. Let's go to the restaurant."

"We can eat out next week," Doug said. He pulled out his phone.

"Let's indulge the over-protective parent in us and stay in. With Pocket."

Martha leaned in and kissed his cheek. "You are the best—the very best. Thank you for being so thoughtful—and indulgent."

Martha grasped the kennel door and slid the latch open.

Pocket jumped to her feet and one eye closed and reopened.

Martha and Doug burst out laughing.

"Did I see what I thought I saw?" Doug asked.

"Pocket winked at us! I'll bet my bottom dollar on it."

Doug logged onto the restaurant's website, and they perused the menu together. When they'd made their selections, Doug placed the order.

Martha went into the kitchen and collected silverware and napkins. "It's a beautiful evening. Let's eat on the patio."

Doug followed her outside, with Pocket prancing at his heels.

"What would you like to do after dinner?" Martha asked.

"I think the three of us should curl up on the sofa to watch a movie," he replied.

"You're assuming Pocket is allowed on my furniture?"

"Oh, come on." Doug rolled his eyes. "Is there any doubt?"

"I guess not," Martha said. "I love cuddling her."

"All I ask is that she doesn't get between us. Saturday night is my turn to cuddle with you."

"That's a boundary I agree with one hundred percent."

"Should we do more training after dinner?"

"I think she's had enough for one day." She finished setting the table and turned to Doug. "Are you genuinely interested in her training?"

Doug nodded vigorously. "I am."

"I'd appreciate your help, and I think it'll be good for Pocket to experience being trained by more than one person. Would you like to join us at puppy club meetings?"

"I'd love to," Doug said. "As long as you don't mind. I don't want to impose."

"Stop! You'd be doing no such thing. It'll be so much fun training her together."

"Sort of like raising a child together—which, at our ages, we'll never do," Doug said wistfully.

Martha rested her hand on his elbow and looked into his eyes.

Pocket spied a rope toy in the grass and leapt off the patio, returning with it in an instant. She pushed the toy into Doug's hand, breaking the romantic spell.

CHAPTER 44

*G*arth

Gina and Craig were here! I smelled Alex as we approached Sylvia's front porch. Somebody needed to change his poopy diaper.

I also smelled something sweet and tangy. Sylvia and Martha were making barbeque. I love the smell of that almost as much as I do beef stew. Or roasting chicken. Or lasagna. It's hard to settle on a favorite —except for Crunchy Cheetos. They're always my favorite.

We walked through the front door to the boisterous greeting we always received at Sunday night family dinners. Everyone hugged each other. The girls raced upstairs to find Sylvia's cat Tibs. He was probably hiding under Sylvia's bed, as usual.

Emily removed my working harness, and I was off duty. I considered following the girls. I'd developed an appreciation for cats since Squeaky and I had become buddies. He was pliable, and cuddly in a way Sabrina and I weren't. And he was smart—every time Emily was near, he either leapt out of the way or squeaked to alert her to his presence. I hadn't realized cats are smart—or, at least, Squeaky is.

I glanced at the stairs but decided to help myself to a drink from the water bowl by the door into the backyard. Martha was standing outside the door. She held her phone to her ear, with her other hand covering her mouth as she whispered into the phone.

"Everyone's here and dinner is almost ready. We'll be seated in fifteen or twenty minutes. I'll make sure the front door is unlocked." She paused, listening intently.

"Yep. You remember correctly. The powder room is the last door on the left. Hide her in there. Give her a handful of treats and make sure she has her stuffed duck. She loves that thing. That'll keep her quiet for a few minutes."

Martha nodded her head as she listened.

"I like that. Going back outside and ringing the bell is perfect. Everyone knows you're joining us for dinner to swap vacation stories. I'll tell them you called to say you've been delayed by an accident on the bridge. That we should start without you."

"Martha?" Sylvia called from the kitchen.

"I've gotta go. See you in a bit. If Pocket doesn't bark when you knock, we'll pull this surprise off." Martha slid her phone into the pocket of her slacks and stepped into the kitchen.

Sylvia opened the oven door, and a blast of hot, moist air fogged her glasses.

I inhaled the heavenly fragrance.

She stepped back, fanning her face with her hand to clear her glasses. She reached up and turned off the oven. "Everything's ready," she said. "I don't want the ribs to dry out."

"That was Doug," Martha said, repeating the story they'd concocted. "He wants us to start without him."

"I hate to do that," Sylvia said. "We can hold dinner for thirty minutes."

"He insisted," Martha said sharply.

Sylvia raised both eyebrows at her friend. "If you're sure? Everyone's enjoying milling around, talking. The girls are still upstairs with Tibs."

"I heard Grant and Craig mention how hungry they are," Martha fibbed. "I'll make a plate for Doug and put it in the oven to stay warm.

To be honest, I'm hungry, too. Smelling those ribs has me salivating. Let's eat."

Sylvia shrugged. She pulled the ribs out of the oven and stirred the beans in the crock pot.

Martha set a large bowl of coleslaw on the counter, together with a fruit salad she pulled out of the refrigerator.

"Corn bread?" Sylvia asked.

"On the table, with plain and honey butter."

I followed Sylvia to the living room, where she announced that dinner was ready and that everyone should get their plates in the kitchen.

Conversation in the living room came to an abrupt end, and the family made a beeline for the food.

I headed into the dining room. The late afternoon sun streamed through the window and created a warm patch on the floor that was the perfect size for a napping guide dog. I settled into place for my dinner-time siesta while the family took their customary seats at the table.

I WAS ALMOST asleep when Sylvia began talking about another guide dog named Lonny. Gina and Craig peppered her with questions about a man named Frank, who was Lonny's owner. I shifted onto my belly and lifted my head. The name Lonny rang a bell in the recesses of my mind. I felt certain I'd met this guide dog they were talking about.

The creaky hinges of the opening front door interrupted my musings. I heard a man and another dog step inside. The man led the dog to the hallway bathroom. I got to my feet and looked at the humans.

They sat at the table, eating and chatting away. No one had noticed what was going on in the hallway.

Emily launched into a recitation of our fun day at the farm the day before. She reported that she and Stephanie were already planning an outing to Sweet Briar Farm in the fall to take a candle-making class.

She invited Gina, Martha, and Sylvia to join them. The women enthusiastically agreed.

I heard faint whining emanating from behind the closed hallway bathroom door. None of the humans commented on it.

The doorbell rang, and Martha got up from the table. "That must be Doug," she said, entering the hallway. "I'll answer the door."

I knew Doug was already inside the house.

Martha reappeared in the doorway to the dining room. "Doug's brought a guest with him," she said, interrupting the flow of conversation around the table. "Is it all right if she joins us?"

Sylvia's eyebrows shot up. "Sure," she said, scooting her chair back from the table. "I'll get another place setting. Grant—will you please bring my dressing table chair down from my bedroom?"

"That won't be necessary," Martha replied quickly. "She won't be eating."

Before anyone could comment further, a golden ball of fluff bounded into the room. She skidded to a stop in front of Craig. Her tail wagged like a windshield wiper at high speed as she raced around the table, greeting everyone.

"A puppy!" Zoe and Diedre cried in unison.

"What's going on?" Emily asked, bending to accept doggie kisses when the over-excited puppy reached her.

"That's a great question," Grant said.

Doug appeared in the entrance to the dining room and put his arm around Martha.

"I—well ... more like we—have become puppy raisers," Martha said. She glanced up at Doug and smiled. "Meet Pocket, everybody. She's a nine-week-old golden retriever from the Guide Dog Center."

"OMG, Mom!" Emily giggled as Pocket continued to baste her neck with kisses.

I averted my eyes. I didn't like this interloper planting her mark on my Emily.

"Grandma!" the girls cried, abandoning the table and running to Martha.

"You'd better sit down and tell us all about it," Sylvia said.

"I want to hear every detail," Gina said. "Craig and I are considering becoming puppy raisers. Now that Alex isn't a newborn, we feel like we'll have time."

"Really, Gina?" Emily said. "I love hearing that."

"When we saw you and Garth, and learned that there's a two-year wait to receive a dog because there aren't enough puppy raisers, well … we knew we had to help."

Martha escorted Doug to a vacant spot at the table next to her.

"I'll go get Doug's plate from the kitchen," Sylvia said. "Don't start explaining until I get back."

The excitement in the room was palpable. Diedre and Zoe returned to their chairs, talking over each other and pointing at Pocket as she took another lap around the table, her tail colliding with chairs and their occupants while she continued to dispense kisses.

Sylvia came back with Doug's plate, heaped with servings of the night's dinner offerings.

All eyes turned to Doug and Martha as they began their tale.

I lowered my gaze, looking for the puppy.

She was on the far side of the room, lowered onto her front legs, with her hind end in the air. Her gaze was locked on me.

I stared back at her.

Pocket's tail twitched. She lowered her haunches and began a stealthy army-crawl toward me.

She was sneaking up to pounce on me. *Was she kidding?* I was at least three times her size. And I saw her coming.

I had a sudden flashback to my early days at the Guide Dog Center. My littermates and I spent many gleeful hours stalking each other. We'd pounce and play-wrestle until we were too tired to go on. It had been a lot of fun.

Pocket had recently been separated from her littermates. She must be feeling homesick. I would indulge her with this game. She'd wear out quickly enough and soon be fast asleep.

I'd been right about Pocket's intentions, but not her stamina. That puppy rassled me until I finally got tired. Energy and tenacity were highly prized qualities in a guide dog, but this had gotten ridiculous. I reached deep into my reserves of energy and outlasted her. A nine-week-old puppy wouldn't get the best of me.

Pocket finally rolled onto her side and breathed deeply.

I got up and crossed through the kitchen on my way to the water bowl.

The humans were still at the table, deep in conversation.

Something familiar caught my attention as I passed by the pantry. I'd never seen anything like this at Sylvia's before. I blinked hard to make sure I wasn't seeing things. There, on the floor, between a case of water bottles and a giant package of paper towels, lay the cheesy orange cylinder I loved almost as much as my Emily.

I looked around. No one was watching me.

Sylvia was a tidy housekeeper. She'd never allow something to remain in her pantry that would make such a mess when stepped on.

I was a helpful guy. A guide dog's highest calling is to be helpful. I did what I needed to do.

THE END

THANK YOU FOR READING

If you enjoyed *Growing the Circle,* I'd be grateful if you wrote a review.

Just a few lines on Amazon or Goodreads would be great. Reviews are the best gift an author can receive. They encourage us when they're good, help us improve our next book when they're not, and help other readers make informed choices when purchasing books. Goodreads reviews help readers find new books. Reviews on Amazon keep the Amazon algorithms humming and are the most helpful aid in selling books! Thank you.

To post a review on Amazon:

1. Go to the product detail page for *Growing the Circle* on Amazon.com.

2. Click "Write a customer review" in the Customer Reviews section.

3. Write your review and click Submit.

In gratitude,
Barbara Hinske

ACKNOWLEDGMENTS

I'm blessed with the wisdom and support of many kind and generous people. I want to thank the most supportive and delightful group of champions an author could hope for:

The many visually impaired people who have willingly shared their stories with me so that this series is accurate and honorable of their lived experiences. I want to specifically thank Anthony Corona and Ron Kolesar for their suggestions and thorough and helpful beta reads;

Teena and Samanth Tabor—and the many puppy raisers they introduced me to—for sharing their insights and knowledge of this important calling with me. You are all the most generous of souls and exemplify the best in us:

Steve Pawlowski for starting me on this most gratifying path—and sharing with me your wonderful father, Frank, as inspiration for a dreamy new character in this series;

My life coach Mat Boggs for his wisdom and guidance;

My kind and generous legal team, Kenneth Kleinberg, Esq., and Michael McCarthy—thank you for believing in my vision;

The professional "dream team" of my editors Linden Gross, Kelly Byrd, and proofreader Dana Lee; and

Elizabeth Mackey for a beautiful cover.

RECURRING CHARACTERS

Recurring Characters

Amelia: Dhruv and Stephanie's newborn daughter in *From the Heart*. Dark hair.

Anthony Cordoba: blind intern who works for Emily's Denver team.

Ava: Zoe's friend at new school. A year younger than Zoe. Deaf. Brainiac. Excellent tap dancer. Mother is Tammy.

Biscuit: Stephanie's yellow lab guide dog.

Bruce Horton: Manager of a business unit in the Denver office of Emily's employer.

Connor Harrington III: highly successful sales executive; Emily's ex-husband.

Dash: a retired guide dog who comes home to live with his puppy raisers—Melanie and Randy.

Dhruv Patel: genius senior programmer on Emily's team; husband of Stephanie; father of Amelia; dogs are Sugar (golden retriever) and Rocco (dachshund). Pari Patel is his mother.

Frank Blake: a retired man who plays accordion in a polka band. His guide dog is Lonny.

Garth: Emily's black lab guide dog.

Gerald: Executive Vice President at Connor's employer.

Howard Kent: Executive Vice President of Systems and Programming at Emily's employer; a champion of Emily.

Irene: Zoe's grandmother.

JOHNSON

Alexander Johnson: son of Craig and Gina Roberts.

Craig Johnson: twin brother of Grant; married to Gina Roberts; father of Alex; veterinarian.

Diedre Johnson: daughter of Grant.

Grant Johnson: twin brother of Craig; love interest of Emily; widowed father of Diedre; architect.

Sylvia Johnson: widowed mother of Craig and Grant; grandmother of Diedre and Alexander; her cat is Tibs.

Josh: experienced puppy raiser in a Guide Dog Center puppy club. His puppy is Fenton.

Julie Ross: counselor at the Foundation for the Blind; her guide dog is Golda.

Karen: works at makeup counter at Nordstrom.

Kari: senior programmer on the cyber security team at Emily's employer in Denver office.

Katie and John: Garth's puppy raisers; their children are Alex and Abby; their cat is Liloh.

Lonny: Frank Blake's black lab guide dog. Looks like and shares lineage with Garth.

MAIN

Emily Main: department head of a top-notch programming team at a technology giant; lost her eyesight when her retinas detached in a riding accident on her honeymoon; divorced from Connor; daughter of Martha; Zoe is her ward; love interest of Grant; Gina is her lifelong best friend: Garth (black lab) is her guide dog.

Martha Main: widowed mother of Emily. In book 6, she becomes a puppy raiser for a female golden retriever named Pocket.

Michael Ward: supervisor in Emily's team of programmers.

Norman Klein: recipient of heart donated by Emily's father (Martha's husband) after he was killed in an auto accident.

Pari Patel: Dhruv's mother.

Pocket: golden retriever puppy in training to become a guide dog.

Rebecca: third grade teacher in classroom next to Stephanie's. New mother of a baby boy.

Rhonda: programmer in Emily's team.

ROBERTS

Doug Roberts: uncle of Gina; love interest of Martha.

Gina Roberts: lifelong best friend of Emily; married to Craig Johnson; mother of Alex; parents are Hilary and Charles.

Hilary and Charles Roberts: Gina's parents (retired); Gina's mother is a breast cancer survivor.

Roger Foley: Connor's boss and Asia Region Senior Vice President.

Ross Wilcox: director of cyber security team of programmers at Emily's employer in the Denver office.

Sabrina: Miniature schnauzer owned by Zoe.

Scott Dalton: Connor's best friend.

Spencer Chamberlain: orientation and mobility specialist at the Foundation for the Blind.

Stephanie Wolf (now Patel): close friend and classmate of Emily at the Foundation for the Blind; third grade teacher; wife of Dhruv; mother of Amelia; guide dog is Biscuit (yellow lab).

Tania: fourth-grade classmate of Diedre.

Zoe: parents killed in a car accident; lives with her grandmother and becomes Emily's ward when her grandmother (Irene) dies, leaving Zoe in Emily's care; dog is Sabrina (miniature schnauzer).

PROLOGUE

Frank Haynes spotted the forlorn-looking creature in the trees at the side of the road. He quickly pulled his Mercedes sedan off the highway and buttoned his cashmere sport coat against the icy fog as he stepped out onto the grassy berm. He walked gingerly in his slick-bottomed dress shoes as he approached the thin calico lurking in the underbrush. The wary animal rose up on her front legs, ready to take flight, and eyed him uneasily.

Haynes crooned softly to her. He pulled his collar up against the biting wind and wished he had grabbed his topcoat out of the back-seat. But he dare not move now. The cat gradually relaxed and cautiously picked her way to him over the frost-stiffened grass. The cat rubbed against his legs in the familiar figure-eight pattern and began to purr—a tiny, tentative whisper that ripened into a deep, throaty rumble.

He reached a cautious hand down to her. She stretched into him, and he knew the bond had been made. He scooped her up and cradled the filthy creature against his chest, shielding her from the cold and stroking her gently, unconcerned about his expensive coat. When she was content, he returned to his car and placed her carefully in the blanket-lined crate that lived in his backseat for just such occasions. "You're safe now," he whispered the assurance. "You won't have to worry about food or cold anymore."

He shut the mesh grate of the cage and was surprised when the cat curled up and went to sleep. Most strays meowed and screamed all the way to the no-kill shelter that Haynes had founded and currently funded.

As he slipped behind the steering wheel, Haynes automatically checked the cell phone left behind in the console and was shocked to see he missed six calls during the short time he had been rescuing the cat. All from Westbury's idiot mayor, William Wheeler. He punched the return call button as he swung back onto the highway. Wheeler picked up on the first ring.

"Frank—where have you been? All hell's going to break loose around here," Wheeler shouted into the phone.

"What's up?" Haynes replied calmly.

"The town treasurer just called and told me the town can't cover the December payments from the pension fund. We're in trouble, Frank."

Damn, Haynes thought. This was coming two months earlier than he predicted. They wouldn't have time to get any of the condos sold by December. "Have you talked to either of the Delgados?"

"I called Chuck to tell him to move money from the reserve account you guys told me about. He said to talk to Ron about it. Ron thinks the reserve account has been 'depleted.' Some accountant and financial advisor he is! How did you guys let this happen? What have you been up to? If the town doesn't make those payments, we're sunk."

"Don't worry about it. I'll call Chuck and we'll get it straightened out. We always do, don't we?" Haynes disconnected the call over Wheeler's sputtering response.

Damn this faltering real estate market and those greedy, careless Delgado brothers. How had they drained the reserve fund so quickly? They must be siphoning money for their own use from the tidy sum that the three of them had "borrowed" from the town worker's pension fund. Fleecing the faceless public was one thing. Double-crossing Frank Haynes was quite another. Wheeler was set up to take the fall, if it came to that. He could make the trail lead to the Delgados, too. Haynes vowed to find out where every nickel had gone. He executed a sharp U-turn and headed back to Town Hall.

CHAPTER 1

Maggie Martin settled herself in the back of the cab as the driver pulled away from the airport and into the thin sunshine of a late February afternoon. She nodded when he leaned back to tell her that Westbury was an hour's drive, and turned her attention to the countryside streaming by her window. She was in no mood for idle chatter with a taxi driver. The dormant farmland lay still and expectant. Occasional clumps of leafless trees were silhouetted against the storm clouds that soon filled the sky. Maggie was glad she had carefully folded and packed those extra sweaters.

She shivered in spite of the heat blasting from the vents and wondered how anyone could live in a cold climate. *Southern California might not have four seasons, but who in their right mind wanted winter?* Maggie chastised herself once again for even making this trip. She was behind in her work—she needed the billings—and she probably wouldn't find any answers, anyway.

As the monotonous scenery sped by, Maggie relived her final moments with Paul in the cardiac ICU. Wired and tubed, he was hooked up to the best equipment modern medicine had to offer. Their children, Mike and Susan, were both frantically making their way through traffic, but neither arrived in time. It had been Maggie and Paul at the very end. In his final moments, Paul rallied. He feebly squeezed Maggie's hand and repeated breathlessly, "Sorry. So sorry. House is for you." At least, that's what she thought he said. She had been crying, and the beeping monitors and wheezing oxygen machine made it impossible to hear.

She had been over this a million times. It hadn't made any sense because she knew their house was hers. Hadn't they just paid it off and thrown a burn-the-mortgage party with the kids? She had tried to reassure Paul, to quiet him, but he had been desperate to make his point. Maggie now understood Paul's deathbed confession. That's why she had decided to come to Rosemont before she listed it for sale. She needed to get answers; to make some sense of her life.

Maggie planned to go straight to her hotel in Westbury to try to get a good night's sleep before she and the realtor toured the house and signed the listing papers the next day. But her plane had arrived forty-five minutes early, the only advantage of the bumpy flight through strong tailwinds. God knows she was exhausted, having spent another sleepless night rehashing her sham of a marriage. But she was far too curious to get a glimpse of Rosemont to wait any longer. As they passed the highway sign announcing the Westbury exit fourteen miles ahead, Maggie retrieved her house key from the zippered compartment of her purse, leaned forward, and instructed the driver to take her directly to Rosemont.

The cabbie, as it turned out, didn't need directions. "Everybody in these parts knows the place," he assured her. "It's been vacant for years," he continued as he caught her eye in his rearview mirror. "Do you know the owner?"

"I am the owner," Maggie replied with an assurance in her voice that surprised her. "Actually, I just inherited Rosemont. I'm going to put it on the market, but I'm awfully curious to see it. Since it'll still be light when we get there, I thought I'd like to see it on my own, before the realtor and I get together tomorrow."

The cabbie nodded slowly, digesting this news, as he flipped on his left-turn signal and turned into a long, tree-lined drive that wound its way up a steep hill. They rounded the final corner and Maggie gasped. At the end of a deep lawn was an elegant manor house of aristocratic proportions. Built of warm limestone, with regal multi-paned windows, a sharply pitched tile roof, and six chimneys, Rosemont had the kind of gracious good looks that never go out of style. Dazed, she handed him his fare, with a more-than-generous tip, and secured his promise to drop her luggage at her hotel and return for her in an hour.

Maggie dashed through the now falling sleet to the massive front door. The key fit smoothly into the lock but wouldn't turn. She tugged and jiggled the handle, to no effect. It wasn't moving. Maggie looked wistfully over her shoulder as the taxi took the last turn at the end of the drive and vanished beyond the trees. Why did she have to insist on coming here tonight? Impatience did her in every time.

She buttoned the top button of her coat, fished the cabbie's card out of her pocket, and unzipped her purse to retrieve her phone. She'd have to call him to come back now. It was too cold and damp outside to even walk around and look in the windows. Maggie tugged off one of her gloves with her teeth and punched in his number on her phone. She brought it to her ear and idly tried the lock one more time. She felt something shift under her hand and the sturdy lock yielded. The door creaked open. Maggie abruptly ended the call and stepped over the threshold.

Even in the gloomy light of a stormy dusk, the beauty of the house overwhelmed Maggie, and she knew, for perhaps the first time in her life, that she was home. And that nothing would ever be the same again.

The mahogany front door opened to a foyer that gave way to a generous living room. A stone fireplace with an ornately carved mantel dominated one side of the room, and a graceful stairway swept up the opposite wall to the second floor. An archway led to a room lined with bookcases. *An honest-to-goodness library, for Pete's sake,* Maggie thought.

She inched forward slowly, like a dog expecting to come to the end of its leash, and peered into the library. Although all of the furniture was draped in heavy muslin covers, the room was stunning with its six-foot-high fireplace, French doors to a patio, and a stained-glass window. "I've been transported to a movie set of an English manor house," Maggie whispered. She set her purse on a round table in the middle of the foyer and unbuttoned her coat.

The fatigue and apathy that had been Maggie's constant companions since Paul's death began to dissipate as she examined this elegant old house she had inherited. Paul had never mentioned owning an estate on fifteen acres in Westbury. At least not until his final moments. Maggie had learned there were a lot of things that Paul had never mentioned. Unlike the others, this one was a pleasant surprise.

The remainder of the first floor was comprised of a large dining room, butler's pantry, kitchen, breakfast room, laundry, maid's quarters, and a large, sunny room whose function she couldn't identify. It had a herringbone tile floor and was lined with floor-to-ceiling windows along one wall. A conservatory, maybe? *Holy cow*—did she actually own a home with a library and a conservatory? The perfect lines of the house were evident at every turn.

With mounting excitement, Maggie found the switch for the chandelier that lit the staircase and raced to the second floor. A spacious landing gave way to six separate bedroom suites. She opened the first door carefully and proceeded with increasing confidence. Each suite was lovely and distinct in its own way, with huge windows and a sitting room and bathroom for each bedroom. One had a balcony, two had fireplaces. "I actually own this place," she murmured to herself in shock. She was considering which bedroom she liked best when she thought she heard a door close below. Was it already time for the taxi to return for her? Could she possibly have been here for an hour?

Maggie tore down the stairs as surely as if she had been running down them all of her life and came face to face with a solidly built man wearing tidy work clothes. With a pounding heart but steady voice, Maggie demanded to know who he was and how he got into her house.

He stepped back and held up his hands. "I'm sorry to startle you, ma'am. I'm Sam Torres. Your realtor expected you tomorrow, and he asked me to come by today to air the house out a bit and make sure that everything was in working order. I've been in the basement for the past three hours fiddling with the furnace. I've got it going now. I'm surprised we didn't hear each other. I didn't mean to frighten you."

He paused a moment to wipe his hands on a rag. He was never very good at guessing ages; he figured she must be in her fifties, but couldn't tell which end of that age range she leaned to. She was wrapped in a down-filled coat and wore those enormous Australian boots that were so popular. His wife lived in hers from October to May. She had a pair of glasses perched on her nose and was now regarding him imperiously through them.

"Welcome to Rosemont," he continued. "I understand you plan to put it on the market right away?"

Something about his polite, calm manner soon put her at ease. Judging by his weathered skin and full head of gray hair, she guessed he must be a few years her senior. She extended her hand to introduce herself and told him that she was most definitely not going to sell this place. Sam looked at her sharply and started to reply but stopped himself. Then, to her own astonishment, she announced, "As soon as my taxi returns, I'm going to check out of my hotel and move in here. Tonight. Permanently." She reached for the banister, as if to steady herself, and turned aside. *What are you doing?* she thought to herself. *You can't just up and move here. Are you nuts? What do you need with a six-bedroom house? Your family is in California, and so is your work.*

Maggie glanced back; Sam Torres was regarding her carefully. She wondered if he could sense that her decision to move into the house that night had been made impetuously on the spot.

"In that case," he said, "I'd better give you a complete tour. You'll need to know where all the entrances, switches, and thermostats are located." He gestured toward the library and began by showing her how to unlock and open the cantankerous old French doors. Sam nodded in the direction of the fireplace. "You won't want to start a fire until all of these chimneys have been cleaned and checked. This house hasn't been lived in for more than a decade." Sam paused and turned to Maggie. "Are you sure you want to move in here tonight? Once the plumbing is in use again, you'll find almost everything leaks. And the place hasn't been cleaned in years. Wouldn't you like to get it fixed up first?"

"No, I can live with all of that for a few days. As long as the furnace works and the electricity and water are turned on, I can cope."

"This sleet is supposed to turn to snow. You might get stranded up here," he cautioned as he produced a business card that read, "Sam the Handyman." "Here's my card. My cell phone number is on there. Why don't you call me when you get back tonight, and I can stop by to make sure that the furnace is still running and you're all set?" he offered.

"Thank you—very kind of you—but no need to drag out here later. I'll be fine," Maggie assured him with a confidence she didn't feel. For some reason, she felt completely comfortable with this concerned stranger. "Truthfully, this is a rash decision on my part."

Sam nodded.

"I can't explain it. I've never done anything like this in my entire life. But every fiber of my being tells me this is the right thing to do. For once in my adult life, I'm going to follow my intuition."

Sam regarded Maggie intently, and a slow smile lightened his worried expression. "In that case, moving in is exactly what you should do. Sounds like divine intuition. You should follow it. And you can always call me if anything comes up. My wife and I live about ten minutes away."

"Thank you, Sam. That makes me feel more comfortable." As they resumed their tour, Maggie was secretly relieved that Sam was making sure all the windows and doors were locked and all the thermostats were set. His instructions were thorough and helpful. It was evident that he knew the house well. The first floor had warmed to room temperature by the time they returned to the front door.

"I appreciate all you've done," Maggie said. "I'm not a dab hand at home repairs, so I'm sure I'll need your help on a regular basis. What do I owe you for today?" she asked as she turned toward her purse.

"Don't worry about that now," Sam said as he reached for the door. "We can settle up later. Would you like me to have the driveway plowed tomorrow?" She gratefully accepted. They said goodnight, and he headed out the door.

***

Later, in the eerie brightness of the nighttime snowstorm, Maggie and the taxi driver wrestled her suitcases and three bags of groceries to her front door. The driver helped her get them all inside and cautiously inquired if she would be okay there. She assured him she would be just fine, but she knew he doubted it, and, frankly, so did she. He had glanced at her in his rearview mirror occasionally on the drive out there and must have seen the waves of emotion surging through her. She went from feeling confident, intuitive, courageous, and spontaneous one moment to terrified, impulsive, incompetent, and irrational the next. She was known for her levelheaded, dependable (and ultimately predictable) nature. Paul said he never wondered what she was thinking, and her kids swore they knew what she would say before she said it—and they were usually right. At times Maggie felt proud of this—she was understood, knowable, transparent. At other times, she felt dull and unimaginative. Well—this decision would surely make jaws drop.

As the taxi crept up the driveway toward her new life, fear and doubt were gaining the upper hand. She cleared her throat and was about to instruct the driver to take her back to the hotel when they again rounded the corner, and there it was. The house. *Her* house. Imposing, dependable, welcoming, strong. She would craft a happy future here.

She paid the driver, walked up the stone steps, and shut and locked the front door behind her. She toyed with the idea of phoning one of her children to let them know she changed her plans but decided against it. They could call her cell if they needed her. She wanted to savor her brave decision and her first night in her new home without the intrusion of their opinions.

Maggie picked up her groceries and headed in the direction of the kitchen. Dusty and in need of a thorough cleaning to be sure, but what a glorious kitchen! Beautiful walnut cabinets adorned with furniture-maker details soared to the twelve-foot ceiling. A huge window over the antique French sink and a smaller window over an old-fashioned copper vegetable sink would make the room irresistibly cheerful in daytime. The appliances and fixtures were outdated and would need to be replaced, but it was still the most beautiful kitchen she had ever seen—much less owned. *People will really have high expectations of a meal fixed here,* she mused. *I used to be such a good cook. I wonder if I can still muster up anything that does justice to this kitchen? I'll practice and get back on my game,* she decided with a bit of her characteristic determination.

Maggie stashed her groceries and dug into the rotisserie chicken and coleslaw that she bought for her dinner. She began a systematic reconnaissance of the kitchen. To her delight, it was equipped with every specialty pot, pan, and utensil imaginable. *I've been lusting after some of this stuff in catalogs for years,* she thought. *What great fun to cook in this kitchen.*

Along one wall was an enormous antique hutch. Maggie found it contained five complete sets of china, including specialty pieces like eggcups, double-handled soup bowls, and tureens. She recognized Colombia Enamel by Wedgwood and Botanic Garden by Portmeirion, but had to check the bottom of a plate to see that she had place settings for twelve of Derby Panel by Royal Crown Derby and a lovely blue-rimmed favorite called Autumn by Lenox. A set of cheerful yellow Fiestaware completed the collection. *Good Lord*—she felt faint. Maggie was a self-described china addict; now she had the collection to prove it. She vowed to use the good dishes every day.

Maggie made herself tea in a Wedgwood cup and wandered through the house to find a place to tuck herself away to enjoy it. The long day had taken its toll; she was exhausted. As she passed through the archway into the library, she found an overstuffed chair in the moonlight by the French doors and knew she had found her spot. Maggie dragged the sheet off the chair with one hand while waving away a cloud of dust with the other and settled into the chair's protective embrace.

An unblemished blanket of snow in the garden looked like frosting on a cake. At least four inches already, and it was still coming down hard. For the first time in months, everything around Maggie was quiet and still, and she felt peaceful. Thoughts of Paul were always crowding her, and they gradually settled on her now. Who was the man that she had been married to for over twenty-five years?

On the surface, Paul Martin was the charismatic president of Windsor College. Charming and handsome, with a killer smile. And laser focus. When he turned his attention on you, you felt like you were the most interesting and important person in the world. She had felt that way for years; had never doubted his integrity or fidelity. Mike and Susan, now both grown and out of the nest, adored their father. Paul's unexpected death at the age of sixty-two had unearthed a number of betrayals. *Were there others yet undiscovered?* He evidently thought he had plenty of time to cover his tracks. Now Maggie was left to cope with it all.

The first shoe to drop was his embezzlement from the college. The interim president discovered suspicious receipts in Paul's desk, receipts that he had been careless enough to leave sitting in a drawer. An audit was hastily done and the results discreetly fed to her. Paul had been submitting fraudulent expenses as far back as they could trace, in excess of two million dollars. Where in the world had he been spending all of this money?

At first, Maggie wondered if Paul had a gambling problem. As she pored through the college's audit, however, it became very clear that the money was being spent in one location: Scottsdale, Arizona. And another fresh hell was born. She would never forget that day, last September, when she had summoned the courage to uncover the identity of the other woman.

Her short flight had been turbulent, and wedged into a middle seat between an overweight man with a dripping nose and a sprawling teenager; she was queasy by the time they landed. Taxiing to the gate seemed interminable. She snatched her carry-on from the seatback in front of her the moment they came to a stop, and shoved past the teen, jostling the woman in the seat across the aisle as she attempted to stand up. "Getting a bit claustrophobic in there," she muttered in a half-hearted apology. The woman huffed and fixed Maggie with an icy stare. She didn't care what anyone thought; she needed to get off of that damn plane. The line in front of her inched along to the door. Why in the hell were people so slow and clumsy with their luggage? Why did they insist on stuffing bags into the overhead bins that they couldn't handle on their own? *Just breathe deeply,* she told herself.

The rental car was waiting for her. Thank goodness for the perks of being a frequent traveler. She settled into the seat and turned the air conditioner on full blast. Maggie fumbled in her purse for the report the private investigator had given her. She double-checked the address, but didn't need to; it was seared into her heart. Maggie punched it into the GPS system, adjusted her mirrors, and began her journey.

It was only ten o'clock in the morning, but near-record temperatures were predicted and heat waves shimmered off the highway. The GPS was reliable, and she was close to the address in under thirty minutes. Maggie decided she needed something to drink and turned into a convenience store to get a giant diet cola and a bottle of cold water. No one was behind her in line, so she took her time fishing out the correct change. Now that she was here, she wasn't so sure she wanted to pick at this scab. She lingered over the rack of tabloid magazines by the door. What was the matter with her? She was just going to drive by a house. She probably wouldn't even see "her." She had come all of this way—she needed to hitch up her britches and do this thing.

Maggie coiled herself into the now oven-like car and burned her hands as she grasped the steering wheel. She took a long pull on her diet cola and set off once more. She drove slowly as the ascending street numbers indicated she was getting close. *Undeniably a swanky neighborhood,* she brooded. *Nicer than ours.* Spacious, new stucco homes with red-tile roofs and soaring arches. Intricate iron gates and ornate light fixtures. Manicured lawns tended by efficient landscapers. No signs of life on this oppressive day. Everyone was safely tucked away.

And there it was. Bigger than the rest—or was she imaging that? It was unquestionably the nicest house on the street. Bile rose in Maggie's throat. If you had lined up photos of all of the houses on that street and asked her which one Paul would have selected, Maggie knew it would have been this house. More grand than their home in California. Maggie drifted across the centerline and caught herself before she hit the other curb. Thank God she was the only car on the street. She needed to get hold of herself; she didn't want to get into an accident right outside the other woman's house. How cliché would that be? She was acting like a stalker, for goodness sake. No one could ever know she had done this.

She turned around in a driveway five houses down and drove past to view it from the other direction. It looked even better. *That bastard.* She tightened her grip on the steering wheel and turned the car around again, trying to find a shady spot along the curb where she could discreetly watch the house. A couple of palm trees provided the only shade available, and she pulled to the curb. The air conditioning was no match for the midday sun, and she felt like one of the ants that her brother would fry under a magnifying glass on the sidewalk when they were kids. Why in the world had Paul done this? Why hadn't they just divorced? Was he that concerned about the effect it would have on his career? Divorce wasn't a stigma anymore. And he evidently had plenty of money, so splitting what they had in California wouldn't have posed a problem. Surely he knew that she would never have gone digging for more. *Or was he addicted to the thrill of living a secret life?* She instinctively knew she had hit the mark dead center.

Her soda was long gone and she was taking the last swig of water, chiding herself that it was demeaning to be sweltering in a rental car outside of the other woman's house—then she appeared.

Maggie crouched over the dashboard, the air conditioning blasting her hair out of her face, and focused on the other woman like a laser. Tall, thin, and pretty—with shoulder-length blond hair and long, tanned legs—she was laughing with two school-aged children as she herded them into her Escalade. She pulled out of the driveway and glanced in Maggie's direction as she turned to say something to the children in the backseat.

Maggie clutched the steering wheel as nausea overwhelmed her. She tried unsuccessfully to choke it back and grabbed frantically for the empty soda cup and heaved violently. Sweating profusely, she fumbled in her purse for some tissues and a breath mint. The tears she had been holding back for months now broke free. This had been a stupid, crazy thing to do. Why had she expected it to turn out differently? She was a mess. Vomit on her cuff and in her hair. The last thing she wanted to do was spend the day here and get back on a plane later. To hell with the one-way drop-off charge for the rental car. It was only a six-hour drive. She'd be in her driveway about the same time as her scheduled flight was supposed to land. And she wouldn't have to see anyone or talk to anyone along the way. She swung the car around and set her course for home.

The minute she uncovered the Scottsdale connection, Maggie had a gut feeling about what she would find. Paul had supported a second family there. The investigator found that the two children weren't Paul's, thank God. But it had been a long-standing relationship and by the looks of the financial records, he had been supporting her handsomely. The most difficult part of Maggie's situation was bearing this knowledge alone; she dared not confide in anyone she knew.

Paul had been acting strangely after he took the post at Windsor College eight years ago. And Maggie had done her best to contrive an innocent explanation and rationalize Paul's odd behavior. But everything now made sense: the weekends away, when he was ostensibly too tied up in "strategic planning sessions" to call home; his trendy new wardrobe and haircut; and his younger, more "hip" vocabulary. When Susan pointed this out, Paul laughed and passed them off as his way of relating to the student body.

He had also become increasingly critical of Maggie's blossoming consulting business as a forensic accountant. At first, she believed he was genuinely concerned she was taking on too much and spreading herself too thin. He was emphatic that he needed her by his side for the numerous social engagements required by his position. Somewhere along the way she realized that he resented her success and her growing independence from him. Paul loved to tell his amusing little story about meeting the shy, studious, plain girl in college and turning her into the beautiful, polished, accomplished woman she was now; that their love story was a modern-day *My Fair Lady. Ugh!* She might not have been a sophisticate, but she hadn't been a country bumpkin, either. Even Eliza Doolittle outgrew the tutelage of Professor Higgins.

The turning point in their relationship was that horrible fight about the black-tie fundraiser he wanted to chair. He would turn up at the event in his tuxedo and make a nice podium speech, and she would work tirelessly on it for almost a year. She had begged him not to volunteer, told him that she simply didn't have the time, that just this once she needed to focus on herself first. She was about to land a lucrative expert witness engagement she had worked so hard to get. It was a fascinating case and would demand all of her time. And would undoubtedly lead to more such work. She simply could not turn it down.

Paul had railed that he couldn't turn the fundraiser down, either. He started on his usual refrain of "whose job pays more of the bills around here" when Maggie quietly pointed out that her income had exceeded his for several years. For the first time in their more than twenty years of marriage, Maggie had put her foot down and told Paul no. Paul had exploded and they had gone to bed angry. This time, however, Maggie didn't give in or apologize just to keep the peace.

They didn't speak for a week. When they tentatively resumed communication, Paul was derisive and demeaning, constantly criticizing Maggie in matters both large and small. But his opinion of her appearance, her job, and her social skills didn't matter much to her anymore. Maggie's friend Helen summed it up nicely: Paul had lost control of Maggie and he didn't like it. She had half-heartedly defended Paul, saying he was a leader and not a control freak, but she knew Helen was right.

Her lawyer negotiated a settlement of the college's claim against Paul's estate in exchange for his million-dollar life insurance policy. The board of regents hadn't been anxious to have their lax oversight of the college's finances exposed, and Maggie didn't want Mike and Susan hurt by a public discrediting of Paul's memory. She needed to get to the bottom of the mystery that was Paul Martin before she brought Mike and Susan into this nightmare. Maggie hired a private investigator that quickly uncovered the truth.

Revisiting these horribly hurtful revelations—so frustrating because Paul was not there to question, cross-examine, rage at—was like watching a tornado relentlessly obliterate her lovingly crafted life. The pain, loss, and desolation were constant companions. But tonight, sunk into this massive chair within the perfect stillness, Maggie removed herself from the starring role and felt like she was watching someone else's tragedy. She let her mind go blank and watched the snow slanting down across the trees outside her window. And she surrendered to a deep and dreamless sleep.

***

Having his office above his liquor store had its advantages; Chuck Delgado was well into the bottle of Jameson he grabbed from behind the counter as he waited for Frank Haynes to arrive on this Godforsaken night. Shortly after two in the morning, someone tapped quietly on the back door below. Delgado checked the security camera and buzzed him up.

Haynes firmly climbed the steps into Delgado's lair and found him slumped in his chair just outside the pool of light supplied by the green-shaded lamp on his desk. Haynes scanned the room, allowing his eyes to adjust to the dimness. The rest of the room was in shadow, and Haynes was glad of it. He didn't care to be accosted by Delgado's collection of crude, pornographic trinkets and toys.

Delgado shoved the open bottle and a highball glass in his direction. Haynes firmly declined. He didn't need to get lightheaded now, and God knows when that glass had last been washed. He cast a dubious glance at the two chairs across the desk from Delgado, and moved a stack of newspapers and a hamburger wrapper onto the floor. *At least he's eating at one of my restaurants,* he thought.

They regarded each other intently. Haynes remained silent.

Delgado nursed his drink and Haynes sat, brooding and impassive.

Delgado finally sucked in a deep breath and began. "Okay, Frank, here's the thing. We ran into an unexpected situation."

Haynes raised an eyebrow.

"Not with anything here. Operations in Westbury are fine. In Florida. It's hard to keep your finger on things from a distance. I sent Wheeler down to check on things, but the bastard spent all his time with the whores in the condos. I understand a guy's gotta have fun, but he didn't do jack shit down there. Bastard lied to me when he got back. If this all goes down, he deserves to take the fall." Delgado gave a satisfied nod and sank back into his chair.

Haynes leaned rigidly forward, resting his elbows on his knees, and locked Delgado with his glare. He waited until Delgado, hand shaking, set his drink down.

"We aren't going to let this 'all go down,' Charles, now are we? We aren't going to let that happen. We had plenty of cushion built in to survive even the Recession. If you hadn't dipped your hand in the till, we wouldn't be having this unfortunate conversation."

"I had stuff to take care of. Those cops down there are expensive and—"

Haynes slammed a fist on the desk and roared, "Silence! I don't care what situation you got your sorry ass into. You know that you were not to bring your sordid business interests into our arrangement. Those condos were supposed to be legitimate investments, not whore houses or meth labs or whatever other Godforsaken activities you've got going in them."

Delgado held up a hand in a gesture of surrender. "You're right, Frank, I know you are. But stuff happens. I'll get this figured out. I may have buyers for a couple of the condos. And I'm expecting money from another associate next week. Enough to fund the shortfall in the next pension payments. Don't go gettin' yourself into an uproar. We'll get things straightened out. I'm on it," he slurred.

"You've got ten days to get this handled," Haynes growled. "I'm going to watch your every move from here on in. You won't want to disappoint me." His tone sent a wave of fear and dread through Delgado.

Haynes rose slowly, turned on his heel, and walked down the stairs, allowing the echo of his steps to recede before he opened the back door and was swallowed by the night.

Delgado held his breath until he could no longer hear Haynes' car retreating. "That guy is seriously unhinged." He reached for the bottle and didn't bother with a glass.

From *Coming to Rosemont*

ABOUT THE AUTHOR

USA Today Bestselling Author BARBARA HINSKE is an attorney and novelist. She's authored the Guiding Emily series, the mystery thriller collection "Who's There?", the Paws & Pastries series, three novellas in The Wishing Tree series, and the beloved *Rosemont Series*. *Guiding Emily* was made into a Hallmark Channel movie of the same name in 2023 and her novella *The Christmas Club* was made into a Hallmark Channel movie of the same name in 2019.

She is extremely grateful to her readers! She inherited the writing gene from her father who wrote mysteries when he retired and told her a story every night of her childhood. She and her husband share their own Rosemont with two adorable and spoiled dogs. The old house keeps her husband busy with repair projects and her happily decorating, entertaining, and gardening. She also spends a lot of time baking and—as a result—dieting.

ALSO BY BARBARA HINSKE

Available at Amazon in Print, Audio, and for Kindle

The Rosemont Series

Coming to Rosemont

Weaving the Strands

Uncovering Secrets

Drawing Close

Bringing Them Home

Shelving Doubts

Restoring What Was Lost

No Matter How Far

When Dreams There Be

Waves of Grace

Novellas

The Night Train

The Christmas Club (adapted

for The Hallmark Channel, 2019)

Paws & Pastries

Sweets & Treats

Snowflakes, Cupcakes & Kittens

Tarts & Turnovers

Workout Wishes & Valentine Kisses

Wishes of Home

Wishful Tails

Back in the Pack

Novels in the Guiding Emily Series

Guiding Emily (adapted for The Hallmark Channel, 2023)

The Unexpected Path

Over Every Hurdle

Down the Aisle

From the Heart

Growing the Circle

Novels in the "Who's There?!" Collection

Deadly Parcel

Final Circuit